THE HOPKINS CONUNDRUM

SIMON EDGE

Published by
Lightning Books Ltd
Imprint of EyeStorm Media
312 Uxbridge Road
Rickmansworth
Hertfordshire
WD3 8YL

www.lightning-books.com

First Edition 2017
Copyright © Simon Edge
Cover design by Anna Morrison
Typesetting by Clio Mitchell

British Library Cataloguing in Publication Data
A catalogue record for this book is available from the
British Library

Printed by CPI Group (UK) Ltd, Croydon CR0 4YY

ISBN: 978-1-78563-033-0

In memory of
Ezio Alessandroni
(25.3.1963–5.3.2017)

I CAUGHT this morning morning's minion, king-
dom of daylight's dauphin, dapple-dáwn-drawn Falcon,
in his riding
Of the rólling level úndernéath him steady áir, and stríding
High there, how he rung upon the rein of a wimpling wing
In his ecstasy! then off, off forth on swing,
As a skate's heel sweeps smooth on a bow-bend:
the hurl and gliding
Rebuffed the big wind. My heart in hiding
Stirred for a bird,—the achieve of, the mastery of the thing!

Brute beauty and valour and act, oh, air, pride, plume, here
Buckle! AND the fire that breaks from thee then, a billion
Times told lovelier, more dangerous, O my chevalier!

No wónder of it: shéer plód makes plóugh down síllion
Shine, and blue-bleak embers, ah my dear,
Fall, gáll themsélves, and gásh góld-vermillion.

Gerard Manley Hopkins

The Lords of the Admiralty received a telegram from Sheerness reporting that a small life-boat had washed up on Garrison Point Beach this morning, containing one man alive and two dead. From the imperfect English the survivor speaks it was ascertained that the boat was washed away from the *Deutschland*, of Bremen. It is supposed this vessel struck either the Galloper or Kentish Knock Sands, at the entrance of the Thames. A tug has been sent from Sheerness to search and afford aid.

The following telegram has also been received from the commanding officer of Her Majesty's ship *Penelope*, at Harwich:

> "The Deutschland, of and from Bremen for New York, with emigrants, grounded on the Kentish Knock on Monday morning. She afterwards knocked over the sand, and is now lying in four and a half fathoms, apparently broken amidships. Estimated number of passengers and crew lost, 50. Remainder landed and under the care of the German Consul at Harwich. The Locust, tug (sent from Sheerness to assist wreck), will pass Kentish Knock on the way to the Galloper."

From *The Times*, London, Wednesday, December 8, 1875

FLORIDA, THE PRESENT DAY
LONDON, 1876

Two men called Barry each read a communication on a Monday morning in May, and each of them frown. They don't know one another, because they have been born a hundred and twenty-nine years apart, one in the old world, the other in the new, which means the two Mondays are separated by five thousand miles and fifty thousand days. And because of this gap in time, only one of the men actually thinks *WTF?* But the other effectively thinks it too.

It is certainly the spirit of Father Aloysius Barry's reaction as he slits open a slim envelope, addressed in a tangled, coiling hand to his employer, at their cramped fourth-floor offices in Davies Street, Mayfair, and unfolds the manuscript it contains. Father Aloysius is used to opening submissions of little merit and is well versed in the various tactful phrases that can be employed when he returns the unwanted material. But this offering is on a different level. Written in the same hand as the envelope, the text looks instantly peculiar, because it is spattered with bizarre dashes and ellipses of a kind he has never seen before. The lines are neatly arranged and legible enough, but the words do not convey meaning in any conventional sense, and no amount of reading and re-reading makes them any clearer, which Father Aloysius is certain is not for want of education on his part. The effort to make something of it causes his head to spin, and it comes as a relief when he gives himself permission to stop trying. Even to his own relatively inexperienced eye, this submission is not just unpublishable: it verges on the insane. And considering the address the package has come from, that could be a matter of more than just literary concern. It will certainly need more careful handling than the usual polite refusal.

Father Aloysius sighs, puts the manuscript at the bottom of his pending pile, and hopes something will come to him by the time he reaches it. Perhaps his editor will know what to say.

For Barry Brook, author of *The Poussin Conundrum*, there are no syntactical thickets to negotiate, no obscure vocabulary or wild system of notation in the message he reads on his iPhone at his large, Mexican-style canal-side home in Fort Lauderdale, Florida. It's just an ordinary tweet among the many from fans who remain enthralled, nine years on, by his murderous conspiracy thriller tracing the bones of Jesus Christ to a cave in southwestern France, and who don't seem as perturbed as he is by his failure to produce a follow-up. They assume he is toiling away on a new masterwork of even greater complexity and have no idea that he sits at a blank screen day after day, month after month, transfixed by a terror that the global sensation which astonished no one more than himself was an unrepeatable fluke. He scrolls through the notifications to see if there's anything particularly complimentary he can retweet to keep his profile up and maintain the illusion he's still in the game.

One message stands out. It comes from a sender called @Wreckileaks, a name that seems to be making some kind of point, although he doesn't quite understand what. It's mildly abusive, but there's nothing remarkable about that. Over the years he has become familiar with invective in all its forms, and at times has been so mesmerised by it that he counts himself a connoisseur. He has managed to offend the religious and the non-religious, the literate and the illiterate, the French (for setting his book in their country) and the non-French (for not setting it in theirs), and he inspires extraordinary creativity in the imaginations of those who wish or threaten on him a violent death, with a strong correlation between goriness and religious fervour (and a touching faith among all who suggest it that they are the first to think of ramming one of his precious set-squares far up his rectum). Whatever his analyst may say, there is something oddly flattering about this frenzy of hatred among people he has never met. It makes him so much bigger and more important than they are, in their sad little bedrooms spewing impotent bile into their keyboards. It makes him feel more secure, not less – although he has naturally spent a small fortune on electronic and other fortifications for his property, just to be on the safe side.

In the present case, the rudeness is pretty mild. It's the content itself that intrigues him. The message reads: *@barrybrook if you want to know the real secrets of the*

Vatican you cynical bastard think shipwrecks not geometry. Interested? More soon.

Maybe he needs to get a life, but he is interested and he does want to know more.

North Wales, 1875

Hopkins woke sweating in the ice-chill small hours, long before the pipes had begun their slow clank into what passed for life. He could tell without striking a light that there was at least an hour to go before the caller did his rounds, opening every door along the corridor to shout *"Deo Gratias"* and not budging until he received the same sleep-slack answer. Usually it was an effort to rouse himself but now, in this unaccustomed wakefulness, he lay staring up at the dark shape of the crucifix on the wall opposite the narrow window, fearful of returning to his dream.

It had started as a pageant of obscene torment. There was a boy from school who had taught him the first of many lessons in disappointment; then a friend's younger brother, running goose-flesh naked during the summer vacation; a coalman's boy, randomly glimpsed during an afternoon walk and preserved in the photograph of his memory, the forehead smudge of grime completing the sense of angelic fall; and finally Dolben himself, not handsome exactly, but captivating, with the promise of a romantic interior world for anyone privileged to enter – and condemning anyone else to a miserable exclusion. In the dream they were on the meadow together, walking beside the Isis as they had done on one of those three perfect, never-to-be-forgotten days; but nothing held its form for long and the scene mutated to some lewder river where Dolben announced his intention to swim. Hopkins himself had also meant to bathe, but when he tried to undress he was thwarted by a stubborn collar stud, buttons that popped back through the hole he had just pushed them out of, knotted laces that were beyond untangling; and all the while Dolben was stripping. The dreamer's depraved subconscious had been more than ready to supply the detail for a body that he had never seen in life: milky white shoulders, surprisingly broad (odd that you could be surprised by something your own imagination had invented, but it seemed you could); a wisp of hair at the middle of a plate-flat breast; a mole on the tender skin at the top of the left arm. Running towards the water, this gangling boy-nymph presented a dimpled haunch and musky cleft, as his observer continued to struggle with his wretched trousers. Hopkins' apparel twisted itself with Gordian spite and he could only look on as Dolben plunged into the lucky pool – alone at first, but then there were two of them. His imagination knew with certainty – because it had invented the likeness – that this was his undeserving rival.

The pair of them splashed together with a feigned innocence, but then the rival was there no longer, ordered away by whatever part of the brain was in charge of this sleep-show, and Dolben was alone in mid-stream, suddenly choking and gasping for breath. There was only the dreamer to watch, helpless from his bed-bound, sheet-wound river-bank, as the water closed over poor

Dolben's head. That was the moment when reason had taken mercy and reminded him that waking was possible. He had pushed gratefully off the muddy bottom of his dream and broken the surface of his lonely little cell, as drenched as if he had really been in the river.

As his breathing slowed, Hopkins inserted an exploratory hand beneath his nightshirt. He was relieved to find that those earlier scenes had not caused any emission. But his pillow was sodden with sweat. He turned it over to use the dry underside. His nightcap was also damp. He peeled it off and flung it aside, pulling the rough counterpane up around his ears, then pushing it away again. Physical discomfort was the only remedy for the desires that had produced that revolting tableau. Forcing himself out of bed, he padded shivering along the oblong of threadbare carpet to his washstand and winced as he splashed water from the ewer onto his forehead. He had a fantasy vision of plunging his whole face into the bowl, holding it under to match poor Dolben, and losing himself to an oblivion where such dreams would never trouble him again. It was of course a sin to contemplate it. Even if it wasn't, he doubted he was brave enough to endure the cold.

And then he remembered that more recent set of drownings, the event everyone had been talking about the day before. The terrible account that Kerr had read from the newspaper, shocking them all because it came so soon after the *Schiller* tragedy, must have put the notion in his mind, and his own wanton fancy had supplied the rest. He shook his head, as if that would dislodge the memory of the dream, and splashed a little more water from the bowl, welcoming its icy jolt now.

Still not striking a light, he ventured off the carpet onto the cold tiles. He lifted the lid of his window seat and groped for the familiar rope handle. They had been told as young novices that any more than twelve strokes was vain-glory. He pulled his nightshirt over his head and knelt at his prie-dieu, below the dark square that would lighten into a portrait of Savonarola, his medieval hero, as the sun came up. With a wild flick, he flung the knotted chords over his shoulder. For a first effort it was feeble – the ropes barely tickled. He put more strength into the next stroke, getting a better reach so that one of the knots whipped round to nick his flank. His breath quickened and he warmed to the task as the force he put into each stroke pushed back the cold of his room and gave his bare skin something else to tremble about. Never. Again. Must these. Filthy. Visions. Come.

He was sweating again as he reached the point of vain-glory, and continued well beyond.

BREMEN, GERMANY, 1875

They were not just expected, which was perfectly natural considering they had written ahead to book their passage. They were actively awaited. The company had grasped that they were coming unchaperoned, and someone had written a note next to their names saying that they should be made as comfortable as possible. It was kind, but also a little alarming. Henrica would have preferred to travel with less fuss and less attention. Perhaps that was always going to be a vain hope.

"There's no need to go near steerage," said the clerk in the offices of the shipping line. He lowered his voice with a theatrical glance at the rougher queue beside them tailing out of the door. "The working man can be boisterous on the crossing. Drink is the culprit. But the purser will do all he can to keep you undisturbed. In first-class we could of course have guaranteed your comfort, and in second-class we can only try. But it's lucky the ship is so empty. One of you will have a cabin to herself, instead of having to share with a stranger."

"Empty?" said Henrica. "Everywhere seems so crowded."

"Crowded?" The clerk laughed. "There's room for eight hundred passengers, but we have barely one hundred today. There are just only six first-class passengers, and twenty-five of you in second."

"Why so few?"

"Nobody likes to travel in December, dear lady, unless they have good reason."

Henrica studied his expression. Was he mocking them? Everyone knew about the 'cultural struggle', as their tormentor called his campaign against them, and it must be obvious from the way they were dressed why they were leaving. But the young man's face seemed innocent enough. "We are much obliged to you," she said. "Thank you, we don't need a porter. We have no other luggage than this."

Until now, the biggest vessels any of them had ever seen were riverboats: massive barges some of them, hauling cargoes across the continent, or passenger liners serving the towns and cities of the Second Empire. But nothing compared to the monster that awaited them, its vast black funnel sandwiched between two towering masts on a deck that stretched as far as they could see. Two of Henrica's companions crossed themselves, and even Aurea stopped her chatter. Everything about the ship asserted its readiness not for a tame inland river, but for the cold, grey sea.

Stevedores were rushing about the quay, dodging between coils of rope as thick as a man's arm, to ferry wooden trunks, sacks of food and bales of cargo into a gaping maw in the iron hull. Departing emigrants gripped relatives in final, grim embraces – tableaux frozen in a different plane to the frantic activity around them. A small boy wound tight in a muffler stopped to stare at a crate of chickens before being pulled protesting away, while just in front of them a liveried youth ushered a black-bearded gentleman in fur-trimmed coat through a rope barrier onto a carpeted stair. Henrica wondered if they were to board here too, but the youth said, "That way, madam," pointing towards the front of the ship without bothering to look at her.

Pressing on towards the far end of the quay, they climbed a ramp that doubled back in a long, gentle incline to raise them to the level of the deck. Henrica had imagined she might feel some pang of anguish at leaving dry land, but the journey from the mother-house had been so complicated – two days by road, with Aurea squealing with excitement all the way and Brigitta gasping at every bump; one night in a rough village coaching inn, and the next in the absurdly plush railway hotel in Bremen itself; the search for their own church in that bewildering, hostile city, so that they could hear their last Mass on German soil; and then the final, short leg to the port by train – that all she could think now was what a relief it would be to find their cabins. Above their heads, rope lines tapered up to the two masts. The sails were still furled on broad yards extending out over the quay. A row of raised skylights, like miniature glasshouses peeping up from the polished pine deck, glinted in the low winter sunlight. Through one of them she saw a vast mechanical wheel, like something from a watermill. An iron bridge straddled the deck at its broadest part, above an engine house built around the funnel. Now they were being ushered away from it towards a doorway that stood proud from the deck, encased in its own hut. Inside was a steep stairway plunging into the ship's innards. Norberta the giantess had to go down backwards, clinging to the banister with one hand and her skirts with the other, with Henrica reaching her bag down after her.

They found themselves in a small chamber, lit by a single small porthole. Trunks and boxes were stacked along the walls and there was an oily smell, seasoned with brine. What hit Henrica most was the din: a steady mechanical roar was punctuated by a regular series of creaks and clangs.

An angular girl in a lace-trimmed cap bobbed to meet them, offering a hand to help each of them down the stairs, and introduced herself as Marta. "Are you all here? One, two, three, four … ah yes, and the tall lady." She was shouting to be heard. "Don't worry about the noise, you'll get used to that. And if you follow me though this door you'll find it's quieter anyway. I've put you in the last set of berths…"

The sway of the ship on the lapping tide was more noticeable in the gloomy interior than it had been on deck. They followed Marta along a narrow corridor and through two doors, and found themselves in a tiny lobby serving the compartments where they were to live for the next two weeks. They were four slivers of rooms, taller than they were wide, but not so very tall either. Each cabin contained two bunks built into the wooden panelling, more the size of cots than beds. There was a miniature wash-stand, a shelf, a narrow bench and a row of hooks. A curtain could be drawn along the front of each bunk, and there was another row of hooks above the mattresses, on one of which hung a white hessian life-belt.

"… and to get into the top one you have this box, under the bed, which you may use as a step. Usually the smaller passengers find it easier to take that one. There are two other ladies coming who will share one of the porthole cabins. The other three are yours. I'll leave you to decide which of you goes where. We sail at half three, with prayers on deck before we leave. Dinner is at six, breakfast at eight and lunch at one. And if there is anything at all… A bathroom? You did see one, madam, but that was for first-class passengers only. You have an excellent jug and basin here, and I can bring you fresh water. Now if there's nothing else…?"

And the girl was gone, bobbing still.

They remained squeezed together in the lobby, the others clearly waiting for Henrica to decide who was going where. She hadn't even thought about it. Should she take the cabin on her own? She had no particular desire to spend the voyage in solitude, so it would be a sacrifice. But the others might assume she was taking advantage. The wisest thing was to think who most needed the extra space to herself, in which case the two obvious candidates were Norberta, who needed it vertically, and Barbara, laterally. As it was, Barbara would barely fit between the bunks and the opposite wall. But Norberta was better suited to being alone. Barbara could take care of Brigitta, who had coped so badly with the coach journey and had turned an ominous shade of green after just five minutes on board, while she herself would room with Aurea and attempt to endure the constant prattle in that throaty Silesian accent that Henrica would never be able to love.

"But there's no porthole," the girl was complaining already.

"We can manage quite well without."

"We've got one. You can swap if you want. I'd rather try to forget we're at sea."

That was Brigitta. She really did look dreadful.

"That hardly seems likely," said Barbara.

This was less than helpful, but Barbara had been like that ever since they set out. With her wide-set eyes, her flat nose and her broad forehead, she was the eldest of the group as well as the stoutest, and perhaps she thought she ought to be in charge. But there was nothing Henrica could do about that. It wasn't as if she had asked to be made leader.

"May we go and explore the ship?"

"Let's settle ourselves first, Aurea dear. You'll have plenty of time to see it all. What can you see from the window?"

"It's a *porthole*. Not much. Lots of people on the quay. Some of them are waving and some of them are crying."

We have no one to do either, Henrica thought.

The door to the lobby opened again and the bobbing stewardess reappeared with a nervous-looking young woman in tow. Introduced as Fräulein Forster, she was no more than Aurea's age. She smiled to reveal too many teeth in a mouth far too small for them, putting Henrica in mind of a colt she had ridden as a girl. Nodding back in as friendly a manner as she could muster, Henrica closed their own door so that Marta could carry on demonstrating the correct use of the wash-stand and the position of the storage hooks to the new arrival.

A little while later there was a further commotion as the last occupant of their quartet of cabins arrived. From the gruff observations that punctuated Marta's babble, it was clear that the elderly lady was not the meek type. Aurea was listening at the door.

"Why doesn't she go first class if she's so grand?" she whispered.

"The Lord is not always kind enough to bestow material wealth on those who believe they most deserve it."

Aurea giggled, then clapped a hand over her mouth as Henrica shushed her, and they both jumped as there was a knock on the door.

It was Marta again.

"Frau Pitzhold and Fräulein Forster are going up for prayers, if you'd like to join them."

"We will say our own," said Henrica firmly.

NORTH WALES, THE PRESENT

The old man wraps his hands around his pint glass but seems reluctant ever to bring it to his lips. He has been nursing this one for forty-three minutes, which Tim knows because he started timing his principal customer's beer consumption a few weeks ago and has found it hard to stop. The first one always lasts at least an hour. The old boy then follows it up with a half, which lasts the best part of an hour too. Tim doesn't know how he manages it. He has tried to speed the process along by pouring the half-pint five or ten minutes before the full hour has elapsed and leaving it sitting on the bar, by way of temptation, but it doesn't make any difference to the rate at which the first one slips down. He has also tried treating his customer to a second full one and only charging him for the half, to see if he can wean his intake up. But that just means the old boy drinks the second one even slower than the first, and the next night is right back to normal, ordering a half. Tim has come to the conclusion that it's the talking that does it. This is an activity that generally makes people thirsty, but in the old boy's case it keeps his mouth so busy, there's little opportunity to use it for drinking.

In the seven months that he has been landlord and owner of the Red Lion, Tim Cleverley has had plenty of time to reflect on the wisdom of coming here. It's hard not to conclude that it's one of the stupidest things he has ever done, which is saying something for someone nicknamed Not-So Cleverley, generally shortened to Notso, throughout his adolescence.

When the solicitor's letter first arrived to say a distant Welsh uncle whose name he can barely pronounce, let alone spell, had died intestate (of cirrhosis of the liver, it transpires) and left him a wholly-owned free house a few miles inland from the coast of North Wales, it seemed like a godsend. His mistake came when he relied on Google Earth, rather than an actual visit, to check out his inheritance. The online pictures, taken on a freakishly sunny day, revealed a quaint, low-roofed structure of whitewashed stone with a large car park that was empty when the Google cameras passed that way (as it is every other day too, Tim later learns). If the cameras could have seen inside, they would have shown an equally empty bar and restaurant, but Tim wasn't focusing on that kind of detail at the time. He was too busy thinking about where he was going to live after his divorce, how little he was earning from his online life-coaching business, and how nice it would be to get away from it all and pull pints for the next few years in a bucolic Welsh idyll, where the pace of life was slow and the quality high. In what appeared in this dazzle of optimism to be perfect serendipity, the sum he would have to give the taxman in order to keep the Red Lion exactly matched his half-share of the proceeds of the flat that he and Nadine had just sold, once the mortgage was paid off and solicitor's and estate agent's bills settled. So when he eventually arrived in his rusting

Suzuki Swift, with the few possessions he had to show for his forty years boxed up in the back, his debit/credit balance was a rejuvenating zero.

Unfortunately his plans for a fresh start have not taken account of the fondness of most of his uncle's former patrons for a cigarette. The smoking ban has kicked in at some point during the old man's final illness, and if it's a choice between stepping into the Red Lion's rainswept beer garden every time those old regulars want a smoke, or staying put in front of their tellies at home, staying put seems to win the day – particularly now they can get six-packs of lager from the local Morrisons for less than three quid. The arrival of a new landlord who can't even speak the language is evidently another reason for them to stay at home, and through most of the winter Tim has shared his evenings with those two or three regulars who don't mind speaking English and whose home lives are clearly even more dismal than his saloon bar.

Having always been Tim's most loyal customer, these days Alun Gwynne is pretty much the only one. Of the other stalwarts, one has died, another is increasingly bedridden, and the third seems to have taken offence at a joke with which Tim was trying to lighten the mood. He still doesn't see why it was offensive, because he heard it told by an actual Welsh comedian on some late-night TV show. But there was an ominous silence when he told it, and when he says the next night that he hopes Old Tom didn't take his idle banter amiss, Alun Gwynne merely rolls his eyes ominously and clears his throat with a rattle of phlegm that makes his ancient black labrador Macca –

short for Macaroni, apparently – break wind in alarm.

He has spent the winter and spring expecting business to pick up when the summer visitors arrive. To listen to Alun Gwynne, who likes to think of himself as a local historian, the area is bursting with attractions, from the ruined coastal fortress built by English invaders in the thirteenth century, to the sacred spring where Henry the Fifth bathed on the eve of Agincourt. But these places are either so compelling that the visitors can't tear themselves away, or Alun Gwynne's idea of a good time is not most people's. Now that summer has nearly arrived, it's clear the passing trade is too busy passing to stop, or is somewhere else entirely. The school holidays haven't started yet, but Tim is already adjusting his expectations downwards. He has become skilled at grunting at his regular's stories without actually listening to them, and is wondering whether he can restart the online life-coaching (yes, he is aware of the irony) from a stool behind the bar. He is also considering offering odds on Betfair for how few pints a country pub can sell in one day and still remain open.

At present the old man is running his fingers through his hair and scratching his scalp. He has a remarkably low hairline for his age, an improbable slate-gray thatch that starts halfway up his forehead and makes him look to Tim, who doesn't want to admit how envious he is, like a slow-witted Mexican bandido. If that makes Alun Gwynne sound exotic, the snowstorm falling on the bar is less so. At the end of every night, Tim sweeps the flakes of dead skin away with a brush and dustpan.

"Do you ever miss your own country, landlord?" the old

boy asks in his sing-song nasal accent.

"This *is* my own… oh, I see what you mean." Tim knows he is an outsider here, but has never quite thought of himself as an expat. "No, not really. I mean, I had a difficult couple of years before I came here, so to be honest I'm glad to get away."

"That's good," says Alun Gwynne. "Because I don't suppose you have much option to go back."

"How do you mean?"

"Well you know, what with all these pubs going bust…" The old boy cocks a shaggy eyebrow and glances significantly around the empty bar. "Nobody else would want to buy it off you, would they? So I suppose you're stuck here."

He chuckles to himself and takes a tiny sip of beer.

"Thanks for that, Alun. Very comforting. But I'm not planning on going bust."

"I'm glad to hear that, landlord. I just thought, you know, when a man doesn't open his bills…" He gives another significant glance at a pile of unopened brown envelopes on a shelf beside the bar. "It's never a good sign, is it? Not that it's any of my business. But I like to have somewhere to go of an evening."

Tim gives him a wintry smile, wondering at what stage it's acceptable to tell your sole customer to mind his own sodding business.

"Don't you worry, Alun. I'm not planning on closing the Red Lion any time soon. Not when I'm having this much fun."

But it's a worrying thought, he acknowledges when

Alun Gwynne has finally shuffled off homewards and he is locking up. He doesn't have many other options so it's high time he found a way of making the damn place work. The alternative – having to slink back to England even poorer than when he left – is too gruesome to contemplate.

North Wales, 1875

The iron-grey sky of the past week had gone and the sea shone blue in the bay. It was a recreation day, and Hopkins had drawn to walk with O'Rourke, a labourer's son known at lectures for asking complicated theological questions in Liverpool-accented Latin. He would not have been Hopkins' chosen walk-mate, but that was the point of these lotteries: there was no choice. In the hazy past before Hopkins had joined the Society, walks had been an occasion for developing friendships and for confidences. Such things were forbidden to him now, and his old life was so long ago that he was sure he had lost the art of expressing feelings, even if he wanted to. Each with their parcel of sandwiches, he and O'Rourke would restrict their conversation to religious subjects and natural phenomena.

They chose to head south, up the valley away from the sea. The college sat tucked in a sheltered thicket on the side of a minor range of hills. Beneath, the valley widened into a gentle saucer that might have been Oxfordshire, were it not for the purple drama of Snowdonia in the distant backdrop. But the hillsides were a tougher kind of country: narrow, winding roads banked with tall hedgerows, behind which rough farms sprawled; fields scattered with spent implements and weeds, where cows and crows were languid companions and the rush of running water was never far away. They passed through the first village, with its mean stone houses and ancient church dwarfed by its guard of colossal yews, and then the second, with St Stephen's more modern tower sprouting from the corner of the spur.

They were heading for Moel y Parc, with its wooded ring giving way to a treeless tonsure that was topped at this season with a cap of gleaming snow. Hopkins was the only member of the community who had taken the trouble to learn that *moel* did not actually mean hill, even though so many of the peaks had it in their name, but 'bare' or 'bald', and was pronounced 'moil'; or that the mutations of the Welsh language came in the initial consonant rather than at the end, so that it could also be *foel*, which you pronounced 'voil'. Of course his enthusiasm had been thwarted by the rules of the Society. He might only learn the language, the Rector had told him, if he planned to convert the locals – and since it was obvious just by looking at the native population that there was no hope of that, he had been forced to drop his formal studies. But he could hardly be accused of disobedience if he continued to observe names and signs while he walked around.

As they turned onto the trail that led up the hill, something cawed from off to their left. Hopkins had heard it before, three identical beats on the same note, but was never sure what it was. *Daa daa daa* came the call, then again *daa daa daa*, purely rhythmic, with no variation in tone. *Daa daa daa*. It could be saying *Ding dong bell*, which was his favourite metrical conundrum. Three beats and three stresses: how did you scan it? You couldn't have more than one stress in a foot, but neither could you have a foot with just one beat, not in conventional metrics anyhow. To Hopkins, that just showed that the rules were wrong. Every child knew the rhythm of *Díng dóng béll*, just as they knew *Óne, twó, búckle my shóe*, and they were unconcerned by the supposed impossibility of the meter. How could it be impossible if you could say it?

"There it is," pointed O'Rourke, and they looked up to see the crow soaring above them. From below, its silhouette was like a cross against the sky, the wings forming perfect broad right angles as they came out from the tail and neck. The bird hovered lower now so they could see its five distinct feathers reaching beyond the end of the wingspan, like heavenly fingers reaching out into the sky.

They stood still and gazed up at it together.

"Do you ever wonder how we know it so easily to be a crow?" said Hopkins.

"Because of its tail. It's fan-shaped, almost stumpy. If it had a pointed tail it would be a raven."

"No, no. I mean, yes of course that's true, but that's not quite what I meant. It's only part of it, anyway. I mean rather, what is the essential crow-ness of it, that makes us know beyond doubt that God is showing us a crow and not, say, a rabbit?"

O'Rourke was grinning uncertainly at him.

"Because rabbits don't fly?"

Hopkins sighed. "I… I'm not explaining it very well. Never mind. Come, have we time to go on higher before we turn back?"

The first time he had come up here, not long after his arrival, the entire landscape had been swathed in the suffocating, cloying grey that was the worst aspect of this part of the world. It struck him then that the hills were suckling the rain from the clouds. But the landscape could not look more different now, as they toiled up through the snow-line, shielding their eyes from the white dazzle. He gasped with the nobility of it as they finally stood at the cairn on the summit. He was grateful for his two jerseys: the one the incompetent village laundress had shrunk, squeezing his chest like a corset, and the replacement his mother had sent, fitting loosely on top, but even that woollen armour under his robe was no defence against the rasping cold. O'Rourke was suffering too, groping for a handkerchief to wipe away a dewdrop.

On the way down they saw a kestrel, floating on the airstream high above the meadow. From their vantage point on the hill path they were almost level with it, and they could see the crook of its neck hanging from its outstretched wings as it scoured the fields for some hapless mouse or vole. A vole on the *foel*. Ha, it worked wonderfully if you spoke it. Now the bird was off, swinging forth on the current to scan another part of the field. That elegant curve brought to mind the young skaters Hopkins had watched last winter on the little fishing lake over the hill. The ones who could really do it swept around as if they were tying a bow on the ice, and here was the bird doing the same on the air. Now it came to a halt again, as if the air beneath it were completely steady, and it stared hungrily down at a hedgerow far below. What majesty and terror all in one.

Other men had not ventured so far, and the recreation room was crowded when the pair of them arrived back. Hopkins took coffee and bread for himself and sat gratefully on one of the stiff-backed wooden chairs. He would never compromise on the length of a walk, however cold or wet the conditions; but his feet ached horribly. Kerr was pacing in front of the low fireplace, so inadequate to heat the tall room, waiting for *The Times*. Now he came over with it, apparently set on reading out the latest reports. But Hopkins had no stomach for them today.

"Really, I'm more than happy to wait my turn."

"If you're sure…"

Kerr took a seat of his own and bent over the paper. An aristocratic Scot who was rumoured to have distinguished himself in the Crimea, he had been a naval commander before joining the Society, so it was inevitable that the maritime disaster would have a fascination for him.

That left Hopkins free to describe the kestrel to Bacon, who could always be relied upon to show interest in his natural observations.

"Did you see it plunge?" the other man asked. Bigger and broader than Hopkins and about five years his senior, he was also a convert, also from London. He had a fresh, pleasant voice, lighter than you expected from a man of his bulk.

"Not while we watched. The hawk went hungry and the prey went free."

Bacon had seen a flock of starlings on his own walk.

"It was a sight that you in particular would have loved, Hopkins. They settled in a row of trees and then at some signal known only to themselves they rose, one tree after another, making an unspeakable jangle and sweeping round in whirlwinds. It was joyous to watch because their cries seemed somehow delighted, as if they were stirring and cheering one another."

"Could they really have been delighted, I wonder?"

"No doubt that was my own illusion, an emotion of my own that I conferred on them."

"I don't know. Perhaps all God's creatures feel the joy of him."

"A controversial thought."

"We should subscribe to Descartes' view that animals have neither souls, rights nor feelings," put in Rickaby, his little monkey face beaming in a way that always irritated Hopkins. "It's better to think of them as automata constructed by God. If they happen to make noises, so does a clock or a steam engine. Thomas Aquinas was also adamant that an animal has no soul. Imputing enthusiasm or delight to them is highly irregular."

Hopkins pursed his lips. He would be prepared to consider a starling equivalent to a clock when the former started striking the hour and the latter learned to fly. But he kept that to himself, knowing that Bacon was right: he was at odds with the Society over this and it could prove an impediment if he held too obviously to the view. But Rickaby was waiting for a reply, smiling as irritatingly as ever, and Hopkins was relieved to have his attention diverted by Kerr, who had finished with *The Times* and was offering it to him.

"What news of the shipwreck?" Hopkins asked.

Perhaps he would pay attention to the terrible details after all.

NORTH WALES, THE PRESENT

Life begins to look up for Tim on the afternoon a rogue tourist wanders into the Red Lion. He's a walker, early thirties, dramatically balding without having clipped his hair short at the back and sides to compensate, so that he looks like he's wearing a clown wig, with t-shirt sleeves flapping uselessly around thin, white arms. But he's clearly tougher than he looks because he's carrying a massive rucksack on his back – tent, camping stove, the whole works, he explains to Tim – and claims to have walked all the way from mid-Wales.

Tim pulls him a pint and makes him a cheese-and-onion sandwich, using the defrost function on his toaster to make the bread seem fresh.

"Looking to get away from it all, are you?" he asks. "You're certainly off the beaten track on this side of the valley. Most people seem to go straight on up to the coast on the main road on the other side. More fool them, of course. They don't know what they're missing."

He beams affably, wishing he could actually mean it.

"Really?" says the walker. "I'd have thought you'd get some literary pilgrims at least. You know, with the poetry connection just up the road. Actually I was hoping you could point the place out for me on my map. I mean, the place where he lived."

Tim is too embarrassed to admit that he hasn't a clue what the guy is talking about. Fortunately Alun Gwynne is on hand, and jumps in with a disquisition on the virtues of the neighbourhood bard. The visitor seems delighted with this expert tutorial. It's only when he has gone on his way that Tim confesses his ignorance. When Alun gets over his elaborate disappointment at this failing – "And to think that I took you for an educated man, landlord!" – he fills Tim in. By the time he leaves, he has provided details of every bush, tree and hill within a ten-mile radius by which the poet is meant to have been inspired. Tim is exhausted by the effort of feigning interest.

Alun Gwynne is clearly fond of the subject, because the next day he brings a paperback of poems.

"I thought you might like to take a look, if you ever have an idle moment."

As ever, Tim is unsure if he is being insulted or teased.

"The ones of particular local interest are here…" Alun jabs a weather-beaten finger at a short poem. "And this one, this one and this one. And of course the *Wreck*."

He flicks through several pages to point to that last poem. It seems to go on forever.

"That's the big one," he says superfluously, "and it was all composed down the road, at the seminal college."

He means the place the walker was looking for.

"It's difficult language, mark you," he adds. "Very complicated. Don't be disheartened if you can't grasp it. A lot of people can't, especially if they don't have a real bent, as it were. It wouldn't surprise me if you couldn't make head nor tail of it, landlord. But give it a try anyway, just to see."

He fumbles in his pocket for a biscuit for Macca, who eats it with one crunch and puts his head on one side in hope of more.

Tim has never had the slightest inclination to read poetry for pleasure. While it's true that he is not exactly rushed off his feet, it would have to be a cold day in hell before he would voluntarily pick up a volume of verse to entertain himself. On the other hand, every man has his pride and he is irritated by the assumption that the writing will be too hard for him – particularly when it comes from someone who is speaking English as a foreign language and has a fairly hit-and-miss relationship with its vocabulary. So, whether deliberately or not, Alun Gwynne has thrown down a gauntlet. After Tim has locked up, instead of flicking through the TV channels to reinforce his conviction that there is nothing on there worth watching, he sits down with the book.

He opens the volume, noting that Alun Gwynne shares his own habit of writing his name and the place he bought it on the inside cover. When he gets to the long poem, the depressing news is that the old boy is right: it's well-nigh incomprehensible. It's full of strings of words that have a slightly hypnotic impact, because they're full of swirling internal rhymes and rhythmic alliterations, but they don't actually mean anything, not to Tim at any rate. According to Alun the poem is meant to be about a shipwreck, and that's what the dedication says too, but you wouldn't know it from the lines themselves. There's no scene-setting, no narrative, and precious little about a ship. Instead it's all about God and – from what little Tim can follow – the poet himself, who seems to be pouring his heart out in an intensely miserable way, although to limited effect when it's so hard to know what he's on about.

Tim's plan to tell Alun Gwynne that he has mastered the poem with no trouble is no longer viable, and he hopes the old boy will quietly forget about it. But he doesn't, of course. It's the first thing he asks about the next afternoon.

"Honestly, Alun, I haven't had a moment," says Tim.

He wishes he were a better liar. He remembers reading somewhere that the real art of being plausible is to convince yourself of whatever you're trying to say before you try it on anyone else. He tries to create a mental picture of what being busy might be like, but no, it won't come.

"Had a late rush after I left, did you?" asks Alun.

That's a cheap shot, and Tim rises above it.

But Alun Gwynne carries on nagging him day after day to know if he has looked at the poem yet, so a couple of nights later he backs down.

"I did, er, finally get round to looking at it, yes," he says. "You weren't joking when you said it was hard. I'm not surprised that some people can't understand a word."

"How far did you get?"

There is a twinkle of merriment, or perhaps mockery, in the old boy's eye.

"Not very far. I didn't want to rush it, you know? Better to take it a bit at a time and savour the finer subtleties."

His customer raises an eyebrow.

"Did you understand any of it?"

Tim sighs.

"Not a bloody word," he says, and they both laugh. It's a relief to be telling the truth.

"There's no shame in it," says Alun. "Some of it is pretty cryptic. Almost as if it's a puzzle."

"Like it's written in code or something?" says Tim. "Yes, I see what you mean."

That thought stays with him for the rest of the day. There's a memory somewhere at the back of his mind that is trying to push through to the front, only it won't come.

It's only later that he remembers, and suddenly it's all flooding back unchecked: the full ghastly detail of the disastrous week that he and Nadine spent in the south of France for their tenth anniversary.

The trip was Nadine's idea, and it would have been fine if they could just have had a normal holiday. But that was never Nadine's way. Instead of drinking Bordeaux by the glorified paddling pool that came with their gîte, as any ordinary couple would have, she made them clamber over ankle-twisting hillsides in the August heat, on an idiot quest for the Holy Grail involving maps, a set-square and a postcard of an old painting. She had just read a book – the book the whole world seemed to have fallen for that summer – and she was on a mission. The result was misery for them both. For Tim, it meant facing up to the fact that he was spending his life with a credulous simpleton. Nadine's discontent took a different form, chiefly her dislike of being called a credulous simpleton quite so loudly and quite so often. He remembers one row in particular, at furious volume in a restaurant full of obviously rubber-necking Brits. That detail is crucial: the restaurant was *full*, just as the hotel was *full* and all the cafés and gift shops in the centre of the village were *full*.

If this were just a function of the hot weather and the dramatic scenery, all the nearby villages would have been swarming too. But everywhere else in the surrounding region was terminally sleepy, places where all the shutters were closed in the middle of the day and you had the creepy sense that everyone had either died, moved away or was watching you from behind them. Their village, by contrast, had something extra: a Unique Swindling Point far more compelling than climate and cheap plonk. And that piece of value-added had been put there by a succession of mutually back-scratching con-artists – he remembers shouting that very phrase as Nadine dripped angry tears onto her crêpe flambée – with each new shyster standing on the shoulders of the last.

Some confected nonsense involving the resurrected Christ, a French wife and a hidden grave had made the village famous and its businesses rich. This wasn't just a matter of luck for those businesses, of happening to be in the right place. This village and its entrepreneurs had made their own luck, by announcing to the world that it *was* the right place. The scam had been going on since Victorian times, but the world had really gone nuts for it when Nadine's favourite book – *The Poussin* bloody *Conundrum* – had turned the whole thing into a thriller. Everyone in the world seemed to have read it and the village had scored big-time.

These memories ought to make Tim shudder: they

certainly always have before. But now they have generated something, the germ of an idea that excites rather than repels him. It's tantalising.

Alun Gwynne says the poem – the very religious poem written on their doorstep – is so bewildering it could be written in code. And codes convey secret messages, don't they? So what if…

Tim spends half the night online trying to see how far he can spin the yarn that is coming together in his head. Old enough to remember the world before the internet, he marvels that there is a page for literally everything, put together by someone, somewhere, so that nothing needs to be complicated or impenetrable any more. And he discovers there is a thrill to be had by clicking on links. Best-selling conspiracy thrillers need powerful people holding life-or-death secrets, and it's a stretch to describe a lonely little priest on a rainy hillside in North Wales as important. But he's a member of the Society of Jesus – *click* – which is part of the Catholic Church – *click* – which is run by the Pope – *click* – who is based in the Vatican – *click* – which has always been a serious player in this kind of yarn. Bingo.

He navigates back to the top of his chain and goes off in a different direction, to see if he can find out more about the poem. How can he doubt it? It's based on a real event – *click* – involving real people – *click* – some of whom were fleeing religious persecution in their native Germany, organised by a bloke called Bismarck – *click* – in response to some initiative or other by the Pope – *click* – of that selfsame Vatican. This is fun! Does it add up to anything? In Tim's excitable imagination it seems to, but it really is getting late, and he has an empty pub to open sometime tomorrow, so he jots down a few key notes to try and clear his brain of the facts that are otherwise likely to keep him awake, and then goes to bed, where he sleeps immediately.

The next step is to try out the fledgling idea on his only available test-audience who, if nothing else, is always up for a rambling tale.

"So let me see if I've understood you correctly, landlord," says Alun Gwynne the following afternoon. He has been listening hard with a frown so discouraging that Tim wishes he had never started explaining. "It's your belief that this vessel was carrying some kind of valuable cargo?"

Tim reminds himself that the scheme is pretty far-fetched, so it's not surprising that it requires patient explanation.

"Valuable *information*. And I don't actually believe it. I'm just hoping that other people might. If I could find the right way to persuade them."

"I see. Information, then. What sort of information?"

"Oh, you know. The kind of secrets that men and women have given their lives for over the centuries, since the death of Jesus Christ."

That doesn't sound bad. Maybe he has a talent for this kind of crap. Or perhaps it's just that something rubbed off on him, in all those years living with Nadine.

"You mean documents, then?"

"It could take the form of documents, yes. In fact I think it's highly likely. Letters sealed with the crossed keys of the Vatican, whose bearers have no idea of their contents and who only know that they can never fall into the wrong hands because the future of the Church of Rome depends on it."

"You know that rings a bell. What was that book called? The Puccini Connection. You know the one?"

"*The Poussin Conundrum*. I do indeed."

The old boy isn't so slow on the uptake after all.

"Wasn't it about the Holy Grail?"

"The very same."

"So you think there was something to do with the Holy Grail on that ship?"

"Could have been, Alun, could have been. That's all we need to establish. Bear with me. Let's say the secrets of the Holy Grail have been passed down from one pontiff to the next, for century after century, and they cannot be divulged on pain of death. But what if…" – Tim finds his own hand tracing a theatrical flourish – "what if some hostile figure had come to power in Europe, threatening the supremacy, the political power, the very existence of the Vatican Church?"

Seriously, this isn't bad.

"And had there?"

"There had indeed. You've heard of Bismarck?"

"I know the name, but that's about it."

"Me too, until yesterday. But let me explain."

And Tim fills his customer in on his new understanding – © Wikipedia – of nineteenth-century political history in Bismarck's Prussia and post-Risorgimento Rome.

"You see, the Vatican was running scared. Bismarck was doing all kinds of things like, erm..." He tries to remember the stuff he has read. "Yes, clamping down on convents and, erm, other stuff like that. Because the Pope had said he was infallible in a papal what-do-you-call-it..."

"Bull?"

"That's the one." Appropriately enough. Boom-boom. "This guy Bismarck was talking about the Catholics as the enemy within, that kind of thing. It could have been the start of some massive backlash, and any self-respecting Pope with a decent sense of posterity would surely have started thinking about getting the things he most wanted to protect away from danger, in other words out of Europe, while there was still time. It stands to reason."

Alun Gwynne is frowning again.

"So the Pope wants to send the Holy Grail to America..."

"That's right!"

"And he gives it to a party of German nuns?"

"Why not? Who would think of searching them for it?"

Nobody, he is thinking to himself, because this is the part where it gets a bit daft, even by the standards of the genre.

But Alun is nodding in agreement. "I see your point, landlord. It's a possibility."

"Really?"

"Oh yes."

Tim has never had much faith in his own powers of persuasion. Maybe he really is onto something.

"But where's the evidence?" Alun is saying. "I can see it may be possible, but to make believe it actually happened you need some sign, you know, a signal, like Puccini with his pentagrams..."

"Poussin."

"Right you are. But you still need something, a clue of some kind that would show the Grail was on the ship."

"Aha!" Tim beams triumphantly and taps the cover of Alun Gwynne's *Collected Works*. "That's what the poem is. It's not surprising it doesn't make sense – it's written in code! I'm sure we just have to look and we'll find all sorts in there. It will probably take some time and effort, but if..."

"You mean like *The treasure never eyesight got*?"

"What's that?"

"Look, it's in here somewhere." Alun picks up the book and scans the long poem. "Here it is. *What by your measure is the heaven of desire, The treasure never eyesight got, nor was ever guessed what for the hearing?* You could say that's a clue, couldn't you?"

"You could indeed. Now you're talking!"

Tim gazes on the old boy with new-found respect.

Alun Gwynne narrows his eyes and scratches Macca's head for him, which he often tends to do when he's thinking hard.

"I can see all this might be a bit of a laugh, landlord, and I like a laugh. But tell me again, what's the point of it, precisely?"

"Well, it could, you know, put us on the map. Not that we're not on the map already, but more so. So that we get lots of visitors like that guy at the beginning of the week, not just stopping for a pint and a quick cheese sandwich, but coming here properly, looking for treasure, kind of immersing themselves in the whole place."

"To the great benefit of any publican, for example, who happens to have premises in the valley?"

Tim swallows, suddenly uncertain how this is going to go down.

But Alun Gwynne explodes into a nasal giggle.

"Good on you, landlord. It's nonsense, but it's valiant nonsense."

He picks up his beer glass and looks surprised to find it's empty.

"Let me top you up, Alun. Half, is it? On the house," says Tim, taking the hint.

"That's very good of you landlord, another pint would go down nicely." He's still frowning hard, but it's much less discouraging now. "So, as I see it, you just have a few loose ends."

"Go on."

"Well, first you need to explain how our local man here in Wales is a party to the high-level secrets of the Pope."

Tim is proud that he has already thought of this.

"He's a Jesuit. The Society of Jesus, they're called. It's shadowy, full of secrets, isn't it? Bound to be. And bound to have a hotline to the Pope. No worries on that score."

"If you say so. And secondly…"

"Yes?"

"Well, if I understand it with The Puccini Connection…"

"*The Poussin*… Oh never mind."

"If I understand it with that one, weren't people looking for the Holy Grail itself?"

"Yes, and the idea is that it's not actually treasure, like people always thought, but the tomb of Christ."

"So if they wanted to do that with your story, they'd want to start diving for it wherever this boat went down. England somewhere, was it?"

Oh bollocks, thinks Tim, because the guy is right. This whole thing is going to need more thinking through.

"And thirdly, how are you going to tell the world about it? You can't just do it yourself on the internet. No offence, landlord, but no one will pay you any attention. Don't you need someone to help you?"

Bremen, 1875

After completing their own Catholic prayers in the privacy of their quarters, Henrica and her party arrived on deck in time to see the crowd on the quayside waving handkerchiefs and throwing hats. The whole population of the ship seemed to be here, shouting or waving back: in the bow, artisans with caps pulled down low against the cold, their wives cradling squalling babies; a few smarter-dressed travellers amidships; and in the stern, beyond a forbidding white line, a small group of elegant gentlemen in silk top hats and fur-trimmed collars and ladies in coats in the brightest reds, mauves and greens.

The five of them found their own place below the funnel to look back at the country they were leaving. Beside them, a white-haired gentleman with mutton-chop whiskers stood silent alongside his wife, neither of them waving. They are like us, with no one here for them, thought Henrica. They had had their leave-taking already, with Mother Clara surprising them by kissing them all, one by one, on the doorstep of the cloister. How far away their little town of Salzkotten now seemed! But there must be no looking back, only forward. She must set an example to poor, trembling Brigitta, and remember that the mission ahead was an important one, and their own personal fears neither here nor there.

A tug was pulling their ship out of the harbour into the river. The low, grey bank slipped by and the crowd began to disperse around the deck as their families on the quayside dwindled out of sight. But the five of them stayed at the rail, looking at the last of their native land.

"We're not moving very fast."

"If we were closer to the shore it would look faster."

"Perhaps."

The tug was heading back to the harbour, but their progress really did seem painstakingly slow. Half an hour passed and they could still see the port they had left behind.

"We've stopped," complained a voice further along the rail, to general laughter and rubbishing.

"No, he's right. We have stopped! Look at the water. You can't see any wash."

Gradually the same conversation travelled along the deck as puzzled men peered and shrugged and relayed to their wives the indisputable truth that they were no longer moving.

A capped figure with brocade cuffs who had been addressing the select group in the stern was making his way forward. It appeared to be the captain himself. He gave a crisp bow of the head as he approached them.

"This is a simple precaution, ladies. We have decided to anchor for a short time to allow the weather to clear ahead of us."

Henrica felt Brigitta stiffen beside her, and Aurea caught her breath audibly.

"Weather? But it seems so fine here."

"We have reports of squalls out at sea, so we are simply letting them blow out. There's nothing to worry about."

"But … if the weather is bad, would it not be better to turn back?"

"Brigitta! The Captain has told us there is nothing to worry about."

"But he said…"

"Brigitta please, remember yourself!"

The captain delicately released himself from their companion's grip.

"Everything will be quite in order, dear lady, I assure you. We'll have a fine passage. Now if you'll excuse me…"

He bowed for a third time and removed himself before Brigitta could pull him back.

"What were you thinking?" Henrica hissed. After three days of trying to understand and sympathise with Brigitta's constant state of terror, fury had now taken over at this display of faint-heartedness in front of the captain.

"I don't want to go! I never wanted to," the other woman wailed. "Once we had left port I thought it was too late. But perhaps this is a sign, and it's our opportunity to turn round…"

"We none of us wanted to come. But you know how difficult everything has become. We can't teach, we can't nurse the sick, the bishop is in prison. None of us wants that, but there is nothing we can do about it. It is God's will that we do his work wherever we are able, and if that means going to a different country, then that's what we must do. Anything else is vanity. And if we do his will, he will protect us. You must believe that. Do try and stop crying. Come on, let's go back down."

Her anger abating, Henrica offered to sit with her distressed companion in her cabin. But Brigitta said she wanted to lie down and it was a relief to hand the unhappy creature into Barbara's care. Sitting on the rude bench in her own cabin, she pulled her wimple over her head and removed the pins from her over-veil, then took off her under-veil and undid the band so that her coif could come off. Some women took the rush as blood surged back to their head as an ecstatic gift from God. Henrica was wise enough to know that, if this was so, it was only because God had forced them into such an uncomfortable garment in the first place. But she was not above enjoying the sensation.

"It's so much more peaceful without the engines," said Aurea, following her lead.

It was true. Since they had stopped, the mechanical hum had cut out. Henrica had not noticed it before, but now that she did, the unmuffled silence was all the sweeter. She closed her eyes and allowed herself to enjoy the peace.

Dusk was falling when the engines finally started up again, coughing and clanking back to life.

"We're moving," confirmed Aurea at the porthole. "I can see from the wash. We must be at sea. I can't see the bank any longer. Come and look."

Henrica got up from her berth. Close confinement was making her almost as restive as her cabin-mate.

"It's mist. Look, you can't see the sea either."

"How will they know which way to go? We may hit

50

rocks."

Henrica thought of the *Schiller*, wrecked just a few months ago somewhere off England, then put it out of her mind.

"There are no rocks on this coast. It's all sand."

"Are you sure?"

She wasn't, but she was not going to admit that to Aurea.

They sat together and read from their breviaries.

An hour later, when it was quite dark, the stewardess knocked.

"Here, Aurea, help me with my veil. Is my band in place?"

"No, come here. There. Now it is."

Henrica opened the door a slit.

"Good evening, madam. Just to let you know that dinner will served at six o'clock."

The dining saloon, on the deck below their own, was a great improvement on their cabins. It had columns painted to look like marble, and the walls were hung with maritime paintings. There were six long tables, only two of which were laid. Frau Pitzhold and Fräulein Forster were already sitting down. The younger woman was wearing her hair up, emphasising her equine profile. She smiled at them nervously. Frau Pitzhold, with a severe pearl choker at the neck, gave a barely perceptible nod. The gentlemen stood up, and Henrica nodded acknowledgement on all their behalf, already feeling the strain of this social encounter. They were to spend two weeks in the company of these people. If only the five of them could dine alone.

On their table was a gentleman in formal dinner attire, who introduced himself as Hamm, and his wife; their children had taken their supper earlier. They were returning to their home in Texas, where Herr Hamm dealt in horses. Henrica learned this from hearing him tell it to his neighbour, a gangling Swede called Lundgren who kept mopping his brow, although the warmth from the saloon's burners was meagre.

Henrica watched Frau Hamm across the table and wondered if she or one of the other women might help them with language lessons on the voyage. If the five of them were to be of any use to the outpost of their order in America, they must master the tongue. Henrica had been trying to study a grammar these past weeks, ever since Mother Clara had told her of her plans for them, and her intention had been to revise a chapter in advance and run a daily class for her companions. But as she listened to the confident chatter around her, with English words dropped casually into every German sentence by these worldly expatriates, her faith in her own abilities faltered. If one of these ladies who had already mastered the language was prepared to help them, it might be much easier. But it was too early to ask now. She would wait to see who was friendly and who was not.

An elderly gentleman got up from the other table and stooped to speak discreetly to Hamm. Henrica recognised him: it was the man with mutton-chop whiskers whom they had stood beside as the ship left the quay. She saw both men now glancing at her, and all her nervousness about their conspicuousness in their headgear, the new

Prussian hostility to their religion and their calling, came flooding back. She looked down, staring hard at her plate and yearning even harder for the privacy of their cabin. Of course none of these women would help with the language. They were far too hostile – and how could it be otherwise, with the present climate of distrust in the country? She risked another glance. The whiskered gentleman was still looking at her and now he addressed her directly.

"Dear lady?" he coughed.

She felt the blood rushing to her head.

"Sir?"

"Would it be…? I hope it would not be a presumption if…?"

Did they want them to move tables? To dine in their cabins? A few moments ago that was what Henrica had wanted too, but that was when it was her own choice…

"…if we asked you to say grace for us?"

She almost laughed out loud with relief. How absurd she was to jump to such pessimistic conclusions. That was the way Brigitta behaved, terrified of everything, whereas she was the leader and she ought to know that the world was not so bad. She bowed her head to cover her smile, as the two tables fell silent and the diners lowered their own heads. She looked up again to survey them all as she started to say the words. Only Frau Pitzhold seemed resistant. Henrica wondered if the old lady clenched her face like that because of some kind of infirmity, or as a sign of silent fury.

Sleep came surprisingly easily. Herr Hamm had told Henrica they were still in the estuary, where the water was relatively calm, and the gentle rocking of her berth was not unpleasant. Perhaps the voyage might not turn out to be as bad after all.

By morning, however, the motion had dramatically increased. They woke to find that it was difficult to stand without holding onto something. Just climbing out of her berth was hazardous for Aurea, up in the top one.

"It didn't pitch so much yesterday."

"See if the fog has gone."

It had. The banks of the estuary were clearly visible now. But the water was swelling and tossing, and the sky was dark with clouds scudding across it in the gale that had blown the mist away.

By eight o'clock the sea was rougher still. Brigitta was deathly pale and only Aurea wanted breakfast. Henrica went with her to the dining saloon so that she would not be left alone, and found the party much depleted. There was no sign of the Hamms, and Frau Pitzhold was also ailing in her cabin. The stewards swayed and danced as they conveyed dishes from the galley, and the coffee spilled over the sides of the cups.

Throughout the morning the seas mounted. Brigitta succumbed, and could be heard through the plank wall retching miserably into a bowl. Not even Aurea could face lunch.

Marta knocked in the early afternoon, to offer flasks of water, fruit from the table and assurance that such gales were normal in December.

"But you're unlucky to have it on your first day at sea. I'm afraid it's because the North Sea is so shallow. It makes the seas rougher. Once this is past, the worst will be over and the rest of the Atlantic will seem calm."

After they had prayed, Henrica knew that she must take some fresh air. Aurea offered to join her, and she was grateful for the assistance as they zigzagged through the deserted saloon, grabbing a handrail here and a column there as the motion of the ship forced them into its staggering rhythm. The companion-way up to the deck now seemed a mountainous assault – the kind of mountain that tossed angrily around.

As soon as they stepped out of the little deck-hut at the top, the wind gathered their heavy skirts and veils and Henrica's scapular flapped up almost into her face. She clutched the foremast with one hand while trying to hold the garment down with the other.

"It's not safe, ladies!" shouted a seaman, woollen hat pulled down low over his weathered face. "You must stay in your cabins when the sea's so high."

"I know, but I must have some air, otherwise…"

Henrica felt the hot bubble rise in her chest. She tried to gulp it back with a draught of cold air, but it was no good. She put her head over the rail, grateful that Aurea spared her shame by looking the other way. The convulsion was shocking in its intensity, and the taste of stomach acid in her mouth and nose was disgusting. The wind caught the foul stuff and carried it off into the churning spray below. Henrica pulled a handkerchief from her sleeve and wiped her mouth, then tried to find a clean side of the linen to mop her brow. Even though it was cold, she was damp with sweat.

She was weak from the forced exertion but at least the nausea had eased. With the urgency of getting to the rail now gone, she saw the seas properly for what they were. Gripping a stay in one hand, she stared in awe at the rolling peaks and troughs that bucked the ship along. If they were within reach of any land, it was nowhere to be seen. The thick grey sky was heavy with snow, and she brushed a sopping flake from her face. This craft that had seemed so large in port was now dwarfed by the watery vastness. Feeling tinier than she ever had, she was grateful that they had God's protection. But she hoped it did not show a lack of faith to be afraid.

Conditions were no better by nightfall. None of them had any inclination to leave the safety of the cabin, and they learned from Marta that both their own and the first-class dining saloon were deserted for dinner. Henrica considered starting an introductory English class as a distraction, but she had no more heart for it than the rest of them. Apart from when they knelt to pray, they took refuge under their bedding, hoping that sleep would provide a release and the storm would be gone when they woke.

Even that small respite was long in coming. The rocking-horse dipping and the creaking of the hull were a far cry from the soothing motion of the previous night, a constant reminder of their vulnerability on the raging sea. She could hear Brigitta groaning and whimpering through the cabin partition. When sleep did arrive, it was a turbulent rest, the movement of the ship and the worry of the passage permeating all their dreams.

Henrica consoled herself with Marta's assurance that the rest of the voyage would seem calm once the storm abated. In a week's time they would be seasoned sailors, looking back on this night and making light of their early terrors.

In the meantime, God would watch over them.

HOLLAND, THE PRESENT

Adjusting her balance to the rhythmic roll of the ship, Chloe Benson climbs a carpeted flight of stairs to the highest level that passengers are allowed to access and heads towards what she hopes is the front of the vessel. As far as the rest of her group are concerned, she has peeled away in search of a toilet and then to get some air on deck, but it's breezy out there and she has no desire to set foot outside. Instead, she is looking for a quiet corner where she can get away from the others and have some long-overdue time to herself. Not that she has anything against any of them. She likes them all, as she generally likes most people, and it really hasn't been a bad weekend as far as these things go. But there's a limit to how full-on Chloe can be.

It is quieter already up here, because there isn't a bar on this level. There are some kids running up and down, and several rows where people have nabbed two or three seats apiece so that they can sleep outstretched. But there are no large, conspicuously drunk groups, which makes a change both from the lower deck and her own experience of the past couple of days. And there, right up at the front, she can see just what she's looking for: a secluded empty seat in the furthest corner, where she can be anti-social for an hour and no one will even miss her.

She has spent the last two days on a hen weekend in Amsterdam. Helen, the bride, was Chloe's best friend in their last year at uni on the south coast and, partly by virtue of their both ending up in Manchester, they have kept in touch throughout the decade or so since. Helen has always had a terror of flying, which for most people would have made a day or two of pampering at a spa in Knutsford or Wilmslow the natural option. But Helen has never done anything by halves, and is particularly unwilling to be outdone by her groom, who has gone on a boys' weekend somewhere in the Baltics. So, on the Friday, they all take a day off work and drive in a minivan bedecked with pink ribbons and balloons to Harwich, then catch the ferry to the Hook of Holland, and on by road to Amsterdam.

It is a novelty on the way over not to have to spend hours waiting around in an airport, and travelling the journey mile by mile without the magic of aviation makes getting there feel like a genuine achievement. Since then, they have been on a vodka cruise of the canals, clattered shrieking around the Leidseplein, cackled at strippers in a gay bar and screeched laughing at Helen trying to grab her own pole and join in (not something Chloe could ever condone in her day job as a health and safety inspector) after one too many hash cookies. There has been some pampering the next day at a Turkish sauna, where Chloe has only just managed to avoid getting herself vajazzled along with bride and bridesmaids, followed by more raucousness involving tequila shots. Save for the vajazzle, Chloe has played her part to the full, dancing, cheering, laughing and whooping whenever required, and she has genuinely enjoyed it.

Half the group are new to her, but she has got on with everyone, even if she's not sure she wants what they all seem to want. Helen, in particular, is clearly letting off a last burst of steam with furious abandon as a prelude to settling with equal determination into family life with Steve, who works in IT at the same big accountancy firm as her. Having flitted from job to job and man to man in her twenties, Helen has her thirties meticulously planned – kids, schools, house-moves – in a way that Chloe could never imagine herself doing. Steve, by all accounts, is a solid, decent bloke who is nice to children and animals, can bake lemon drizzle cakes as well as strip down an engine, and also finds time to keep himself impressively buff (they have all seen the pictures on Facebook) at the gym. Chloe is genuinely pleased for them both and is looking forward to the wedding. But she is equally clear that their kind of manicured marital life isn't for her. The one thing she has learned from the three significant relationships she has had in her adult life – two decent but unfulfilling, one scarily tempestuous – is that she is drawn to misfits, to people who stand outside convention in some way. The only question is whether she falls for another bastard misfit who will make her life a misery (like number three) or whether she will finally latch onto someone who is both decent and exciting.

For the moment, however, she is exhausted. This return journey in a thrumming, swaying vessel is the last thing she needs after all that tequila, and she would give anything for the relative comfort of Schiphol and Ryanair. But her refuge in the upper bows does at least give her the chance to escape into the kind of luxurious pampering she most adores. Settling in her seat, she rummages in her rucksack and pulls out the volume of poetry that seems all the more appropriate for the journey, because of the North Sea connection, and which she hasn't had a chance to open until now.

As she opens it and begins to read, she feels a warming thrill more profound than anything on offer in the Turkish sauna.

North Wales, the present

There is a storm in the night, with the wind and rain rattling the windows of the Red Lion in their frames. Tim is fully expecting to find slates torn off the roof and puddles on the floor of the bar when he gets up in the morning. But the sun is out again and, aside from the brimming water butt next to the back door, there is no trace of the night's weather. From the kitchen window, he can see all the way down the valley to the coast. Some days, this is a view to slit your wrists to, little more than a low stack of grey lateral bands representing sky, sea, hill and vale, more or less blurred depending on whether it's raining or merely about to do so. But this isn't one of those days. The sea is an improbable shade of blue, the sun is bouncing off the tower of the stumpy little cathedral in the novelty city (pop. 3,500) that passes for the local metropolis, and he is almost glad he came here. Emphasis on the 'almost' – let's not get carried away.

Still thinking about Alun Gwynne's loose ends – so much more annoying when he knows the old boy is right – he goes for a stroll to see if he can get his scheme any clearer in his head. He takes the road up the spur of the hill behind the pub. There are dog-roses in the hedgerows and meadow pipits flitting between the trees. He can see himself getting to like the place, especially if he ever becomes solvent. That strengthens his resolve to make this off-the-wall idea work. It would be genius if he could bring it off, so there has to be a way.

He casts his mind back once more to that disastrous French holiday. He recalls that Nadine had a guide-book, as well as the preposterous thriller. It was the focus of one of their many arguments that week, with Tim quoting extensively from it to back up his contention that there was nothing too stupid for Grail-hunting conspiracy theorists to believe. After they came home, it ended up on Nadine's dressing-table shelf, where its spine was the first thing he saw when he woke up every morning. That was until they stopped sharing a bed, in a sequence of events that Tim still finds painful to contemplate. With an effort he pulls himself out of that memory wormhole, forcing his attention back to the guide-book. If he had it in front of him now, it would tell him that the Grail Trailers are not *just* interested in one particular village in the Dordogne. It is certainly the highest-value location in the gullibility Top Trumps, but the disciples of the creed are also encouraged to visit Poussin's birthplace in Normandy and the crumbling studio in Rome where the painter is meant to have worked on the canvas that contained all the clues, and where enthusiasts can view the pentagrams and other geometrical giveaways carved into the stone walls.

This is the obvious answer to Alun Gwynne's point about diving the wreck. The visitors who will make Tim rich are tourists, not treasure-hunters, and they simply need to be pointed in the direction of the compulsory sights. For Tim, the task is to think what their poet might have carved into the walls of his room, what telltale graffiti he might have etched on the back of a chapel pew. There must be something – and if there isn't, it cannot be beyond a mildly dishonest imagination to make it look like there is.

But he is getting ahead of himself. The far bigger question is how he is going to transform this crazy fantasy nonsense in his own head into the kind of crazy fantasy nonsense that lots of people believe – or are sufficiently interested in to come and check the place out for themselves.

The lane curves away to the south now, over the brow of the hill, but there's a fingerpost on the bend indicating a footpath in the other direction, down towards the sea. Tim climbs over a stile that has seen better days and strikes out across a field where cows, sheep, hens, a few crows and an old JCB are calmly sharing the same pasture. On the other side of the field is a copse which he is almost certain marks the boundary of the big old house, the "seminal college" which was home to their man nearly a century and a half ago.

He would like to see the place for himself. Having a proper sense of what it looks like will surely fire that imagination and give him some more definite ideas. But when he gets to the end of the field, the path goes around to the right to skirt the copse. After a few yards, there's a smaller path going into the trees. He follows it for a while, but it soon peters out into thick undergrowth and, as holly branches twang in his face, he realises that he isn't going to get any view of the place this way. He retraces his steps to the main path and then strikes off away from it, up through the field, in the hope that he can look down on the college from above. But it's the kind of hill with fake horizons where he can never get high enough, and when he does, he has somehow got on the wrong side of the crest and can't see the house from there either. Footsore but determined, he goes back across the field in what he imagines is the direction of the lower lane that serves the house itself, scrambling over a wall and snagging his jacket on a barbed wire fence to reach it. Completing a full circle around the hidden place, he makes his way up the narrow lane, past a private property sign and into the drive of the college, where he gets as far as a gatehouse cottage and some outbuildings. He can just about see the grey corner of the house itself, with a row of narrow Gothic-arch windows beneath a slate roof, angular gables and a cluster of towering chimneys.

A figure appears in the gatehouse door.

"Can I help you?"

It's an old man in a flat cap, a more gnarled and hostile version of Alun Gwynne, with the same high intonation that makes him sound like most of his voice is coming down his nose.

"Hello there. I was looking for the footpath. Have I missed it?"

"There's no right of way here. This is a private road. You'll have to go back down to the lane and up to the right to find a footpath, if that's the one you mean," says the gatekeeper.

"Really?" says Tim. "To be honest I was just hoping for a glimpse of the house. I couldn't just…?"

This is where the old man will take a shine to the charming young Englishman, young*ish*, and invite him to have a look around, maybe even bring him into his lodge afterwards for a cup of tea and some authentic yarns.

But the man hasn't read that script.

"There's no right of way here," he repeats. "You'll have to go back down to the lane. There's a footpath down there."

Tim holds his gaze for a second, giving what he imagines are puppy eyes. But it's clear the old boy is not about to relent.

"Right then, yes. Not to worry," he says. "Thank you. Thanks very much."

Is his foreignness in Wales turning him into the most clichéd Englishman, profusely grateful in circumstances that don't merit it? But he also wants to emphasise that he has no ulterior purpose, and that he will be just as happy taking a pleasant stroll on the lower footpath.

In reality, nothing could be further from the truth. He is determined now. He has to find a way of seeing inside the place.

On his way back he finds himself wondering what Barry Brook would do. Inasmuch as Tim has ever thought about the author of *The Poussin Conundrum*, it has always been with loathing. As the peddler of hokum to gullible creatures like Nadine, Brook is personally responsible, in Tim's view, for some of the worst episodes in his marriage. Now, however, the situation is different. Tim is trying to peddle even more cynical hokum than anything Brook has managed, so perhaps it's time he thought of him in a fresh light. Oughtn't he to be Tim's role model? It's a depressing thought. Is this how far he has sunk? But the truth is that he and Brook are on the same side now.

Then it hits him. It's so obvious, he can't think why the idea hasn't occurred to him before. Brook has millions of eager, gullible readers who must be desperate for another instalment of Grail nonsense, yet in ten years or so the author himself hasn't produced anything. Rather than trying to emulate Brook, Tim should be roping him into his scheme. Brook can then construct the story – which, let's face it, he will do much better than Tim could – and pass it on to his massive, expectant audience all over the world. If Tim can only persuade him, he will be in business.

How do you contact celebrity authors? Tim has a vague notion that this once used to be done via literary agents or publishers, but there must be an easier way in this day and age. When he gets home, he boots up his laptop and does a quick search for an author site. There is one, complete with a contact form, but it looks impersonal and the site is probably maintained in a publisher's office, or by some fan club, and Tim wants his message to reach Brook directly, not relayed via a third party. Then he remembers Twitter. Isn't that the kind of place where even the richest and most famous people run their own accounts?

He himself has a moribund account that he once thought might help promote the Red Lion. He logs into it – thinking that he really ought to change his password-for-everything, which is still N8dine – and does a quick search for Barry Brook. Sure enough, the guy is on there too, clearly never passing up an opportunity to market himself. By the personal tone of some of the replies, it looks like it really is him.

Tim's Red Lion account isn't suitable for making contact. If he is serious about convincing readers of pulp thrillers that there is something special about his valley, he can't risk anything that would source the story back to him. So he needs a nice, new, anonymous account, and it also needs to have an attention-grabbing name. Coming up with one proves easier said than done, and for a while he is stumped, staring out of the window and looking for inspiration in the sheep pasture. The name needs to say 'conspiracy' while also making it clear that he's not a nutter – with maybe a hint of Victorian poetry thrown in. He sighs, doodles for a bit, stares out of the window again and is wondering if this is just a form of procrastination, when it suddenly comes to him and makes him laugh out loud. He carries on chuckling as he registers the new name. Now, identified only as @Wreckileaks, he is ready to go.

For starters, he follows Brook. It looks weird that he is only following one person, but if the guy notices, maybe it will make him feel special. Then, rubbing his hands for inspiration, he returns his two index fingers to the keyboard.

He is not used to writing in the 140-character format and it's a shock how quickly he runs out of space. He also wants to make the tone as arresting as the name of his account, for which he reckons a degree of abruptness may be required, just to make sure the writer sits up and takes notice. And he needs to work out whether he wants Brook to believe his story, or just to come into cahoots with him. That's difficult when he doesn't know how the guy thinks. Is he as gullible as his readers, or as cynical as Tim is becoming?

After several attempts, and a lot of pruning to get rid of surplus words, he finally ends up with:

@barrybrook if you want to know the real secrets of the Vatican you cynical bastard think shipwrecks not geometry. Interested? More soon.

With that wording, he reckons he is acknowledging that the guy doesn't actually believe in the nonsense he expects his readers to buy into. But by suggesting that the Vatican does have real secrets, he is planting the idea that there is a mysterious truth out there and the Holy Grail project as a whole isn't entirely nonsense. That way he hopes he is covering both bases and he can reel in either cynical Barry or credulous Barry.

But who knows? He is running on guesswork. He stares at the screen for a few more minutes, then hits send.

And now it's a matter of just waiting. He doesn't know much about the etiquette of Twitter, and he has no idea how likely he is to get a reply. He does notice from Brook's account that the guy tends to reply quite a lot to tweets from readers, even hostile ones.

At first he checks back every couple of hours, but then he remembers there's a time difference and he mustn't be too impatient. He forces himself to stay away and lets a day go by, and then another, without logging on. Before he knows it, he has developed a phobia of doing so. He tells himself he has been far too rude and aggressive in his approach, and Brook is bound not to reply. Why would he? He wonders if he should delete the original tweet and send a politer version. He's not even sure if you can delete.

He finally logs on to check whether he can do that or not, and he has done such a good job of talking his own expectations downwards that he is astonished to find he has ten notifications. Barry Brook has followed him back – prompting a flurry of other random accounts to do the same – and has also sent him a direct message.

@wreckileaks, tell me more it says. The message includes a private email address.

Tim does a little jig around the kitchen. This really could happen.

He has to think about opening up the pub soon, but he also needs to plan what he's going to say, now that he has the luxury of as many characters as he wants in a proper email message.

"There's no need to rush into it, landlord," says Alun Gwynne when Tim tells him the good news. "If the chap is interested, he'll wait. Take your time over what you say to him, that's my advice."

Tim decides the old boy is right, and he needs to get this right.

The first task, he resolves, is to buy a copy of *The Poussin Conundrum*. It will nearly kill him to do it, but it's the pragmatic option, because it will give him a clearer idea of who he is dealing with. He discovers that they have it in stock in the tiny bookshop in town – of course they do – and he spends every spare moment in the next couple of days skimming through it. At first it triggers another bout of Nadine Rage – had he really planned to spend the rest of his life with someone who thought *this* was a work of genius? – but by the end it starts to draw him in, which makes him even angrier. He finishes reading it at three in the morning, hating himself for not being able to put it down.

At least he now has a decent idea of what will float the conspiratorial boat. Geometry, maps and numbers – especially the kind that can be dressed up as code – are The Holy Trinity of the Gospel According to Barry. And that brings him back to the place where he started. It's no use just asserting vaguely that the poem looks as if it might be written in code: he needs to come up with some kind of plausible demonstration of how it might be.

Alun Gwynne referred to it as cryptic, like a puzzle. That makes Tim think of crosswords, which he has always been hopeless at. He is vaguely aware that they are based on conventions which are a mystery to the uninitiated but obvious to anyone who does them all the time. That sounds far too crackable for present purposes. He needs instead to show that the words of the poem could be a kind of cipher. It could be a simple letter substitution, but he's not sure anyone would be convinced of that: these words of the poet's may be hard to understand, but they do at least look like proper words and sentences, which a cipher wouldn't. One thing he does know about poetry is that the number of syllables is important. A youthful phase of composing comedy haikus taught him that, and he has learned from his nocturnal research that one of the ways the poet offended Victorian convention was the wild variation in the lengths of each line – which in poetry terms means the number of beats.

Acting on this whim he gets out his *Collected Works*, which now falls obediently open at the right page, and starts counting.

There are thirty-five verses, each with eight lines, and he discovers they all have the same rhyme scheme: ABABCBCA. There the regularity runs out. The eight lines of the first verse contain 5, 7, 6, 6, 12, 11, 10 and 12 syllables, whereas in the second verse it's 4, 7, 9, 7, 11, 14, 8 and 15. It's not always clear how many syllables there are in a word: Tim has memories of having to sing Victorian hymns at school where 'power' was pronounced 'pah' and 'hour' was 'are', and he isn't sure if 'lashed' is one syllable or two. But even without those variants, it's still totally irregular. He dips at random further in; verse 31 comes out at 9, 9, 12, 9, 15, 21, 13 and 23.

This must be a nightmare for anyone trying to make sense of the poem in a literary way. But for Tim as would-be cryptologist, it is gold dust.

He opens a fresh document and starts to create a table:

1.	5 7 6 6 12 11 10 12
2.	4 6 9 7 11 14 8 15
3.	5 8 10 6 14 10 10 16
4.	4 7 9 9 16 12 8 15
5.	4 8 9 6 11 13 9 16...

It takes a while and it's a boring task, but when at last he concludes with...

31.	9 9 12 9 15 21 13 23
32.	9 8 13 12 13 11 5 14
33.	7 7 14 7 15 13 9 17

34. 7 6 9 8 12 15 10 18
35. 4 6 16 9 24 13 9 14

...he gazes with pride at the mesh of digits.

It doesn't mean a thing, of course, but it wouldn't be hard to convince the credulous that it does. It could be a simple letter substitution. At first glance, it looks like 8 is the most frequent, followed by 11 and 7, which means they would be the commonest letters: E, T and A or N. He starts to fill it in on that basis, to see if any words emerge, but then he remembers that this should be Barry Brook's job. In any case, it could be more complicated than that. Instead of letter substitutions, the numbers could be map references, or bible verses. Yes, that's more like it! You could plot each line on a graph, which might give you the profile of a hillside or the course of a path. Or what if you cut a hole in the grid for every 5 or 8 or something and overlaid it on some significant text? There's no end to the Grail-seeking fun you could have with it, no more ridiculous than half the nonsense in *The Poussin Conundrum*.

Confident in his mission now, Tim is ready to draft his approach to Brook. He opens a Gmail account in the name of Wreckileaks and creates a new message:

Hey Barry
Good call, buddy. You won't regret it.

Have you ever heard of a poem called The Wreck of the Deutschland? *Well you have now. It's your next pot of gold.*

It's about a bunch of Catholic nuns, emissaries of their order, on a mission to the New World, because everything's going tits-up in the old one. But their journey doesn't go well, and that's what the poem is all about.

The poet himself is an insider. He has no literary credentials and has never been published before. He's a member of a highly disciplined religious order, the Jesuits, where the guiding principle is obedience, and he does nothing that hasn't been cleared on high. He is asked to write a poem about the nuns. But instead of being published, it's suppressed. I've researched this myself and I can tell you his own order won't touch it in their official magazine, and it doesn't see the light of day for another forty years.

The official version is that the writing was too difficult and no one understood what he was trying to do. It's certainly heavy going, as you'll see if you've got it on your screen. But is that really why they sat on it?

You and I can see there may be a better explanation. If you're looking at it now, go to verse 26 and look at the last two lines. What by your measure is the heaven of desire, The treasure never eyesight got, nor was ever guessed what for the hearing? Treasure! Not literally – I don't think we're talking jewels and gold doubloons, because these were nuns from a poor order who had renounced worldly possessions. I think he's talking about metaphorical treasure, as in the ETERNAL SECRETS of the Vatican!

Think about it. If the Catholic Church believed it had suddenly become vulnerable in Europe, it stands to reason they would try and spirit some of their most valuable relics or documents out of the eye of the storm to the safety of America. But what if they got lost en route?

That's where our poet comes in. What if he was trying to leave a message for the world, just as Poussin was? (Brilliant *book by the way. Big fan!) It's all there for anyone who cracks the code. I reckon that's what the guy was trying to tell us when he put himself in the poem. Go back two verses, to the start of number 24.* Away in the loveable west, on a pastoral forehead of Wales, I was under a roof here. *That's where he was, and that's where I am now, just down the road from this pastoral forehead, and if you climb the next hill you can see the roof he's talking about. That's where we need to start looking, and the rest of the clues are all in the poem.*

Check out the numbers I'm sending you, which correspond to the number of syllables in each line of each verse, and tell me that's not intriguing! This is Victorian England, man, when poetry was supposed to be totally regular, so this stuff is totally crazy. They said it was off the wall, but what if there was a method in the madness that no one has ever noticed before? Bible references, that's my best guess. Word to the wise: start looking in the Book of Job – that was all about a shipwreck.

If you're looking for a subject for a sequel, trust me, it's right here, on my doorstep.

He signs it 'WL' and reads the message through. It's bloody good, even if he says so himself. The Book of Job is a particularly neat touch – for which he has to credit Alun Gwynne and his chapel background. The old boy has his uses.

He attaches his page of numbers and has just hit send when he hears a customer entering From the lack of groaning, wheezing and sniffing, it isn't Alun Gwynne. That feels like an omen. Maybe Tim's luck really is changing.

North Wales, 1875

There were times when Hopkins wished he could bring some of his old friends here, just so he could convince the doubters what a good life it was.

But it was undoubtedly an inward-looking one. The college routine of prayer, meditation, lectures, disputations and lottery-walks was designed to keep a theologian's mind empty of all but what ought to be there, namely the contemplation and understanding of God's work. Even the recreations were policed, and then there was basic housekeeping: sweeping his room with sawdust every third day, and carrying out his slops. Amid all that, *ad lib* moments were few and far between. You couldn't just go and write a letter, to his initial frustration when he first entered the Society, and to the ongoing frustration of those who cared about him in the outside world.

He barely heard a word nowadays from his old Oxford friend Bridges. When he did, the letters groused about the tardiness of his last reply or about correspondence being opened. That last part was certainly true, but it was only a formality, and it was absurd to think that the Rector actually *read* Bridges' accounts of treating patients or the health of his stepfather. Nevertheless, it got in the way. Although they had been drawn together in their student days by their shared interest in the High Church revival, named after their university as the Oxford Movement, Bridges had his mind firmly set against Rome and had taken Hopkins's conversion hard. Hopkins' decision to join the Society, against which Bridges harboured all the usual prejudices, had increased the distance between them. Naturally he had done his best to try to dispel those prejudices. But an unfortunate occasion in his early days as a novice, when Bridges had made the effort to visit him, only to be turned away because it was outside approved hours, had cemented his view that his friend was a prisoner of dangerous cultists.

The last time they had met they argued about doctrine, and the memory rankled. Perhaps it was an inevitable disappointment of adulthood that coming-of-age friendships did not last for life, however much you hoped they would.

It mattered twice over with Bridges, because a connection to him was a connection to his young cousin, Dolben. *Where are thou friend, whom I shall never see, conceiving whom I must conceive amiss?* Those lines that Hopkins himself had written years ago still came back to him, although he had burned the poem itself. *Or sunder'd from my sight in the age that is.* Had he really rhymed *is* with *amiss*? It took a particular kind of fool not to see that 'is' ended with a phonetic 'z' not an 's', and if anyone else had done it, he would've swooped on them. His only possible excuse was extreme distress at the time, after the terrible accident.

It had been hard to mourn for the boy, because Hopkins had no position. He did not even qualify as a friend, and he would have made himself ridiculous if the depth of his grief were known. He had drafted a mean little letter of condolence to Bridges, praising Dolben's beauty of character and person, but he had added that he found it difficult to feel the loss on such a fleeting acquaintance. He doubly regretted that now, both for the untruth itself and the denial, which felt like a betrayal of the boy in his grave.

But all that was long ago, in another life and another world.

Here, in the actual one, the college was abuzz with the prospect of the Sunday evening debate. Because it was close to Christmas, a light-hearted motion had been allowed, "the sooner the Welsh language dies out the better". Rickaby was to be the proposer, seconded by Splaine, and the entire college gathered before supper to listen to them. Their contributions – received with much seasonal hilarity – were full of the usual complaints that the locals spoke English perfectly well and only lapsed into their own tongue to make incomers feel excluded. Splaine got a good laugh when he produced a blackboard and started chalking up words consisting mainly of l's, w's or y's, in an attempt to justify his case that this was a nation of obdurate boors whose chief pleasure in life was baffling those who relied for communication upon the occasional vowel. But Hopkins did not like the mockery. Since Clarke and Purbrick, who were meant to be opposing the motion, were also playing to the gallery with some mean-minded sneering of their own – Purbrick contended that the facility to converse in a closed group prevented the Welsh from bothering anyone else – he raised his own hand to speak from the floor.

"I hate to bring such tedious matters as logic and fairness into play and spoil an otherwise perfect entertainment," he began, against a background of giggles and then some shushing when someone noticed the severity of his expression. "But isn't there a basic contradiction between the proposition that our Welsh cousins are a backward people and the complaint that their language is too difficult for us to grasp?"

He had made a good point and they were actually listening now.

"I am proud to consider myself half-Welsh," he continued, emboldened. Actually he had never found any Welsh ancestry, but his surname was surely a Celtic one, so he could be permitted the exaggeration for an honourable purpose.

"Mr Splaine is laughing, as if I had by that admission renounced my right to an opinion or my claim to an intelligence. But I may be the only man in the room with the qualification to speak on the language, since I have at least learned a little of it. I will not dwell on its euphony, because there is none for those who will not hear. Nor will I trouble you with the peculiarly complex grammar, which the 'simpletons' of this parish somehow manage to master from an early age. But what I hope may surprise you, if you are prepared to open your minds to it, is the richness and sophistication of the Welsh poetic tradition. For example, where we alliterate in English, we repeat the same initial letter, as in 'Rickaby's rotten reasoning'…"

He paused, waiting for his satirical barb to hit home, and was gratified by the ripple of laughter he got – with him, this time, not at him.

"...But the Welsh poet repeats an entire alliterative phrase. The effect is to bind the two halves of a line together, as in "Splaine did it splendidly", so that you are using 'spl' and 'n' and 'd' twice over. I use the phrase rhetorically, you understand, not as a commendation of Mr Splaine's arguments tonight."

More laughter.

"Another device the Welsh bards have is to divide the line into three parts, where the end of the first part rhymes with the end of the second part, while the second and third are bound together by alliteration. Thus we might say "Henry Kerr / went too far / walking", so that *Kerr* rhymes with *far*, while *went* and *walking* are linked by alliteration, and of course the last word, *walking*, would rhyme with the end of another line using the same system. When this system is repeated line after line, it produces a hypnotic effect, as if one were being swirled in a vortex of language. Let me give you one more example..."

But the attention he had won at Rickaby and Splaine's expense now ebbed, and his words seemed to be having a hypnotic effect of their own on his audience. While Kerr, the honest sea-dog without a line of verse in his soul, was frowning with the effort to follow, the rest of the theologians had either glazed over or were sniggering like first-year novices.

The debate went overwhelmingly the other way.

As the hungry theologians filed out in search of supper,

the Rector called Hopkins back.

He had only become aware that his superior was in the room towards the end of his peroration, and it had occurred to him that he was openly admitting his disobedience in continuing to learn Welsh, as well as his continuing interest in poetry. Now he braced himself for the reprimand.

But the Rector's eyes were smiling.

"That was an interesting discourse, Mr Hopkins," he said. He was an Irishman and his voice still bore the mark of his origins.

"Thank you, Father. I fear you are being kind to spare my feelings. I bored where I sought to enthuse. And the debate was roundly lost, so my advocacy is proved failed."

This was not false modesty. He was embarrassed by his headstrong performance.

"You do yourself disservice. It was a passionate advocacy."

"Please don't think I mind about these things as much as I may have given the impression."

"No, Mr Hopkins, I don't believe you mind about the Welsh language as much as you argued." The Rector used his authority gently and his scrupulous politeness was difficult to read. "But poetry, I fancy, is another matter..."

He left the suggestion hanging.

Hopkins looked at the worn carpet in search of inspiration.

The Rector was moving towards the door.

"This shipwreck in the Thames is a terrible business," he said, holding it open. "Have you been following the reports?"

"Dreadful. It has been a terrible year at sea."

It seemed like only the other week that the *Schiller* had gone down. They had all been gripped by that event too, although on that occasion it was the sheer number of casualties that had shocked them, not the fate of religious women of their own persuasion.

"God truly works in mysterious ways, but he has his reasons for everything," sighed the Rector.

"It is not for us to question his purpose, only to accept that he has one."

"Quite so, Mr Hopkins. Would that the ill-educated masses would see it that way. In these atheistic times, such tragedies, as the newspapers call them, are wont to play into the hands of the godless."

"It is therefore incumbent on us to explain…"

"Yes, Mr Hopkins, to explain! That is precisely what we must do. A short poem might be fitting, don't you think? Just a few lines, to put the present human suffering in the context of God's majesty? It's merely an idea."

And without another word, the Rector turned and strode away down the broad, low corridor, the wings of his robe flapping behind him.

North Sea, the present

Chloe cannot precisely explain why she is so discreet about her passion for the poet. Keeping quiet about it has just always come naturally. Perhaps it's because she was hopeless at English at school and she studied biochemistry at uni: she is not the kind of person who is meant to like serious literature, and deep down she has an unspoken fear of being ridiculed for daring to entertain such pretensions. Of course that doesn't stand up to any kind of scrutiny – it's years since she has seen anyone from school, and even if it weren't, it's hard to imagine any of them giving a toss what she reads – but the habit of hiding her interest away has become ingrained. It's something she has got used to keeping in a box marked private.

But the poetry is no less important to her for that. She loves the guy's work, positively adores it. She especially loves the idea that she can read the same lines over and over again and carry on finding new meanings, depths, subtleties in them. That's so different from her experience of reading a novel where, if she really likes it, she can't read it again for ages because she already knows what's going to happen, and instead she has to start searching for something fresh that she likes as much, which is often easier said than done. With the poems, the re-reading is the best part. They start off so blurred as to be totally incomprehensible, but then, as she gets to know them better, the picture comes magically into focus, like when she takes a photo on her phone using the zoom setting, or the way the view through a misted-up morning windscreen gradually clears. She is reassured that this also seems to be most people's experience of the poet. In fact, none of his work was published until long after his death because he was so far ahead of his time, and his own age was baffled by it. Knowing that has deepened her sense of affinity: she likes the idea of coming to understand someone who was generally misunderstood by everyone else. Of course she knows he is no longer viewed as baffling or unpublishable, quite the contrary. Perhaps that's another reason for keeping him private: so that she can convince herself he really is her own personal challenge.

Her capacity to memorise huge chunks of the work comes as a surprise to her, because she has never shown any other aptitude for rote learning. That reinforces the impression that she has some kind of special relationship to the poet, and reciting him by heart has become a particular pleasure. It took her months to crack the masterwork, but she got there by dint of determination and plenty of practice. She knows she probably ought to get out more, but it's more creative than binge-watching box sets, which is what most of her friends seem to do of an evening. And she at least has something to show for it – a party piece, as it were, although it's nothing of the kind because she has never been to the kind of party where she would dream of performing it.

Crossing the North Sea by ship has an unsettling

effect on her. Warm and secluded as she is in her hiding place in the upper bows, she can't resist going out on deck once she has re-read the relevant stanzas. She is well aware that this beery, boxy, ro-ro car ferry has as little in common with a nineteenth-century passenger steamship as she does with a nineteenth-century German nun. Whenever she tries to picture the nuns themselves, she sees them walking these wide carpeted corridors with their sturdy metal doorways, and it's very hard to detach herself from these surroundings. But once she steps onto the deck and gets a blast of wind and rain, she really does feel plunged into the world of the poem. It's not actually possible to lean over the side of the ship – for reasons she would thoroughly approve of with her professional hat on – but there is scarcely anyone else out here, and if she immerses herself in the weather, she can blank out most of her twenty-first century surroundings. At this remove from the waves, it's hard to judge how big they are. But staring out into the night, with just a few distant points of light from other ships, she can imagine the fear anyone might feel if the elements chose to assert themselves. She doesn't believe in God or an afterlife, but the loss of her own father to cancer nearly ten years ago has left her with a powerful sense that the memory of the dead can live on, as long as those remembering them want it to. Out here, she feels as if she can commune with everyone on that ship, including the poor passenger she had read about who survived a massive shipping disaster on the same route only a few months earlier and then found himself reliving the same experience. He was either incredibly unlucky to be shipwrecked twice in one year, or incredibly lucky to survive twice. Maybe it doesn't have to be either/or: he was both at the same time. Chloe is coming to realise that life is like that.

She shivers, and realises she has been away from the rest of her group for far too long. They are probably worrying about her. As she steps back inside through one of the big metal doorways, she has decided she owes it to the memory of those poor creatures to be a bit less secretive about her literary interest. Who knows? There may even be some like-minded souls somewhere who really would appreciate her party piece.

When she gets home, she holds to her resolution and does some googling. Sure enough, there is a fan club – it describes itself in more sober terms, but that's basically what it is – which every now and then meets up in locations relevant to the poet's life. She even discovers that the next event, just a couple of months off, isn't so far away. It's a weekend occasion, so there's no reason why she shouldn't go. She wonders who she can ask to go with her, but she rules all her friends out as fast as she can think of them. 'Dead poet' and 'lecture' are less-than-thrilling prospects for most normal people. But she still wants to go, and there's no earthly reason why she doesn't drive over there on her own. She knows North Wales from family holidays when she was a kid, and the roads have got much better since then, so she could get there in an hour and a half on a good day. And she will still be obeying her resolution even if she does go alone, because she will no longer be solitary once she gets there.

Sending off her cheque and keying the date into her calendar give her a tingle of excitement. It would not be most people's idea of adventure, but it's oddly satisfying to be following her own nose for a change, just to see where it will lead her.

NORTH WALES, THE PRESENT

It is four days since Tim sent his email to Barry Brook, and he is getting concerned that he hasn't received a reply. The guy is usually pretty prompt, so it doesn't feel right that he hasn't come back now. If he were up for the idea, surely he would want to know more and reply immediately. That means he has cooled on it. Either that, or Tim's message hasn't got through. It has got lost in the ether or gone straight to junk, or Barry just hasn't noticed it among the screeds of communications he must get. But the name Wreckileaks is eye-catching, and Barry ought to have been looking out for it. So that brings Tim back to thinking that the guy's heart isn't in it any more.

In that case he will just have to win him round.

As he thinks about that, his mind keeps returning to the phrase in the poem that he has highlighted for Barry: *under a roof here.* He thinks back to the unsmiling old gatekeeper who turned him away at the entrance. The bloke is probably only doing his job, but there's nothing like being told you're not allowed to see something to make you want to see it all the more. It's tantalising. Of course it's ridiculous for Tim to get reeled into his own inventions, but it is frustrating to have come close enough to see that roof but no further. And somehow it seems important now, as if getting inside will boost his chances of finding something to rekindle Barry Brook's interest.

This evening he has one customer, who has been nursing the same drink for the best part of an hour. Unusually, it's not Alun Gwynne, but the gloriously named Hugh Pugh, a pensioner with bloodhound bags under his eyes and the kind of beard-and-no-moustache combination that has become fashionable among the young, but which makes Hugh Pugh look like a Confederate general. After a long absence, he has rallied from illness and managed to complete the short distance from his cottage to the Red Lion – Tim could genuinely throw a stone and hit Hugh's front door – with the aid of a gleaming motability scooter, which is currently the only vehicle in the car park aside from Tim's Suzuki.

Tim tries to get Hugh to tell him everything he knows about the college. But unless the whole village is engaged in a conspiracy of silence (actually it's a thought – he makes a mental note to try it on Barry Brook), what he knows is very little.

"There must be some stories about that old place, eh?" Tim nods encouragingly.

Hugh Pugh shrugs. "It's a big house with a lot of Englishmen in it. Catholic Englishmen, from the look of them. They keep themselves to themselves, which suits me very well."

"But surely… I don't know… someone from the village works there, or delivers the milk, or cleans the chimneys? You know, stuff like that – and they tell stories about it?"

Hugh Pugh takes a long swig of his beer – perhaps he'll even order another one – and wipes his mouth on the back of his hand. His brow is furrowed with a frown of deep thought.

"Well, yes, I suppose they do," he says eventually. "Griff Wynne from over the hill delivers their milk, I imagine. But he delivers mine too. Has done for thirty years. And I don't imagine he has many stories to tell about me. Or am I missing something?"

Tim shakes his head and admits sadly that no, he probably isn't.

If this were a proper, thriving pub in a proper, thriving village, there would be some customer who knew the college well, with a sister who did the laundry or a nephew who mended the boiler, and who (crucially) would understand the concept of gossip. But if it were a proper, thriving pub in a proper, thriving village, Tim wouldn't have to invent a crackbrained scheme to entice a writer of pulp thriller trash over from America just to keep his business going. As if to prove the point, Hugh Pugh downs the rest of his drink and lowers himself laboriously off his stool.

"Time to call it a night, I think, landlord."

It's all of eight-thirty.

"Right you are, Hugh. Mind how you go."

When Alun Gwynne eventually shows up, he isn't much help either.

"The Roman Catholics have always kept themselves to themselves," he says, "and everyone in the village is either chapel or English. No offence meant, landlord."

"None taken."

"So there's not a lot of crossover, as you might call it. I can ask around for you if you like, but I'm not hopeful. Nobody is very interested in them, you see."

Tim did see, but it was maddening. How could people not be interested in a mysterious all-male society of outsiders who had been living among them, with their weird clothes and weirder haircuts, for a century and a half? At least he imagined they had weird clothes and weird haircuts. The truth was, he had never knowingly clapped eyes on one of these outsiders either. To Tim, that heightened the mystique; to Alun and Hugh, not so much, clearly.

"There is one thing you could try though, landlord," says Alun Gwynne, draining his pint glass and nudging it with subtle but definite intent across the bar.

"Let me get this one for you, Alun. Half, is it?"

"That's very good of you, landlord. I think I'll have a pint, if you don't mind."

"Not at all," smiled Tim through gritted teeth. "So what's the other thing I should try?"

"Well, have you thought of looking the place up on the internet? You can find all sorts on there, you know."

It's true – amid all that research, he hasn't actually googled the place. If he weren't wasting his life trying to make chirpy conversation with two of the most depressing old men in North Wales, he might have had a chance to do so. But he can never remember the name of the college, so he doesn't quite know what to search for. Lots of l's, y's and w's and not a single vowel, like pretty much everything else in the area; that's all he knows. So he makes Alun Gwynne write it down, and when customer and mutt have eventually departed, he closes up, pours himself a generous double measure of good Scotch from a private stash of his uncle's that he has found in the cellar, and boots up his laptop.

Sure enough, the place has a website. It isn't completely shut off from the outside world: you can go on retreats there. Tim is not entirely certain what a retreat is, but from the descriptions, it's plain he would have to do a lot of Bible study, and not just the Book of Job. Tim isn't sure he's capable of masquerading as any kind of devout Christian, let alone a Catholic. There are also some pictures of the interior: the chapel, the library, a day room. It's all pretty austere and institutional, although there is a surprisingly ornate garden with formal terraces and paths climbing the hillside and views out to the Irish Sea. The site offers some of the building's history too, with a mention of their man. Nothing about hidden carvings, secret passages or mysterious underground chambers, but you can't have everything.

He checks his emails before shutting down. Joy of joys, there is actually a reply from Barry Brook.

Hey man, it says, *I have to say I'm intrigued. The story sounds a blast and I really appreciate that you brought it to me. Of course I have some questions, like, what's in it for you? What are you looking for? I can maybe offer you a modest tip fee if it comes to something, but only if it does. And it would help if you could give me more about the place itself: some atmosphere about this valley of yours, and of course anything about the building where the guy was writing. Priests' holes, secret inscriptions, geometric layouts – you know the score. I'm sure you know the place well, so give me what you've got as soon as you can. I'm listening.*

BB

Tim punches the air.

"Game on!" he says to himself, and wishes he had someone to share the moment with. He'll tell Alun Gwynne about it tomorrow, but somehow that's not quite the same.

Later, however, the email keeps him awake. It's clearer than ever that he needs that last clinching element, the piece of treasure-hunting mumbo-jumbo from inside St Vowelless's that will convince Barry it really is worth signing up to the scheme. Previously, it was just an indulgence of his own making, but now Brook himself is demanding it.

"Can I make another suggestion, landlord?" says Alun Gwynne the next afternoon.

"What's that?"

"It would make life a lot easier if you didn't insist on seeing the inside of the place in person."

"Go on."

"Well, this Holy Grail of yours. It's made up, isn't it?"

"Yes, it's made up."

"So why don't you make something up now? It's not as if you're really going to find pentagrams carved into the walls, or am I wrong? Just tell Barry Brook that you've found some fascinating detail."

"I've thought of that. But what if he comes over and wants to see it for himself? Anyway, I want to have things that visitors to the area can come and see for themselves."

"But look here. If the place is so hard to get into, you're

never going to be able to put it on your tourist trail, are you? The people that run the place will never stand for it. So you don't actually need to find anything there, you see?"

"I know, but…"

"You just want to go inside, don't you? Because you've stirred up your own curiosity for some made-up nonsense."

Alun Gwynne cackles, which leads to a lengthy coughing fit. At his feet, the slumbering Macca glances up to check his owner is all right. Once Tim has given Alun a glass of water and the spluttering has finished, the dog farts and goes back to sleep.

The old boy is right, though, both about the curiosity and the possibility of making something up. Tim is aware that he is obsessing about minor details which he ought indeed to be capable of making up. Is he really worried about Barry Brook wanting to see the evidence for himself, and about disappointing marauding Grail Trailers? Or does he simply not have the imagination to invent something? That would be ridiculous: he has got this far on the basis of a creative imagination that would put most professional con artists to shame. He can surely come up with a Gothic detail or two.

With that reassuring thought in his head, Tim goes to bed in a much more relaxed frame of mind and sleeps soundly.

The next morning, with the sun remembering it's meant to be early summer and attempting to make an appearance, he wakes up with a plan. He is going to write back to

Barry Brook and tell him he has found the words "the treasure never eyesight got" scratched inside a pentagram on one of the ornamental steps leading up the hillside terrace. Alun Gwynne is right: it doesn't matter what Tim invents, because neither Barry nor the hordes of tourists are ever going to get inside. And if that ever changes, he will just have to sneak in one night and try and carve the inscription himself. That's the virtue of putting it in the garden, rather than in one of the turret bedrooms.

He is certain this is the kind of killer detail that will ensure he has his man on the hook. Unfortunately, his laptop has other ideas. It makes the familiar chime and the screen lights up blue, but halfway through it changes its mind and goes black. Tim plugs it into the mains and hits restart, but that makes no difference, and after ten minutes of pressing, prodding and pleading, he snaps it shut.

This is doubly frustrating, because he has the exact form of words in his head that he wants to write to Barry. After another diversion searching for a working biro, he jots his message on the back of an envelope and allows himself a pause to take stock. If only he had remembered to get some coffee in, now might be a good time for a cup.

He glares out of the window, wondering why life is so determined to thwart him in everything he does. He has resolutely refused to ditch his museum-piece Nokia in favour of a smartphone, because he doesn't see why he should pay a small fortune every month just to be chained to the internet. This is one of the few times he regrets it. He has no idea where you go to get a laptop repaired in this part of the world, but in any case that could take days – even if the machine can be fixed. By that stage Barry Brook may have written him off as a time-waster.

On the other side of the valley, where the better road heads into the mountains of Snowdonia, he can make out a tour bus appearing and disappearing through an avenue of trees. It's a brutal contrast to the narrow, deserted lane on their own side, which he can just see entering the village in the cleft of its deep hedgerows. That's where Alun Gwynne lives, in a low pebbledash terrace built down from the road towards the river. He tries to remember if Alun has his own computer. It's possible – and even if he hasn't, he can surely introduce Tim to someone in the village who would let him send an email.

He grabs a waterproof from the peg behind the door – he has learned from experience not to trust a rogue hour of sunshine – and stuffs the envelope with his scrawled message in his pocket. He feels as conspicuous as ever walking through the village, feeling unseen pairs of eyes following him around. He has imagined them watching him ever since he arrived here, and at first he brushed the thought away, telling himself that this is his own townie prejudice against small places, and everyone has much better things to do than sit around spying on him. He has almost convinced himself of this when Alun Gwynne will say, "I hear you've been to the supermarket, landlord" or "Did you enjoy your walk up the hill?" – which is enough to make him barricade himself indoors. Today, as ever, there is no one in view as he strolls past the net-curtained windows with their brass ornaments on the ledge, an odd form of ostentation which can only be for the benefit of passers-by.

Alun's cottage is the last in a row of three. This small terrace is as nondescript and unpicturesque as most of the rest of the village. Tim has never visited before, and only took imperfect notice early on when he asked the old boy out of politeness where he lived. The door is around the side, through a plain wrought-iron gate. A path of slate stepping stones leads across an unkempt lawn where the remains of the spring's daffodils are drying up in sorry, wilted clumps. He is reassured he is in the right place by the large tin water bowl on the doorstep, which must be for Macca. He presses the doorbell, which chimes with horrible chirpiness.

"Can I help you?"

The woman on the doorstep is nicotine blonde, with heavy eyeliner and tight jeans. She could be seventy, but she's looking good for it. She looks as if she has lived life more than most folk in these parts and still survived to tell the tale.

"Oh, I'm sorry. I was looking for Alun Gwynne. I must have the wrong house. Is it the one at the other end?"

"No, you're in the right place. Come in a moment and I'll give him a shout. He's in the greenhouse with his dahlias."

Tim is stunned. Alun has never mentioned a wife. Or maybe he has and Tim wasn't listening. But he just assumed. The guy has lonely old bachelor written all over him.

"*Alun! Mae dy ffrind yma i dy weld di.* Landlord *y* Red

Lion."

Tim hasn't picked up much Welsh since his arrival, but the one thing he does know is that the language is spattered with random bits of English, giving you a brief window onto what is being talked about. Now he at least knows that he's not paranoid, and everyone really does know who he is.

Alun Gwynne appears in the doorway.

"Well, landlord, this is a surprise! And an honour, if I may say. I see you've met my wife. Will you have a drink?"

It's not yet eleven o'clock, which is early even by Tim's standards.

"Well that's very kind of you but…"

"Cup of tea? Or we may have some Nescafé if you prefer?"

"Oh, I see. I'm all right, thanks."

He is gasping for a coffee, having run out again. But he hasn't drunk instant for fifteen years and isn't about to start now.

He sits as bidden on the edge of a shiny leather-effect sofa and explains his mission to Alun Gwynne, who stares into mid-air for a few moments and then shakes his head.

"I don't have a computer, landlord. And I can't think of anyone here who would want, er, that's to say, who would be at home during the daytime, you see? And in the evening… well you have a pub to run, don't you?"

Tim is tempted to suggest leaving Alun Gwynne in charge, while he nips out to whichever villager will let him send the email, just to put the old bugger on the spot. He wants to force him to say what he was originally going to say before he stopped himself, that no one would want to help Tim out.

But before he has a chance, Alun says: "You could try the library in town. They have machines for the public to use, I know that for a fact."

It's an idea. And he can finally pick up some decent coffee from Morrisons while he's there. He thanks Alun for the tip and makes his way back to the Red Lion to pick up his car keys.

"I'd get a move on though," Alun calls after him. "The traffic can be murder down there at lunchtimes."

Tim must be adjusting to rural life. When he first came here, he thought it was hilarious that the large village down the valley calls itself a city, owing to the little cathedral which is also (proudly) the smallest in Wales. But now, as he joins the snarl of traffic curling through the centre and scouts for a space in the pay-and-display, it really does seem like a seething metropolis. What is happening to him?

The library is little more than a room at the back of the Tourist Information. They don't really have any books or do any of the other traditional library stuff, like telling people to shut up, but you do get fifteen minutes of free log-on time. Tim has to wait for a pair of muscular Poles in track-suits to finish using the only two computers, so he kills time running his eye over the second-hand DVD shelf, with its array of kids' films and thrillers that almost certainly never made it to actual cinemas. Above the shelf, there's a notice-board with flyers for Pilates classes, Boxercise and aquarobics, and Tim is about to turn away to see if the Poles have been timed out yet, when he glimpses a familiar-looking word semi-obscured under a notice for the Bowling Club junior league. Could it be…? He lifts the Bowling Club notice away, and yes, it really could! It's a flyer for a lecture about the poem, *his* poem, and its connection to the local landscape. But the main thing is the venue. It's in the college itself, St Vowelless's, and while it would normally be just his luck if the event turned out to be last week, it isn't, it's *next* week.

Nadine would say it's a sign that all this is meant to be and Project Barry Brook is destined for success, which of course is bollocks of the first order, just like anything else Nadine has ever uttered. But that being said, the discovery feels highly auspicious. Tim may as well go and check the place out. His email about the inscription on the staircase can be a fallback Plan B if all else fails.

Forgetting about the computers – the Poles still haven't finished – he steps out of the library to find it is drizzling. But instead of grousing, he finds himself applauding his own forethought in wearing his jacket. Is this what it is like to be a glass-half-full person? He could grow to like it. He is in such a good mood that he almost goes to buy himself a celebratory pint in the pub across the road. After all, it's nearly lunchtime. Then it occurs to him that if he is going to sit in an empty bar subsidising a beleaguered landlord's profits, it may as well be his own. In any case, he is mindful of Alun Gwynne's warning about the hellish traffic.

North Wales, 1875

The old Welshman in the gatehouse tipped his cap as Hopkins and Splaine, his companion on today's lottery walk, made their way out of the college and into the lane.

"Good morning, Ieuan," said Hopkins, shivering in the December chill and hunching himself under his muffler. His breath steamed in the air.

"Morning Father, morning Father," said the old man, once for each of them.

"What did you call him?" whispered Splaine when they were out of earshot.

"Ieuan. It's his name."

"His name is Yayan? Really? And that's Welsh? Honestly, it sounds more heathen than Christian."

"It means John. Is that Christian enough for you?"

"Good heavens! How on earth can they mangle John into Yayan?"

He was actually spluttering, Hopkins observed to himself. *Splaine spluttered.* Such linguistic serendipity could not be entirely accidental. Could it?

"No wonder they have it as their private tongue," his companion was saying. "No one else in their right mind would bother to learn it."

"*I* have bothered to learn it," countered Hopkins. "And you expect them to learn our language, and to know how to pronounce *though, through, rough, cough, thought* and *bough*. If theirs is impossible, what is ours?"

Splaine laughed.

"I should remember never to argue with you, Hopkins. You always win." He clapped him on the shoulder as they reached the valley road. "Now which way shall we go? North or south?"

Hopkins glowed in the compliment. He knew he should not take pride in it, but it was true, he was good in argument. In fact his brain felt more alive than he could remember, fizzing and frothing with phrases for his poem. As they headed south towards the village, ideas continued to search for matches in sound and tonal shape, and the serendipity of the spluttering Splaine was a mark of how well they were finding them. Now they turned east on to a farm track up the little hill behind the college. He liked to think of it as a forehead facing down the valley towards the sea, suspended in eternal contemplation. Nowadays his own brow wrinkled with the pleasant burden of creative endeavour. His companions on these walks must doubtless be puzzled to find him quieter than usual.

Sometimes it was an effort to hold onto these snatches of silent sound. It was not just that they might soar away before he could get them down, but also that there were so many of them, far too many to fit into the few lines the Rector had indicated. And at the moment, cramping them up was a cruel waste. This was all about spreading long-folded wings.

He had his first line: *On Saturday sailed from Bremen.* Happily, *America* had the exact same rhythm as *on*

Saturday. So it would be *America outward bound*, ti-tum-ti-ti-tum-ti-tum. But there was an ugly elision between those first two words, and it was in danger of sounding like *America routward*. A solution might be to turn *America* into *American*. It wasn't grammar – but if the whole thing were made into an adjective, and joined up with hyphens to show what he was doing, to become *American-outward-bound*, he could get away with it.

Of course, a rhythm like that was unsustainable. What would set this ode apart would be its willingness to engage theologically, to grapple with questions of awe-inspiring complexity, and for that purpose an altogether more sophisticated scheme was required. His trump card, he decided, would be to play with the pace of each stanza by varying the lines within it, not just a little but enormously. Those lines would steadily lengthen as the stanza became more contemplative, but they would still be bound together by a rhyme scheme that would tie the first line to the last. *Bremen*: stamen, lemon, day-men, pay men, maim in, tame in… It wouldn't be easy. But at least with lengthening the lines, the occasional imperfection would be far enough from its pair not to jar too much.

An envelope arrived on Christmas Eve in his mother's careful, sloping hand, and he was pleased to see that it was stuffed with newspaper cuttings. His pleasure waned when he saw that one of them was a duplicate, and she had omitted to send the most important article. He made time to write back immediately, asking her to check for it, because he would need the details it contained for his crescendo. There had been something about a brave sailor going down on a rope to try and save a child, or was it a woman, and the awful things that had ensued. Perhaps his memory was enough. *Handy and brave … from the rigging to save … handy and brave … pitched to his death at a blow … see him for hours … di-dah di-di-dah … swinging to and fro … and the something something, dah-di-di dah-dow …* no, that wasn't it, there must be a C rhyme as well as an A and a B … *in the burl and the swirl of the wave.* Yes, once he had the rhyme scheme as a skeleton, he could flesh out the longer lines at his leisure.

Christmas was always a time of mixed emotions. The midnight Mass was his favourite moment of the year, when he felt only pity for those who would never experience the intensity of the religious life for themselves. But on the twenty-fifth, he naturally pined a little for his family, as he was sure everyone in their little community did for theirs, only it was always the great unspoken, there being a tacit understanding that one shouldn't bring the mood down by dwelling publicly on such matters. It made him melancholy to think of all the rest of them back at Oak Hill – not quite all of them, because Arthur and Cyril were married now and Milicent was in a convent – but it would be a cheerful gathering, with a walk on the Heath after lunch and then charades or some other game. It was strange not to be a part of that, to know that he never would be again, and it didn't become any less strange as the years passed. Not that their own day at the college was entirely without jollity. There was a second glass of wine with dinner, and afterwards a spelling bee. Hopkins came within sight of winning, but was felled at the last by *allegiance* (odd – he had always put an extra *i*, as in *allies*, and but for this game he might have gone on doing it for the rest of his life). It was a maddening error, not just for the losing to Clarke; the five-shilling prize would also have done very nicely for a volume of Welsh poetry to aid the process of composition. His vow of poverty had seemed a trivial concern when he first set out on this journey: he would be fed, clothed and roofed, often in splendid surroundings, so what more could he need? He had not foreseen what it would be like not to be able to buy stamps for letters, or books. He could and did appeal to his mother, but it was like being caught in permanent childhood, all the more frustrating when he was the eldest.

There were extra full-day holidays at this season, and on the Wednesday after Christmas he took advantage of a more relaxed attitude to the normal rules and set off alone over the hill. He followed the rolling road across the countryside, which could never seem to decide quite what it was. It was almost as if Surrey had been picked up as a giant picnic blanket and thrown over a strew of unruly rocks so that it kept the pastoral aspect but took on the rugged shapes. As he descended for the last couple of miles, he admired the herds of towering pillow clouds, with one great stack knoppled all over in fine snowy tufts, until he reached the spot where the sacred spring burst from its hillside overlooking the twin estuaries.

It never ceased to amaze him that the star-shaped well in its spindle-pillared chapel, taller than it was wide, had escaped the desecration that every other Catholic shrine in these islands had suffered. They said Henry the Fifth had prayed here before Agincourt, although Hopkins was more taken with the story of Saint Winifred, who had her head cut off here when she refused the advances of the son of the local prince; the spring burst from the spot where it fell, so the legend related, and their own college was named after the uncle who later restored her to life. The first time he had come here, the place was mobbed: a few days previously a boy of eleven who had gone deaf and dumb after a fall from a crane had been restored to hearing and speaking after bathing twice in the well, and pilgrims and locals alike had been queuing at the inn above the well just to see the room where he had stayed. It was good to know that Catholicism was alive and well in England and so unafraid to express itself. But it was also nice to enjoy the place in the tranquility of winter, when he knew he would have the pool to himself.

He presented himself to Father Di Pietro, a tiny, ancient member of their own society who was in charge of the premises and had perfectly decent English when he chose to use it, but scant inclination to do so. Today was no exception. He returned Hopkins' compliments of the season, but there was barely any other conversation as he let him into the chapel, where new wooden changing cabins had been installed.

Hopkins undressed and walked three times through the bath adjoining the main spring, before moving to the outdoor pool. The lukewarm water steamed in the chill air, and he allowed it to wrap him in its comforting embrace. You were meant to kneel on the saint's stone, but it was too tempting not to wallow a little while here. Manoeuvring himself onto the lowest of the underwater steps that had been provided for the comfort of pilgrims, he sat with his chin resting on the surface of the pool and peered through the warm fog that clung to it. To think that this was purely natural, heated by the earth, not by boilers.

By and by his favourite phrase came to him. *Díng dóng béll*. It was because of where he was sitting, of course. *Pússy's ín the wéll*. Once again, he thought how odd it was that when you were a child you accepted it perfectly as verse, even though that first line broke all the laws of metrics that you were taught as soon as you were old enough. The important thing was that it worked, with no offence to the ear. Where did that leave the supposed laws? What if they were simply explanatory theories, like in the natural sciences? When you observed some phenomenon of nature that didn't fit the theory, it proved you needed a new one. Couldn't the same be true of poetry? It would be much better if *one stress made one foot*.

The delight of his discovery made him shout out loud.

"Eureka!" he cried. He had always wanted to discover something in a bath so he could use that phrase in its proper context.

Father Di Pietro looked over at him through the window of the chapel.

"It's nothing," Hopkins called happily. "I've just worked something out, that's all. Too complicated to explain."

If the little priest was disappointed not to be enlightened

further, he did a good job of hiding it.

Hopkins was too excited to care. The glory of his theory was not just that you could have one beat per foot, so that *Díng dóng béll* was perfectly good trimeter. You could also have three or four, provided only one of them was stressed. The more he thought about it, the more he liked it. *Térrible bútchery, fríghtful slaúghter* was a four-foot line (you would call it two dactyls and two trochees in the conventional scanning), but so was *Térrible bútchery, féll swoóp* (which the old scanning would insist was three feet not four).

"Ha," he said, and again louder: "Ha!"

Father Di Pietro did not even look up.

NORTH SEA, 1875

Henrica was dreaming she was on kitchen duty in Salzkotten. She was stirring a large cast-iron pot, and someone who looked very like her mother – only that couldn't be right, because her mother had died years before she entered the convent – kept adding vegetables and water. Henrica told her they had enough and the pot was going to overflow, but her mother ignored her and actually it didn't overflow, but started growing instead. It got larger with everything her mother added, and now Henrica had to climb a stepladder to stir it, begging her mother to stop, because they didn't need so much soup, and if she didn't look out the whole thing would get too big for the stove. But her mother wouldn't stop, and the range was beginning to buckle under the weight. Henrica saw it start to go and knew she had to get back out of the path of the scalding broth. She was running out of the door when the crash came, the metal screaming as if the range had ripped itself open…

"What was that?"

She was awake now, groping to remember where she was. The rocking of her berth reminded her, and now she saw the shape of Aurea's white shift as the younger woman started climbing down the ladder from the top bunk.

"Did you hear it?" whispered Aurea again.

Henrica shivered and pulled the thin blanket closer around her. A true leader was always on duty, ready to take charge, to reassure, show an example. She wished Mother Clara could see her now. See, you should never have picked me!

"Can you see anything?"

Aurea was at the porthole.

"Not a thing. It's still pitch black."

There was a knock, and the stout figure of Barbara was in their doorway, candle in hand. Her hair hung loose around her broad face and she had thrown her tunic over her nightclothes. "Are you awake? Did you hear it? What do you think it was?"

Henrica forced herself to life, swinging her legs out of the tiny bunk and reaching for her coif. Heavenly mother, it was cold. "What time is it? Light the lamp, Aurea."

"I'm trying to. My fingers won't work."

"Rub your hands to get the circulation going."

A smaller figure appeared in the doorway, pushing herself in. "I knew it! Oh, I knew it, I knew it! We should have turned back when we had the chance," wailed Brigitta, struggling into her own coif. "We should never have come."

"Hush, Brigitta, you'll wake the whole ship."

"Nobody is asleep after that noise. What was it?"

Henrica had to stop them panicking. She was frightened too and she could easily start wailing herself if Brigitta carried on like that. "Is Norberta awake?" she said, as steadily as she could.

"Here she is."

Norberta's angular face appeared, yellow in the flickering light of Barbara's candle. With Henrica and Aurea kneeling on their bunks, they all managed to squeeze inside and shut the door. Now the lamp was lit and they could all see each other properly. Henrica reached beside the hard, narrow pillow for her pocket watch, a gift from her father long ago, back in a world that didn't pitch and toss and put you in fear of your life in the middle of the night. It was five o'clock.

"It was so loud," said Aurea. She was excited as well as afraid, Henrica realised.

Barbara dropped to her knees. *"Ave Maria, gratia plena…"*

Aurea still wanted to know precisely what had happened. "It was like metal ripping," she said, peering fruitlessly again out of the porthole.

"Dominus tecum…"

"The motion isn't so bad now, though." That was Norberta, the first thing she had said.

"Benedicta tu in mulieribus et benedictus fructus ventris tui…"

It was true. The ship was swaying much less than it had been when they went to bed.

"But what about the noise?" Aurea wouldn't give it up. "Listen!"

"Sancta Maria, Mater Dei, ora pro nobis peccatoribus…"

"I can't hear anything," said Henrica. Apart from Barbara, she might have added.

"Exactly. The engines have stopped."

She hadn't noticed, but it was true. The ever-present distant roar was gone, and instead there was complete, eerie quiet.

"We should dress properly," Henrica resolved.

"What was that?"

There had been a soft bump.

"And again!"

Now came a third bump, much less soft, and the ship listed abruptly. Brigitta screamed as they grabbed one another for support – being squashed in so tight was good for that, if nothing else – and even Barbara stopped praying.

"Come on, everyone get dressed," repeated Henrica, in a tone that she hoped sounded brisk rather than panic-stricken. "Then I'll go and find out what's going on."

Before the others could go back to their own cabins, there was a knock at the door. Henrica opened it as much as she was able and found Marta. Her cap was crooked and her hair uncombed, as if she had also roused herself in a hurry.

"Good morning, ladies," she said with a cursory bob. "I'm afraid I must ask you all to put on your life-belts."

"What has happened?" demanded Brigitta.

The girl's hands were clenched tight.

"I'm sure it's nothing to worry about. The life-belts are just a precaution, but the captain has asked for it."

"O sweet Blessed Mary!"

"Try not to be alarmed, madam. Please just put on your life-belts and stay here until you hear further instructions."

"But what should we…"

"I'm sorry, madam, I really must go and tell the other passengers. I came to you first, but I do have to get round everyone as quickly as I can. I'm sure you understand."

Henrica was sure the smile had gone before the girl had properly turned away.

There came another dull metallic thump, bigger again than the other ones, making the whole boat lurch once again. Brigitta yelped, and they all clutched each other for support.

Henrica broke out of the embrace. "Come on, let's do as she says. Finish dressing and then let's put on our life-belts." She could hear the tremor in her own voice.

The other three went back to their own cabins to dress. That gave them more room to move, even if they were trying to do it on a slant, but the unwieldy belts were a further encumbrance over their thick layers. As she and Aurea struggled into them, there was a sharp report above their heads, and then another.

Aurea peered up through the porthole. "They're sending flares."

It was serious, then.

Barbara was back in the doorway, looking broader than ever in her bulky life-vest. Behind her, Henrica saw Frau Pitzhold's door open a crack, and then shut again.

She made a decision. "I'm going to leave you for a short time. Barbara is in charge. I suggest you pray."

"Marta told us not to leave the cabin!"

"We need to know what's happening. Don't worry, I'm wearing my life-belt. Get the others together now and ask for Our Lady's assistance. I fear we need it."

Frau Pitzhold's door opened again as she passed, and she saw Fräulein Forster's frightened eyes looking out at her. Henrica offered a smile of reassurance that she did not feel.

It had not been so obvious in the tiny cabin, but the empty saloon was listing alarmingly. It was difficult walking at such an angle, and harder still when the floor was jolted by another thump. It sent her tripping to the bottom side of the room, where she used the wall to steady herself. At the foot of the companion-way, she met Hamm. His topcoat was visibly soaked and he was breathing heavily.

"What's happening, Herr Hamm?"

"We must try not to be alarmed, sister. I'm sure everything will be fine. Have you seen my wife?"

His shirt was not fastened properly at the neck, and his damp hair was blown wild around his bare head.

"I haven't seen anyone. Only the stewardess and a glimpse of Fräulein Forster."

"She's still in the cabin, then. I left her trying to keep the children calm."

"What's happening?" pressed Henrica.

"I… I'm not sure. We'll have to wait for the captain to tell us. Did the girl tell you to stay in your cabin? If that's what she said, I'm sure that's what you should do."

"Not if nobody will tell me what's going on." She threw her arm forward to grab the companion-ladder.

"Don't go up, sister. It's really not safe."

"If nobody will tell me what's going on…" She was surprised to hear herself raising her voice to a man. But urgency and fear made her bolder. She knew now that she would have to assert herself if she had any chance of guiding her party to safety. "Please understand, we are five women travelling alone. In parties fortunate enough to have the protection of a man, it may be possible to spare the women the worst of the news. But we do not have that luxury, and keeping us in ignorance is not a kindness. If you know what is happening, you must tell me."

He shut his eyes for a moment, then said quietly: "We have run aground. We have lost our propeller, so we can't go back. That was the noise that woke us all up. It has sheered clean off. Those big thumps – there, like that one – are the waves hitting the side of the hull. Normally the ship would move with the impact, but now we're stuck fast. I'm afraid it means the situation is grave."

Henrica struggled to take the information in.

"But… if we are aground, what land have we hit? We've left Germany behind, surely, so where are we? Holland? Or England?"

"Neither," said Hamm. "We're on a sandbank in the middle of the Channel. The nearest is England, but it's fifty miles away. I'm sorry." He put his hand to his head to tip the hat he was not wearing. "Please excuse me, sister. I must attend to my family."

He hurried away and Henrica turned back to the stairway. Hamm had told her not to go up, and it was the last thing she wanted to do. But she needed to see for herself what was happening, even if it was only from the safety of the deckhouse. Slowly she began to haul herself up, holding her skirts away from her feet and struggling to hold onto the handrail when the ship lurched with another thump.

Pushing the door open at the top and gasping in the sudden cold, she looked out onto a chaotic scene. The deck tilted at the same alarming angle as the saloon. In the light of lamps at the base of the masts, sailors braved the incline, and the hardier of the male passengers shouted questions at them as they clung to whatever they could grip onto. There was another thump, and a wall of white water broke over the higher side of the ship that faced her, surging over the whole deck. She gasped as it swilled into the deckhouse and around her clogs. Slamming the door shut in panic, she leaned against it. She was trembling with fear and cold, but she could not go back down yet. She must find some hope, something to take back to them. Summoning all her courage, she opened the door again, slipped outside and pushed it closed behind her before the next wave could come. Away from the shelter of the doorway, the wind grabbed her veil and jerked her neck back. She caught hold of the flapping cloth, pulling it round her face for protection against what she realised was driving snow, and clutched onto a rope stay with her other hand. She fully expected to be shouted at, to be ordered back below forthwith, but in the commotion the men all had greater concerns.

On the bridge above her, she could make out the trim figure of the captain leaning forward and shouting instructions. The command was passed along the ship, gradually becoming intelligible as it came closer: "Launch the lifeboats!"

She strained to see, still gripping onto the rough rope stay, as a group of seamen in the stern surrounded one of the lifeboats in its cradle. Ropes were unfastened and the canvas top-cover was pulled off. Was it time to fetch her companions? Surely they would be told when to come up. In any case, Henrica could not imagine trusting herself to such a tiny craft, so what chance was there of persuading Brigitta? It had always sounded so gallant, letting the women and children go first, but there seemed nothing chivalrous now about men despatching the weak and defenceless into the storm. She watched as the boat was winched from its housing and lowered the short distance into the angry sea from the side of the ship that was nearer the water. One of the sailors was inside it now, then passengers were being handed in, first one, then a second, both gentlemen. One of them was holding his hands out, and Henrica now saw a small female group huddled in one of the aft companion-ways. It must be priority for first class, which was why her own party had not been summoned. Or perhaps Marta was in their cabins now, telling them to come above. But it was madness, surely, to set foot in such a flimsy vessel. The gentlemen were beckoning frantically to coax the women on, and one of them gingerly advanced. But suddenly, as Henrica watched, the boat was torn from its rope and disappeared on a ridge of white water. It happened so quickly, she could hardly believe her eyes. She saw frantic arms waving on the surf, then the tiny craft disappeared in the trough of a wave. Once again it came up, and then it was gone for good into the darkness. The last she saw was the three men aboard struggling to raise a sail.

"Launch another boat!" came a cry alongside her.

Surely not? Who in their right mind would get into a lifeboat after seeing that? But the canvas cover was already being stripped off and the second boat was raised out of its cradle and lowered towards the water. Another seaman was about to step in when a wave broke on the side of the ship behind them, and the boat was tossed away amid the froth of white water, whatever ties holding it fast snapped clean away. This time, at least, there was nobody aboard. Crossing herself, Henrica could not watch any more. Letting go of the stay, she lurched in the direction of the deckhouse. It was only a few feet away but she muttered a prayer of thanks to the Blessed Virgin as she felt the door handle in her palm and pushed herself inside.

Two women she recognised from the other table at dinner were in the saloon, sitting side by side in chairs that must be fixed to the floor, otherwise they would have slid down to the wall. They stood in alarm when they saw Henrica's bedraggled state.

"Sit down, sister," said the younger of the two, wisps of blonde hair framing an angular face. "Catch your breath."

Henrica did as she was told, consciously staving off the moment when she would have to return to her own companions. The women looked at her expectantly. What should she say? She ought not to spread alarm, but she had to tell someone what she had seen, and somehow it was easier with strangers. She started to tell them about the scene on deck, the launch of the first boat, the terrible moment when it was ripped loose, and then the loss of the second one. It was all so awful, and the captain surely couldn't expect any of the women to…

"Ulrich!"

A gentleman had appeared behind her, and the older woman sprang up and took his hands. His head was as wet as Henrica's robe.

"What's happening, Father?" the younger woman pleaded.

The man looked dazed. "There's nothing to… Everything will be all right. That's to say…"

"Come on Ulrich, don't give us that," said the older one, pulling away from him. "They want us to get in boats where we will certainly be drowned. The Reverend Mother here saw it with her own eyes."

Henrica dimly remembered a world where she might have been amused at that wild over-estimation of her status.

The gentleman put his hand to his brow. "Another t two boats were lost after that," he said slowly. "They were both empty, thank God for that at least. They've g-given up launching them. Now they are throwing cargo overboard to make the ship lighter, and they're going to raise the sails. The captain says the wind may lift us off the bank. All the men are asked to help with the pumping. I was coming to tell you, my dears, that you must wait in your c-cabin and try not to worry. They promise they will have us off here, and if they do not, help will come soon. They have sent flares."

When Henrica re-entered their little suite of cabins she had settled on what to tell the others.

"The captain has decided against putting us in the lifeboats. They are very small, and we should not have liked to get into one, so that is no loss," she said briskly, after explaining that they were aground. She related the plan to sail the ship off the sandbank. "For the moment, the best we can do is pray that it works."

To her surprise, they accepted this without fuss. Brigitta had been crying, but was at least calmer now, and Barbara seemed to have done a good job with them. Aurea was more subdued, which was no bad thing, while Norberta's expression of gloom was not so different to normal.

At nine o'clock, four hours after they had run aground, Henrica ventured outside the cabin again to join some of the other second-class passengers in the tilting saloon. She heard from the stammering man called Ulrich, whose surname was Meyer, that the captain's attempt to sail off the sandbank had driven them further onto it, so the sails had been furled. Now that it was fully light, the wind dropped further and the seas abated. It was still icy cold on deck, but Meyer said there was a friendly spirit, with gentlemen from first class rolling up their sleeves alongside labourers from steerage.

"At least t-two steamers have been sighted, which means they must have seen us t-too," he added. "Help will c-come."

"As long as it comes before nightfall," said Lundgren, pulling at his long, pale fingers. "The tide will come up again tonight, and she will not stand another battering."

"Not in f-front of the ladies, old man," Meyer muttered with a glance at his wife and daughter.

Henrica was glad the rest of her own party had chosen to stay in their cabins.

North Wales, the present

It is the day of the literary lecture. Tim has been planning to close the pub while he goes off to the college for the afternoon. It's not a good precedent, but neither will it make any difference to his takings. In the event, however, Alun Gwynne offers to help him out.

"I can keep the place open for you if you like, landlord. You can teach me how to use the pumps. As long as we don't get a rush, I'll be fine. Don't worry, I don't want paying. A free drink or two will do just as well."

Tim can't immediately think of anything obvious that could go wrong, so he goes ahead and teaches Alun how to pull a pint, makes sure the number of his Nokia is taped to the side of the bar in case of some massive emergency, and heads off on foot to St Vowelless's.

He has made such a big deal of getting inside that he is actually nervous as he walks up the drive. He is imagining another tangle with the gatekeeper, but the old man has clearly been primed that outsiders are expected this afternoon and gives Tim a nod that might almost count as friendly as he passes through the gate. Rounding a clump of ancient rhododendron bushes, he finally gets a proper look at the place.

Having seen pictures on the website, he already has a good idea what the college looks like, but he is not prepared for how forbidding it looks in real life. The tall limestone walls with their small arched windows wouldn't look out of place on a borstal, and the monotony of the stern grey face overlooking the front lawn is unbroken by any adornment or even a doorway.

The entrance is inside a central courtyard, an enclosure so resolutely colourless that it could be in the most unforgiving urban tenement, rather than on a tree-lined Welsh hillside. The door is open, and he follows a gaggle of other obvious interlopers into a long, low hall, its ceiling punctuated by broad-slung whitewashed arches. There's a whiff of polish that takes him back to his school days, all grim respectability and no outdoor shoes on the parquet. A sign on the staircase warns that the upper floors are out of bounds, which ordinarily wouldn't deter Tim. But there's also a woman in a steward's badge and tweed skirt waiting to take their entrance money and make sure he goes where he's meant to, so if he's going to nose around, he'll have to do it later.

He follows the other visitors into another whitewashed room with sombre black beams crisscrossing the ceiling. There is a low fireplace at each end and nothing on the walls. From the inside, he observes, the windows look much larger than they do from the front: each group of four arched apertures forms a larger bay. It means that there is plenty of light flooding in from the front terrace and a good view down the valley towards the sea: surprising, considering how hidden the building itself is. The room is arranged with functional plastic chairs in a double horseshoe around a speaker's lectern. There is a photocopied handout on each, and a table at the side with a tea urn and a plate of custard creams. About a dozen chairs are already occupied. The crowd consists of a pair of shrunken elderly women with sticks, two or three ruddy couples in jumpers with daypacks, and assorted single men, several of them in clerical collars. Tim is swamped by a wave of gloom as he contemplates the afternoon ahead. What possessed him to get so excited about coming here?

Everyone else is poring attentively over the handout, which seems to consist of handwritten notes entirely in block capitals on the lecture they are about to hear. To Tim, the notes are all but incomprehensible. Instead he turns his attention to the structure of the room. He looks up at the lattice of beams on the ceiling. That might be a good place for a poet doubling as a secret agent of the Illuminati, or an unscrupulous publican with a flair for invention, to locate a hidden inscription or cryptic geometric clue. Those windows, too: there is surely something mystically significant about the way the four small arches create a larger fifth one, and then are repeated in the same pattern over and over again all over the building. He could imagine counting the windows of all the rooms from the inside, then making the same count on the outside and finding they don't tally, which leads to the discovery of a secret tunnel in which can be found…

He should be doing this himself, he thinks, instead of talking Barry Brook into it. He has just as much of a flair for conspiratorial cliché. All he lacks is the publishing deal and the worldwide following of hundreds of millions of gullible fans.

One of the men in clerical collars – small, round, bald, sixtyish – has got up from the front row and is now standing behind the lectern surveying the room with a beatific beam.

"Welcome, friends, to this annual gathering, where today we celebrate the extraordinary genius of a man who lived here nearly a century and a half ago, and who within these walls composed what is now widely regarded as one of the greatest poems in the English language…"

Really? Tim sneaks a look around him and everyone else is nodding away reverentially. Perhaps it's true, and he has completely underestimated how famous his guy is. All the better for Project Grail.

"…And what I propose to focus on in the next hour or so, before I take questions and then release you for tea and biscuits…"

Most of the audience murmur polite amusement at the notion they should need releasing.

"…is its setting in the Welsh landscape, and particularly of course its Jesuit perspective. And it's with the theological aspects that I propose to begin, so if I can draw your attention to the first note on the sheet that you should have found on your chair…"

The speaker is as good as his word. The talk is very religious, very literary and thoroughly baffling. There's a lot about 'inscape' and 'instress', and everyone else is nodding away, as if they know what those words mean. For Tim, it's an effort to stay awake. He keeps sneaking a regular look at his watch, but he seems to have entered a zone where time slows to a crawl – a spooky supernatural concept for a pulp thriller writer, perhaps, but a depressing discovery for anyone having to suffer this torture in the real world. It doesn't help, with these west-facing windows, that he is sitting in a patch of warm sunlight. He stifles the third yawn in quick succession. It would be brilliant to be able to drop off now and wait this ordeal out in a nap. But he has never been able to sleep in a chair without support for his head, and these seats barely come up to the small of his back.

He glances at the people around him to see if the rest of them are as bored as he is. They all seem entranced, nodding and laughing at pleasantries that aren't by any stretch of the imagination proper jokes. A helmet-haired old lady closest to him is bent over a notepad, meticulously recording the speaker's every pearl.

That's when he sees her. She's on the right-hand side of the horseshoe near the furthest window: a dazzle of red hair swept back into a pony tail, skin so white it could almost be blue, high cheekbones, no makeup and various bits of clanky jewellery at ears, neck and wrists. Only a fool would say she looks like Nadine, but she could be Nadine's much hotter cousin. She must have come in when he was staring at the ceiling or plotting priests' holes in the arched windows. Otherwise he would have noticed.

Finally, the talk comes to an end. There are ten minutes for questions, which is another ordeal, but then, mercifully, it is over and Tim can hit the tea urn and the custard creams.

There is actually a crush for it and, as soon as he has his tea, someone jogs him and he ends up with milky slop in his saucer. Pouring it back into the cup, he looks around for his redhead.

"Did you enjoy that?" barks a voice at the level of his chest.

It is the helmet-haired old lady who was taking notes. Gripping his arm, and standing close enough to spit crumbs in his face, she says urgently: "I adore Hopkins. When I taught him for A-level I used to take my class into the woods to eat bluebells to help them understand the difference between inscape and instress."

"And did that... help?" says Tim, edging backwards to see if her grip on his arm will ease. It doesn't.

"Wonderfully," she bellows. "It was all about the *being* of a bluebell, which you couldn't understand just by looking at it."

"And did they find it easy? The poem, I mean?"

He is still physically ensnared, so he has to say something.

"Good heavens, no!" she cackles, in another shower of spit and custard cream. "Utterly mystified by most of it. But the cleverer ones began to get it in the end, and that was part of the fun. Even the ones who didn't understand a word seemed to like the sound of it. In a sense, I think that's the whole point, don't you?"

Tim is groping for something non-committal when she releases his arm abruptly and turns her back on him. He assumes that she is just raiding the biscuit plate again and will return to him, but she is now clutching someone else to tell them about the bluebells. This strikes him as rude, but it at least gives him a chance to look for the redhead, who turns out to be behind him, nodding away at one of the clerics. He takes a step towards them and stands there, hoping she'll invite him into their conversation. She doesn't, and he's wondering if he'll have to back away again when the cleric comes to his rescue.

"Are you a Catholic too?"

"Me? God, no," says Tim, then remembers he shouldn't sound so dismissive. Or blaspheme. "I mean, not that there's anything… Erm. Are you?"

He addresses that to her, obviously.

"Originally," she says. "The hair's a giveaway, right? Irish parents. I was weaned on potatoes instead of milk."

The cleric – praise be! – excuses himself in search of more tea.

"It went very deep at one stage," she is saying. "Until the age of nine I genuinely wanted to be a nun when I grew up. But don't worry, I got over it."

Her voice is unexpectedly robust. Ballsy, he might even say. And northern. Please don't let her hate southerners. At least she's also English, so he's not going to fall foul of that particular local prejudice.

He has shown no interest in other women since Nadine. That is the emasculating effect Nadine has had on him, he tends to tell himself: she has put him off for life. But now, as this freckled beauty smiles up at him, he can feel he may not be completely past it. He looks into her laughing blue eyes and grasps that he's in with a chance here, more than a chance. Even Tim, cursed with a woeful lack of confidence in his own sexual allure, can see that he must represent by far the most eligible prospect in this room.

"Have you been to one of these before?" he asks.

"Do I come here often, you mean?" She is laughing at him. "Actually it's my first time. But I'm a big fan of the work, especially the *Wreck*, which is why it's awesome that they focused totally on it today."

No argument there.

"And you?" she asks. "A big fan?"

"Oh completely. And I'd have to say the *Wreck* is my favourite too."

He hasn't read a line of any of the guy's other poems so it's technically not a lie.

She grins.

"What's your favourite stanza?

Panic.

"Stanza?"

"You know, verse."

"Oh right. I don't think I've got a favourite one. I mean it's all so...." He fumbles for the word, any word.

"Rich?"

"So *rich*, exactly, that it's hard to pick out... I mean there are phrases, obviously. Erm, *On a pastoral forehead in Wales*, for instance. That always stands out because I live round the hill and I'm always looking at the same forehead."

"Oh yes! And the wonderful double-meaning as well!"

Trying not to let the renewed panic show, Tim angles

his head in a way that's meant to show he is far too gentlemanly to interrupt her flow, and that she should continue.

"You know, he mentioned it in the talk? A place full of both sheep and priests."

He hasn't noticed that, which is embarrassing, because he now sees you'd have to be thick not to. And he certainly doesn't remember that bit from the talk. Maybe he really did nod off through part of it.

"Of course! Marvellous, isn't it?"

Marvellous? What's getting into him? He doesn't normally sound like such a southern arse.

"Any other favourite lines?"

He now desperately wishes he had paid any attention at all to the speaker.

"Oh loads, of course. Erm. *Thou mastering me God*, obviously." Yes, he can actually quote the first line! There's hope for him yet. "And then there's *The treasure never eyesight got, nor was ever guessed what for the...* something." No!!! Surely he didn't just say that? He is getting so carried away that he has managed to draw attention to the one thing above all else that will mark him out as a charlatan, a shallow intruder with no culture who has insinuated himself inside these walls for the most mercenary of reasons. He must think of another line quickly before she has time to...

"*The treasure never eyesight got...*" she repeats, eyes narrowed. Even her eyelashes are red. "Remind me where that comes?"

"Verse twenty-six," says Tim too quickly. "Or

thereabouts."

Her beautiful brow crinkles into the slightest of frowns then smooths as her eyes brighten and she recites the entire verse. Then she laughs, a great throaty guffaw, as she sees him gaping.

"Sorry, I'm such a show-off," she says. "Did I get it right?"

Putting his tea-cup to one side, he has pulled Alun Gwynne's *Collected Works* out of his canvas knapsack to check. And yes, she has got it word for word. More than that, she has made it sing, so that he really does begin to see the seductive power of the swirling, rhythmic sentences. He can even convince himself that he understands the sense – of the first bit, at any rate, which seems to be about the clouds parting and the sun shining through on a nice day. And is it his imagination, or does she widen her eyes suggestively on the word *desire*? He is in danger of reddening like a teenager.

But he is also quite scared. What kind of a machine must this creature be to know a great random chunk of the poem from memory like that?

"Can you do the whole thing? I mean, completely off by heart?" he stammers.

"No, just stanza twenty-six. You got lucky."

He's relieved that she's not such a machine after all, and maybe there is something special here if the line he identified as his favourite comes from the one verse she knows off pat. Then he realises she's laughing at him again. Of course she knows the whole thing – why the hell would she just know that one part?

"It's a freak skill," she shrugs. "I guess it's so, like, hypnotic, it's hard not to remember it. I know loads of the shorter poems, but the *Wreck* was the real challenge. Like Everest. You know, I had to do it because it was there?"

Tim has never had any idea why anyone would brave avalanches, frostbite, lack of oxygen and the chance of death at the slightest false step just to say they've climbed a mountain – although on balance he would rather endure all that than try to learn this ridiculous poem. But he keeps that thought to himself.

"How long did it take?" he asks instead.

"I built it up over time. I found I knew bits of it and then started joining them together." She laughs again. "I don't get out much."

"I bet you do," says Tim, then realises how creepy he sounds. He has been out of this game too long.

"So, what is it about that line in particular for you?" she says.

"What line? Oh, you mean *the treasure*? Nothing really, when there are such a lot of other... Like I say, you can't really choose when the whole thing is so *rich*, can you?"

"But there must be something that made you..."

He panics again, but at that moment rescue appears in the unlikely form of the helmet-haired old lady, who grabs each of them by the arm and announces once more, with no apparent inkling that she has already said it to Tim: "You know, when I taught him for A-level I used to take my class into the woods to eat bluebells to help them understand the difference between inscape and instress."

"That's brilliant!" says Tim's new friend. "Inscape is

all the things that make it unique, because God never repeats himself, and instress is the way we experience it, which can include tasting it, because that's part of its uniqueness too. You didn't poison the kids, though?"

"Oh no, bluebells are quite safe to eat. We only lost one or two who got carried away and started eating wolfsbane. But they were trouble-makers anyway."

The woman laughs and turns abruptly away.

"She is joking, isn't she?" says Tim.

"I hope so. I'm Chloe, by the way."

She holds her hand out. Her skin is soft but her handshake firm.

"So you live around here?" she says.

Tim tells her about the Red Lion, accentuating the bucolic aspects and playing down the catastrophic business performance of the empty pub.

She says she has come over from Manchester way and has to be getting back soon because she doesn't like driving in the dark. She's also worried about falling asleep at the wheel and wishes they were serving coffee rather than just tea. Tim kicks himself that he still hasn't picked up any ground coffee for his espresso machine. Idiot.

"I'm sorry, otherwise you could have stopped by on your way," he says. "Unless…"

"Yes?"

He has remembered he has a fridge full of Red Bull.

"It's disgusting stuff, I know, but it's full of caffeine, so it keeps you awake."

"Actually I quite like it." Her eyes are shining with merriment. "Especially with vodka. But yes, thanks very much. I'll take you up on that."

Tim is glowing with pride as they make their way to the car park so she can give him a lift in her yellow Fiat Panda. For the moment, Barry Brook and all his works are completely forgotten.

He is relieved to find that Alun Gwynne hasn't burned the Red Lion down or flooded the bar. In fact he has managed to drum up a couple of customers, Hugh Pugh and another old boy in a flat cap. From the way he is slurring, he may also have broken his pint-and-a-half habit now that he can pull his own for free.

All three men's eyes are on stalks when they see who Tim has brought with him.

Hoping against hope that none of them will give voice to the smut that they are clearly thinking – or if they do, that they will have the decency to do it in Welsh – he gives Chloe a quick tour. The place isn't looking too bad in the afternoon sun and she says nice things about the ancient beams – not like the hideous Victorian ones at St Vowelless's – and the view down the valley. He does his best to keep her away from Alun and the other two, and he almost manages it. But he has to turn his back on her for a moment while he roots in the back of the fridge for Red Bull – there isn't normally much call for it – which is all the time that Alun needs. When Tim stands up again, she is getting the full works: slurred facts about the 800-year-old yew tree in the churchyard in the next village, the oldest brick-built house in Wales just down the valley, the prehistoric caves over the hill…

"To be fair, most caves are probably prehistoric," Tim

butts in, "and I'm not sure Chloe wants to hear…"

"Oh I do, it all sounds wonderful. I'd love to come back and see it all properly when I've got more time," she says, turning pointedly to Tim, whereupon Alun winks and leers and gives him a thumbs-up over her shoulder.

Tim takes her by the arm and steers her away from Alun before she can turn round and see, knowing that the old bastard will be wanting free drinks all week as his reward. But Tim is so pleased with the way the day has turned out, that he may even provide them.

As she is about to go, Chloe proposes leaving him her email address. Tim can't find anything to write on behind the bar and she follows him back into the kitchen – as much to avoid being left alone with Alun Gwynne as anything else, he suspects. Leaning over the kitchen table to jot it down, she spots his copy of *The Poussin Conundrum*.

"Christ, you're not seriously reading this crap are you?" she says. "And I thought you were a man of good literary taste!"

Tim laughs, pleased that she shares his own gut reaction to Barry Brook's conspiratorial drivel. She really is no Nadine. But it's equally clear that he must not tell her why he has a copy of the book. That would mean coming clean about his real reason for turning up at the lecture today, from which she would immediately infer that all the stuff he fed her earlier about how much he loves the poet is a pile of crap. He's not sure where this unexpected turn of events is going, but it would be a shame to mess it up needlessly. That's the kind of thing the old Notso would have done, and Tim is trying not to be Notso any more.

"Trust me, I hate it just as much as you do," he says. That's almost true: he hated himself for not being able to put it down. "No, er, someone left it in the bar the other night and I just brought it through. I haven't chucked it out or anything because they may come back and I can't bear to throw books away, however trash they are, you know? But yeah, no. Not me. I'd never, erm... No way."

"Good to hear it," she says. "Okay, handsome. I'll be in touch."

He grins to himself when she is gone. Sometimes he really isn't so incompetent after all.

North Wales, 1876

Now that he had his scheme and his form, lines came to Hopkins at all hours of the day, and he developed a habit of jotting a note down as soon as he could, then pulling together the fragments whenever he had some *ad lib* time. The occasion of the poem was tragic; he must of course not lose sight of that. But it was thrilling to feel that he was putting his magpie mind to decent use at last, marshalling all those quirks of language that he had observed and collected so painstakingly over the years.

He remembered trying to explain his personal theory of language, transcending etymology and onomatopoeia, to Dolben. Like everyone else, the boy had found it hard to grasp. Now finally this was his opportunity to demonstrate it properly, not as a linguistic theory, on which score he had failed to convince, but as a poetic tool. He would organise it into something majestic that would be truly worthy of its subject matter.

Of course, it got in the way of everything else he was meant to be doing: study, contemplation, prayer and society with the rest of the college. He was distracted, and although he did his best to hide the fact, it really was hard to focus on some of the day-to-day affairs. This project was so much more engrossing. If he had a nagging voice in the back of his head telling him that his explosion of personal creativity was against the rules, and this wasn't what the principle of obedience was supposed to be about, he managed to drown it out in the ferment of his own excitement.

On the work grew, in a ramshackle rather than a linear way, with bundles of phrases here and there that were not yet enough to be stanzas, but had the clear makings of a path through the poem. Leaving them to germinate at their own pace, he put his greatest effort into polishing the early part, so that he would have a proper, confident template with which to continue. He had also realised that he was starting in the wrong place. *On Saturday sailed from Bremen* was a decent opening line for a stanza, but not for the piece itself, not as he now conceived it. If his ode were a painting, the shipwreck must of course occupy a significant area of it. But the frame should also surround a broader panorama, establishing God's role as the Maker before narrowing in on the manner and mystery of this particular Taking Away. The theme of the enterprise, he saw clearly now, was knowing God. And since God was everywhere, there was no need to start in Germany.

After three or four weeks, he was bold enough to try a section on Kerr as they walked on the steep path that linked the hillside terraces behind the college. Hopkins had written four or five stanzas out on foolscap which he had stuffed discreetly under his gown. Now he retrieved them and read them out in a shy voice, keeping his head down so that he could watch his step as well as follow the words. When he looked up, he thought he caught a look of panic in his friend's eye.

"Shall I read it again?"

"Yes, old man. I'm afraid you have to make allowances for the slow brain of a literary simpleton. Read it out one more time, if it's not too much trouble."

They rested on a seat on the top terrace, looking out at the valley under great rafters of clouds holding up the sky. If he were alone Hopkins would have wanted to sketch the formation, but not now. He started over on his recital, going slower this time, emphasising the stresses more boldly, as authorial pride overcame performer's modesty. The intensity of it gathered inside him and he was moved by the sensual power of the words, as well as by the force of the feelings they described. He had to close his eyes when he got to the end of the last stanza of his little extract, not wishing Kerr to see how they brimmed with emotion. He disguised a swallow by clearing his throat, as if the recital had left him with a frog in it.

When he opened his eyes, Kerr was frowning into his lap.

"Oh dear," said Hopkins. "Is it so very bad?"

"No! No, no, no, by no means bad. Quite the contrary, not at all. It's just that…"

"Go on."

"You know I'm a lummox about these things, old man, so you mustn't mind me. I don't know where I got the idea… But I thought you were writing about the wrecked ship."

"I am."

"Are you?"

"Yes."

"Ah. I'm afraid I haven't the brain for it, because I didn't understand shipwreck from any of that. I heard some nautical words but I fear I missed the wreck altogether."

Hopkins smiled with relief. "The first part is autobiographical. I'm still quite a long way off the wreck."

"Autobiographical? I suppose that explains the first line, *O God my master.*"

"*Thou mastering me / God!*... The line runs over so God is the first foot of the next line…"

"*Thou mastering me God,*" nodded the other. "Much better the way you put it. It has a proper ring. That's why you're the poet and I'm the lummox. Carry on…"

"*Giver of breath and bread…*"

"Got it. That's God. Easy to understand, even for a lummox. And then?"

"*World's strand, sway of the sea, Lord of living and dead…*"

"Ah, now that's where I begin to have trouble. Why is God the world's *strand*? To my mind that's a beach."

"Yes, it's German for beach, and we ourselves say 'stranded', meaning beached or marooned. It can also mean a thread, you know, as in a strand of cotton, but in this case I am using it to mean 'that which is beyond or around the world', just as the strand is beyond and around a lake. Are you with me?"

Here he was, explaining it all over again.

"Just about, old man. But *sway*? I know the sea sways about, but what has the sway of the sea got to do with God? He causes it, of course, but the words don't say that. They seem to say he *is* it."

"Well, yes, the sea does sway, and of course that's apt given the subject of the poem. But it also means to influence or to govern, you know, as we say that someone holds sway, so it's a way of saying that God controls the waves."

"But – forgive me, old man – that's not quite the same part of speech. If you hold sway, that means you hold influence, so the sway is what you have, not what you are. Sorry, Hopkins, I don't mean to carp. I'm just trying to explain why I find it all so hard. If you take liberties with grammar, there's a danger that no one will know what you mean.

Hopkins pulled out his watch. They had the Rector on Canon Law at three. "It is all about the impression," he said. "You can convey a complexity of meaning without being slavish to grammar. Come on, we're going to be late."

"I'm sorry, old man. I say this with the best of intentions. I hope you're not put out."

"Of course not. I'm very grateful."

Hopkins turned to lead the way back down the steps. After so many years of not writing, he had forgotten how irritating it could be to show other people one's work.

As he lay in bed that night waiting for sleep, he imagined reading the same five stanzas to Dolben. Would that dear, lost youth have argued over syntax like a dull Latin master correcting fourth-form prep? He hoped not. Dolben was by nature rebellious, much more than Hopkins himself could ever be. He had scandalised his school and his family by roaming the countryside in the garb of a barefoot medieval monk. And even if his poetry tended to the trite, he was a dreamer, a creature of the spirit, who knew the value of letting his soul take flight and would surely have understood the point of turning a noun into a verb. He would never allow himself to be tethered by the stultifying conventions of English grammar.

From imagining Dolben listening to his poem, it was a short step to walking arm-in-arm with him in the gardens of the college and enjoying the cloudscape. This happy caprice, unhindered by more realistic memories, such as Dolben refusing to reply to so many of Hopkins' letters, carried him into a contented slumber. For once, Hopkins' conscience allowed him to dream freely and untroubled, swimming in the warm well – *díng-dóng-béll* – of imaginary rapture.

NORTH SEA, 1875

The stricken ship might be aground on a sandbank fifty miles from the English coast in the icy cold of December, but the cooks had still managed to keep the kitchens going. At midday Marta knocked on Henrica and Aurea's door to tell them all the women and children of the ship were invited to eat in the first-class saloon, while food would be sent to the men on deck or pumping in the hold.

Henrica heard her young companion's excited intake of breath without needing to turn round, and sure enough, when the stewardess had gone, Aurea clapped her hands with delight.

"The first-class saloon!"

For the first time in many hours, Henrica found herself laughing. The girl was so childish and had far more interest than she should in material luxuries. But she was indomitable. Unlike Henrica, she had not seen lifeboats washed away in the storm with helpless people inside them, so she did not have the same sense of the gravity of their plight. She had not heard from Lundgren, the agitated Swede, of the dangers that awaited them at high tide; for the moment, Henrica was keeping this intelligence to herself. So she was still able to enjoy those aspects of this nightmare that could be considered an adventure. If her so doing helped all of them keep their spirits up, so much the better.

The first-class saloon was a larger and more luxurious version of their own dining quarters, with a softer carpet, plusher upholstery and fine gilding on the acanthus leaves of the painted marble columns. The steerage passengers shuffling in ahead of them were visibly awed by the finery, and they had to be encouraged by the serving staff to move into the room and not crowd the doorway. Henrica heard a fur-clad dowager complaining loudly that she had not paid through the nose to mix with riffraff, and she noticed the odd hostile glance in their own direction from some of the poorer women. But in the main the mood was of stunned exhaustion.

There was room for everyone, because the ship was so empty, and the semblance of normality conferred by sitting at table made it almost possible to forget the gravity of the crisis. But the tilt of the gilded apartment was a constant reminder of their peril and, apart from Aurea, only the children seemed to have appetites. The young Hamms, a boy of six and a girl of four, were making the most of the opportunity to gorge on roast beef, suet puddings and an array of cakes that was wheeled out of the galley in brave defiance of the conditions.

By the end of the meal, the collective gloom had dampened even Aurea's spirits, and afterwards Henrica and her companions returned to their cabins and alternately dozed, prayed and read from their breviaries. Sleep remained a refuge from cold and anxiety, and from the incessant thump of waves on hull – softer now the storm had calmed, but always there.

Henrica woke in the early evening to find the daylight gone. Lighting the lamp, she saw that it was five o'clock. That meant it was exactly twelve hours since they had run aground. It seemed so much longer. It also meant, ominously, that dusk had come and still no rescue.

From somewhere above them came the same sharp report they had heard in the early hours of the morning.

The noise roused Aurea too.

"What was that?"

"They are firing rockets again."

"Because nobody has come."

It was a statement, not a question.

Henrica tried to read from her breviary, but it was difficult to concentrate and she got up from her bunk. Donning her veil and wimple, she returned to the tilting saloon in search of news and found the menfolk, looking tired and bedraggled, on a break from pumping.

"What's the matter with the English? Where are their lifeboats? Or do they only save their own ships?" Hamm was saying. He spoke freely in front of her now, Henrica noticed.

"They have lifeboats," said Lundgren quietly.

She wondered how he came to speak with such authority.

"So they will come," said Meyer. "We must be p-patient."

"I hope you're praying for us all, sister," said Hamm.

"Of course we are, Herr Hamm. And we can be confident the Lord is watching over us."

"He may be watching, but what is he doing to help us?"

"It is in darkness that his light can best be seen."

It was the answer Mother Clara liked to give when times were tough. She wished she could sound more convincing when she said it.

She returned to their little group of cabins to assure the others that the English had lifeboats and help would eventually arrive. Barbara had her arms round Brigitta and seemed to be making more effort now to keep her calm, while Norberta was praying silently on her own. She was such a solitary creature, Henrica observed. She knew from Aurea that the pair of them came from neighbouring villages in the east, and she remembered that they had arrived at the convent within a few months of one another. But whereas Aurea had adapted easily to the life of the cloister, it had clearly been more of a struggle for Norberta, who seemed shy even of opening her mouth. She had told Aurea she had always been the outsider at home, teased and then shunned for her height – a girl who nobody would ever want to marry and good only for a nunnery. But joining the order did not seem to have made her any more comfortable in her own skin. Henrica knew that she ought to work harder to integrate her into their group, but for the moment it was enough to lead them through their present danger. If the Lord spared them, she vowed she would make it a priority to draw Norberta out of herself on the rest of their journey.

A little later, Marta came knocking again to say that the women and children were once more invited to dine in first class, as the men continued to work shifts at the pumps.

"There is also some good news," she said. "Our flares have been seen. A rocket was fired from a lightship in the mouth of the Thames, and another from a different light vessel further out to sea. It means they know about us."

"So rescue will come?" said Aurea excitedly. "We will be saved?"

"Not before morning," said Marta. "No ship can approach at night. But yes, it means they will come."

Henrica wondered when she would finally have to tell the others what the Swede had said about the perils of a high tide. Not yet, anyway.

None of them had any heart for a meal, even with these encouraging tidings. They remained in their cabins, reading and praying.

Henrica did not dare undress when it was time for sleep. It was better to be ready for any eventuality, and neither she nor Aurea had any inclination to remove even their life-belts. Bulky as they were in the cramped cabins, they offered a certain reassurance, and the two of them also kept their tunics on, as well as their coifs. The tight head covers were uncomfortable, but they at least deadened the thump of the waves.

"I wonder who she will send instead of us," said Aurea in the darkness. Her voice was slower and sadder than Henrica had ever heard it.

"Who?"

"Mother Clara. When we are gathered, she will have to send a new team to St Louis. The hospital needs the hands."

Henrica suddenly felt an overwhelming need for her

mother's embrace. But now was not the time for giving up.

"Mother Clara won't need to send replacements," she said, as calmly as she could manage. "We are going to America ourselves. Tomorrow help will come, and we will all be in St Louis by Christmas. I promise you. Now try and get some sleep."

MANCHESTER, THE PRESENT

Chloe has no regrets about giving Tim her phone number. She doesn't buy for a moment that he is the enthusiast for the poet that he professes to be, and she has no idea what really brought him to the literary lecture that afternoon. She is curious about that, of course. But she is not hugely bothered that he has over-egged his love for the work. She has had far worse lies from men at first acquaintance, and this one was so laughably inept, it is hard to hold it against him or consider it in any way sinister. If anything, it's endearing.

After the long drive from home – slowed by roadworks, a wrong turn on the motorway bypass round Chester, and another on a featureless dual carriageway system somewhere in Flintshire – she walked into that room at the college and was immediately underwhelmed by the sight of her fellow poetry-lovers. With hindsight she is not sure what she expected, but this sparse array of retired teachers and soapy clerics was really not it. She had been more excited about this occasion than it warranted, and the gathering itself came as a deflating contrast to the way her imagination had dressed it up. In that context, the sight of a tall, elegant man with raffish eyebrows and a dress sense verging on the beatnik represented a sudden, dramatic improvement. If it came with a sizeable dollop of bullshit on the side, that is a level of reality check that Chloe is prepared to accommodate.

When they chatted, he made her laugh, sometimes intentionally, and afterwards she was charmed to see his empty old pub, which some people might consider sad and depressing, but for Chloe it's more a question of unrealised potential. The sorry tale of ineptitude that had brought him there was equally endearing, and she was even amused by the ancient, red-faced trio propping up the bar. Leaving her contact details was a very natural next step.

He emails first, and they only speak on the phone once she has given him enough tacit reassurance that she won't brush him off or fail to pick up. When he calls, she takes mischievous pleasure in his obvious nervousness, and she is in no hurry to help him through the silences that punctuate the conversation whenever his confidence falters. Eventually, however, she takes pity, and she is the one who suggests coming over for a visit. He jumps at the suggestion with such eagerness that she is once again struck by his lack of guile. Whatever he is bullshitting about, it doesn't feel dangerous.

She thinks more about this on the drive over. She has chosen to turn a blind eye to the obvious nonsense that he is peddling about his interest in the poet, and she has decided to treat it as an entertaining foible rather than a cause for concern. She will get to the bottom of it in the end, she has no doubt. But as someone who spends her working life encouraging other people to evaluate risk and avoid obvious pitfalls, it would be as well to have some idea of what her rubicon, the limit of her indulgence, ought to be. She doesn't mind if he is nowhere near as keen on the poet as she is. She knows that already and, to be fair, she has set the bar pretty high. In any case, she can always educate him – and he clearly has some openness to being educated, otherwise he would never have been there that day. The only point at which she really might have to draw a line and start backing out, she concludes, is if he turns out to be some kind of shameless manipulator, because if there's one thing she doesn't like, it's a cynic. But the idea of someone so obviously inept and see-through as Tim manipulating anyone makes her smile. It really isn't something she is going to have to worry about it.

At this point she notices that she is approaching the confusing set of roundabouts where she took a wrong turn last time, and she realises she needs to stop thinking about far-fetched hypotheticals and concentrate on the road.

He makes her laugh as soon as she arrives. He has planned a programme of sight-seeing before lunch, and the itinerary includes all the places that Alun Gwynne promised to show her. They discover, on a tourist information notice headed 'Fascinating Facts', that the church in whose graveyard the 800-year-old yew tree stands has been the site of religious worship since the sixth century.

"How *fascinating!*" says Chloe, and it becomes their giggly catchphrase for the afternoon.

They learn that the earliest brick-built house in Wales was erected in 1567 by the man who helped found the

London Royal Exchange.

"*Fasc*inating!" says Tim.

It's childish but fun. Inspecting these modest little landmarks in mock earnestness carries the implicit assumption that sight-seeing isn't the real reason she has driven all the way here, and she likes that. It makes her feel like a teenager.

The sun is out and there are small brown birds with white tails darting around on the wind as they walk up the hill behind the village. It's wonderful to breathe the air and gaze back down on the valley below, with the sea glistening in the distance.

"Here, let me give you a hand," he says, as they climb a rocky bit towards the top of the valley. Once she has put her hand in his this first time, it's an easy progression towards entwining their fingers as they walk side by side.

"You don't really regret moving here, do you?" she asks.

"Less so now than I did last winter. You being here helps."

"Oh yes?"

He reddens. "I mean, seeing it through your eyes. I spend so much time worrying about paying the bills for a failing pub that I forget to look around me."

"Don't worry, I know what you mean."

They fall silent.

"I'm sure it's got potential though," she resumes. "Location, location, location and all that. If it's in a good place, which it certainly is, there will be a way of making it work. You just have to find it."

"Trust me, I've been looking."

"What are the options?"

He starts to say something, then he seems to think better of it and a cloud crosses his face, breaking the mood. It's only a small change, but she is pretty sure she is not mistaken. As if to confirm she is right, he looks at his watch and says they ought to be getting back because there is food in the oven.

He has made a decent stab at roasting half a leg of lamb. It's partly burnt on the outside, and he hasn't pre-boiled the potatoes before adding them to the roasting tin, so they're still hard. But she appreciates the effort, because it's clear that this kind of thing doesn't come naturally to him.

The poet barely comes up. That *Complete Works* is still lying on the bar and Alun Gwynne – who turns up midway through the afternoon – is keen to chip in references whenever he spots his opportunity. But Chloe doesn't especially want to discuss the work. The day is going well, conversation with Tim is flowing on all sorts of subjects, and she doesn't want him to ruin it with a flat-footed attempt to flout his fake literary credentials.

It's clear that they will kiss when it's time for her to leave, and when they do so it's warm and nice. He tastes of beer and mint sauce, but she probably does too.

"It's been great, it really has," she says. "I'd invite you to mine for a return visit, but it's so much nicer here."

"You're welcome here whenever you want," he says.

She savours the thought all the way home.

North Wales, 1876

The days and weeks went by for Hopkins in the obedient rhythm of the community. There was a freeze in early January, although not cold enough to prevent wettings to the waist for two reckless young theologians who skated too far out on the fishing lake. Then the thaw came, and with it a flood that made the entire valley glisten. Milk and eggs fell scarce as the local farms suffered, making a table that could barely be any plainer suddenly even more so. The sky took on a permanent drear, giving the surrounding hills a depressing sameness of colour and tone, and blanketing out the farther peaks. The only virtue of the heavy cloud cover was that the breath no longer steamed so obviously at early meditation. But when the first lambs were at last spotted, there was a lightening of mood all round.

He was normally the most excited of anyone at this season. He still set distance records on his afternoon excursions, but now he was less inclined than ever to make conversation with his companions. Head down, in the modest way that they had been taught as novices, he was occupied with word-lists: same-sounding, same-meaning, same-initialled. His discoveries had convinced him that he was tapping a new seam of poetic wealth. Was it not extraordinary that *lush* and *plush* both brimmed with the same rich bounty, a bounty that might *gush* or *flush* if it burst out? Convention obliged the poet to place each of the rhyming words at the end of a line. But a revolutionary poet with a new system of metrics would jam them together, quite separate from the rhyme scheme, in a quick-fire series.

Soft, sift; goal, shoal; wheel, whirl; was *whorl* a word?

"Hi, Hopkins! Oughtn't we to turn back now? We'll be late."

Yes, yes, as you wish.

Beat, bank, bow, beam. Breast, braid. Flange, flame, flood, flesh, fall.

"Look, daffodils!" the companion went on – Clarke or Purbrick, O'Rourke or Bacon, it scarcely mattered who it was. "Spring has well and truly sprung!"

Spring, sprung.

"Sing a song that spring has sprung," Hopkins beamed suddenly.

"I'm not sure the Rector would approve of singing," said Clarke, or Purbrick.

That made him giggle.

"I didn't mean you should. I simply liked the sentence."

There were times when he found his fellow theologians aggravating. One Sunday evening after the dominical sermon, the talk in the recreation room turned to walking holidays. Someone had received a letter from friends planning an expedition to the Dolomites. This prompted general reminiscences about trips they each had made before joining the Society, and Hopkins threw in his twopenn'orth about his own happy tour of Switzerland.

It didn't do to express regret that all that was behind them now, because it would lower everyone's spirits. But Barraud said he would love to see the Loire valley again, and Clarke chipped in to say it would be the Pyrenees for him, whereupon O'Rourke said he had always had a hankering to see Germany.

"Not a country you'd want to go to nowadays," said Hopkins, assuming general assent.

"Why ever not?" said O'Rourke.

"Surely, the persecutions. Everything Bismarck has been doing against Catholics."

"But that's politics. It doesn't stop me wanting to see the country."

"Nobody who cherishes religious freedom should visit the place so long as the Kulturkampf persists," said Hopkins, looking around the rest of the company for support.

"What's Kulturkampf?"

That was Reeve. How could he not know?

Hopkins continued to address O'Rourke. "International disapproval is a powerful tool. A stand needs to be taken, and if people like ourselves don't take it, even at the hypothetical level, then who will?"

"Kulturkampf is the name that Bismarck uses for his campaign against the Catholic religious life," Rickaby explained to Reeve.

"It's not a campaign, it's a persecution," said Hopkins, feeling he ought to get his hackles back down, but unsure how to do so. "Bismarck says it's his response to the Vatican Council, but that's tosh, utter tosh, because

156

it's just an excuse to turn against Catholics. And it's the reason so many are fleeing Central Europe, especially from the religious orders."

"I don't think it's got anything to do with the Vatican Council," said Splaine. How he loved to show off his superior grasp of everything. "The doctrine of papal infallibility was the Pope's response to Garibaldi's provocation in Rome, and had nothing at all to do with Catholics outside Italy. Bismarck isn't stupid, he knows that perfectly well, so I agree it's an excuse. But I don't even think it's about persecution. Bismarck's coffers were empty and this was a good way of getting his hands on monastic property. It was about balance sheets, not sovereignty."

"Be that as it may," said Hopkins, "he has turned brutally against our counterparts in Germany and we can't pretend it's not happening. Some of the consequences have been tragic. Need I remind you that emigration by sea can be a perilous business?"

The dissent fell away, but he knew he had been too passionate.

In his room afterwards, trying to ignore the pain in his eyes, he sat up late poring over a copy of *The Tablet* that he had sneaked from the recreation room. It contained an account of the requiem Mass after the shipwreck, which by uncanny coincidence had been held very close to his own birthplace in the East London suburbs. He had tried to picture the church, which should be less than half a mile from their house. They had moved away just before his eighth birthday, giving him excuse enough not

157

to remember, but he was disappointed with himself: it would have been nice to think that he had some latent Catholic sensibility even then. It had taken his mother to point out in a letter that the church was probably a more recent construction, because she herself would certainly have remembered it. And given it a very wide berth, she might have added.

Hopkins rubbed his eyes. The relief it gave was treacherous, because once you started rubbing you had to carry on and on, but there were times when the temptation was irresistible.

Cardinal Manning himself had preached the sermon. Life and death were the same to them, he had said of the blessed deceased: when a means of escape was at hand, they allowed others to take their places. Amid the agony, the despair, the piercing cries of their fellow passengers, a divine calm pacified the souls of these holy victims. Hopkins frowned. Hadn't the eyewitnesses told of terrible cries from the deceased themselves?

Laying the paper aside, he leafed through the pile of cuttings his mother had sent. Straining to make them out in the hopeless gaslight, he unfolded and refolded each one. Yes, here it was, he knew he had seen it! According to the survivors, the tallest figure had called: "O, my God, make it quick! Make it quick!"

The gas flickered.

The report said the voice was so loud it could be heard clearly above the storm. Hopkins closed his eyes and imagined looking down on the ship. In his mind's eye, the cry curled upwards around the mast and into the night-time clouds, like a twisting plume of smoke. It was no longer a cry so much as a roar, the roar of a great creature … a wonderful, powerful animal …

Like a lioness breasting the babble.

Yes, that was rather good, because *babble* naturally gave him *rabble*, which neatly dealt with the masses in the rigging too. And that was the key, yes, of course it was. These creatures were of the weaker sex but they were strong in spirit – and where did that strength come from but their faith, their absolutely certainty? That was what enabled them to rise above the most intolerable physical hardship. Oh, this was working now… They were yearning for death not because it was a lesser evil than their earthly torment, but because they knew that what lay beyond death was better than anything the earth could provide, and so the roar must be born of … joy? … excitement?

Ha!

For once he barely noticed the cold as he changed into his nightclothes. Kneeling, he offered his thanks for the divine guidance that had at last given him eyes to see.

NORTH SEA, 1875

It was now Tuesday, only the third day since they had left Bremen and less than twenty-four hours since they had struck the sandbank, but it already seemed an eternity since this nightmare had begun. They slept through the start of the cold night, but Henrica was roused while it was still pitch dark by a commotion in the lobby outside. She heard Marta rapping on one of the other doors and calling an urgent instruction. This was repeated twice more before the knock sounded on their own door, which opened before she or Aurea could reply.

"Ladies, please hurry. The captain has asked all passengers to come on deck without delay."

Henrica sat up in the flimsy covers that she had wrapped over her bulky clothes and life-belt. "What time is it? Has help arrived?"

"It's two in the morning."

It was too dark to see the girl's face, but there was nothing reassuring in her voice.

"Come to the aft saloon as quickly as you can and you'll get further instructions. And don't forget your life-belts."

"We're already wearing…"

The door closed as abruptly as it had opened.

"Henrica?" came a terrified whisper from the upper bunk.

"It's all right, my dear. Try to be strong."

Shivering, Henrica got out of the bunk and opened the

door a crack. The lamp in the lobby was burning, and Barbara's face appeared in her own doorway. Her face was swollen and her eyes shrunken small.

"What's happening?"

"Maybe rescue," said Henrica, wishing she could believe it.

A third door opened and Frau Pitzhold emerged, wrapped in a fur-trimmed coat which was so bulky she must be wearing it over her life-belt.

"Come along, sisters. It sounded urgent." It was the first time she had spoken to Henrica directly. Fräulein Forster emerged from the cabin too and scuttled after the older woman.

"What should we do?" said Barbara, struggling to attach her band.

"We must do as she says."

The door opened wider, and Brigitta's pale face appeared behind Barbara's in the lamplight. "I can't go on deck, Henrica, I just can't."

"Our only hope is to pray, and I prefer to do that here," said Barbara.

"Who says there's no hope?"

"If help had arrived the girl would have said so."

"This is senseless. We must all do as the captain says and go to the back of the ship."

Henrica had known her authority might be challenged at some point on the journey, but she had not imagined it would be so soon, and in such circumstances. She must try to assert herself without undermining what little morale they had left.

Fortunately, Aurea was in no mood to stay where they were. Henrica persuaded a trembling Norberta to join them, and the other two were eventually induced to finish dressing and follow Marta's bidding. Pinning veils seemed to take an age, and Brigitta drew blood from Barbara's scalp in her attempt at haste. But at last they were ready.

Emerging into the listing saloon, Henrica saw that it now pitched more obviously from front to back than from side to side, so that they had to climb uphill as they joined the frightened passengers filing towards the stern. The burners were working in the aft saloon, so it was warmer here, but the room itself was a wretched sight. Huddles of steerage passengers, easily recognisable because they had no life-belts, camped on the floor and bedraggled the finery, but nobody seemed conscious of the trespass any longer. The refugees were too consumed by the danger to be awed, and the dowagers whose territory they were invading looked long past caring. There were men here, as well as women and children, which must mean the pumping and shedding of cargo had been abandoned. As a lost cause, or because salvation was imminent? There was no sign of relief on any faces, only fear and exhaustion. A baby was crying, and many women were sobbing too.

Henrica spotted a dazed but familiar face.

"Herr Lundgren, what's going on? Nobody has told us."

The Swede seemed at pains to avoid her eyes.

"The waves have done a lot of damage. Now the tide is coming in, the bow is sticking to the bottom and only the stern is rising. Once enough water gets in, that may sink too. Our survival depends entirely on how high the tide comes."

Henrica clutched her rosary tighter and checked to see if the rest of her group had heard, but they were too far away. Aurea was helping a steerage mother calm her children, and the other three stood in a tight group below a crystal wall-light, its opulence ridiculous now.

"That it could happen again. Again! Why, sister?" The Swede looked at her directly now, and his eyes were red.

He must be thinking of the *Schiller*. It was the great unspoken dread for all of them, but she had been at pains to avoid any mention of it. It was the last thing Brigitta needed. She hoped she could rely on the Swede's good sense. Men could be such frail creatures.

"The Lord will take care of us."

"You're right, sister. I'm sorry for my moment of weakness. Forgive me."

A blond-bearded steward was moving through the saloon.

"Ladies and gentleman, you must all prepare to go on deck. If you have one, make sure you are wearing your life-belt, then move up towards the stairs at the entrance to the saloon. Try to go calmly, there is plenty of time for everyone to get out. But you must understand that this saloon will be submerged at high tide, and the captain has given the order to batten down the hatches, so everyone must come above. Once you are on deck, members of the crew will help you fasten yourselves onto the rigging to keep you safe from the wind…"

"Fasten us to the rigging?"

"So we are not swept away," said Lundgren. He was

still ashen pale.

Now Barbara's hand was gripping her arm.

"I can't do it, Henrica. I simply can't. How can they expect us to go up there?"

"Please, Barbara, we must show a lead. If you and I are not strong, how can we expect the others to be?"

"I will not be lashed to a mast. I'd rather take my chances in here."

"Our Lord submitted himself to greater indignities. And you heard what the steward said. This saloon will be submerged."

"Then it is God's will."

The parties of steerage passengers were picking themselves up off the floor and moving back down towards the entrance to the saloon, where there was a companion-way up to the deck. Grabbing Barbara by the hand, Henrica pushed against the flow to where the others were huddled.

Brigitta was in the worst state. Her eyes were wild and she was struggling to breathe. "We should never have come," she gasped. "We should never have left the mother-house. It was madness to travel at this time of year."

Henrica grasped her hands to try and calm her. Couldn't Norberta have done this?

"There is nothing we can do about that now. We have to make the best of the situation, obey instructions and bring comfort to those who need it."

"I'm frightened."

"Me too, Aurea. Everyone is frightened."

"I don't want to go on deck. It's too dangerous…"

"I don't want to go either, but we have no choice. It's even more dangerous here."

Most other occupants of the saloon were moving towards the companion-way, where an officer was urging them not to push, and to let the men of their party go up first, so they could look after their women and children at the top. But who would attend to their own party? On the other side of the room, Frau Meyer was shepherding her youngsters back down towards the companion-way, the poor little ones looking tiny and vulnerable in their life-belts. Only Lundgren lingered, his breathing nervous and shallow. "Ladies, I beg you to follow," he said. "Please believe me when I assure you I know what I'm talking about. It's your only chance."

"Thank you, sir, but we are resolved to stay," said Barbara. "We are content to put our trust in the Lord."

Henrica tried to control her fury. She must not succumb to the sin of pride, and leadership was not necessarily about getting her way whatever the circumstances. But Barbara had no business making decisions for the group like that. Everyone was frightened, and it was utterly irresponsible to stoke the fear rather than try to quell it. Before she could say anything, however, there was a commotion at the stairwell. A woman from steerage was staggering down from the deck, her clothes sodden.

"My husband! My husband!" she screamed.

Lundgren tried to calm her as she lurched towards them.

"He will look after you if you stay on deck."

She turned to him with a wild expression, as if her eyes barely saw him.

"He's gone!" she screamed. "The wave took him. One moment he was there and… I reached out but I couldn't…"

She threw herself down in a heap of skirts, sobbing and pounding on the soiled carpet with her fists.

Henrica knelt to comfort her, feeling the damp of the carpet through her tunic. "The Lord has taken him. His suffering is over and he is in a better place. But now you must save yourself. That's what he would surely want. Please, my dear. This gentleman will look after you now."

The Swede was bending over the keening woman to help her up.

"You will follow, sister?" he called back to Henrica.

But her companions were kneeling, and it was clear they would not obey her even if she tried to command them. Their terror of the deck was too great.

"Will you lead us in prayer?" said Barbara.

Henrica knew she could not refuse. She sank once more to her knees.

"*Pater noster qui es in coelis. Sanctificetur nomen tuum.*"

She was on her fifth Ave Maria when Aurea screamed. Henrica opened her eyes and saw that water had appeared at the lower end of the saloon.

The blond steward was still there, appealing to the few small huddles of passengers who had not gone up. There was desperation in his voice now.

"Ladies and gentlemen, please. I must ask you one last time to come on deck. The weather is harsh, but everyone will survive if they are safely attached, and in the morning help will come. Our position is known, and rescue will be on its way as soon as day breaks. But if you stay here, you will drown. This saloon will be under water in another hour. The navigator has made precise calculations, and there is no doubt of it. If you do not come now, you will have no chance later."

In the corner opposite them, an exhausted Frau Pitzhold rose slowly to her feet, followed by Fräulein Forster. Henrica had not noticed they were still there. A young steerage couple got to their feet too, the trembling woman clutching a baby to her breast.

The steward held out his arms to help them. "Very good, sir, you've made the right decision. Take care of the lurching, ladies. Try not to be afraid, someone will help you at the top. You too, madam, step this way. The baby will be quite all right. You hold him, and someone will hold you and make sure you are tied fast. Yes please, madam, this way…"

She started at a touch on her arm. It was Marta.

"You must come up," the stewardess pleaded, her eyes glistening. "The captain says if we can survive the night we will be saved. So I swear to you there is some hope if you go on deck. If you remain down here, there is none."

"You go, Henrica, if you want to," said Barbara, remaining on her knees. "We will stay here."

What could she do? They were petrified, and she was not a military commander, ordering troops into battle. Not even Aurea would meet her eye.

Henrica understood their terror of going outside, but

she herself was terrified to remain. She had been on deck, so it was not the unknown quantity to her that it was to them, and she knew the crew were right about being safe if you were lashed on. For her, the real threat was the grave-cold water lapping into their refuge. But she was their leader. If they were set on staying in the saloon, she must remain with them.

"You go, my dear," she said to Marta. "I cannot. You've concerned yourself enough about us, and the Lord will thank you for it. But it is time to save yourself now."

Turning away so that she would not lose her composure in front of the girl, she crossed herself.

She shut her eyes and thought of her father, his new wife, her younger brothers and sisters. They had all been so worried about this journey she was making, and she had brushed away their concerns. They would all still be at peace in their own beds at this hour. Soon, in the next day or two perhaps, they would hear the terrible news. Who would break it? Would they read about the shipwreck in the newspaper, or would the shipping line send someone? She remembered her poor father's grief when her mother died. He had suffered so much then, with a young family to look after as well as classes to teach in the parish school, and now she would inflict it all on him again. She thought too of Mother Clara, left behind with the other sisters to fend for themselves in the worsening political climate. The Reverend Mother would blame herself for their deaths. It would be a torment for her, Henrica could see that with perfect clarity, and there was not a thing she could do to change it. She could only hope that the pain of loss would ease, as it surely would, and they themselves would eventually be forgotten. Better that than they be remembered as disappointments who had failed to discharge their mission.

It took another half hour for the water to arrive at the top of the saloon. They were not completely alone. Around a dozen passengers in total had refused to go on deck. When they found their ankles soaked, some of these now changed their minds, wading back towards the stairwell. But they had left it too late. The lobbies were already submerged, and there was no way they could find their way through, even if they could bear the biting cold of the water. These people now began to wail, crying out for help to those whose advice they had earlier spurned.

"The skylights! We can get out through the skylights," a woman shouted. "Bring the table."

The two remaining men in their beleaguered group dragged the heavy piece of furniture from the side of the saloon to the middle, directly under one of the apertures.

"Find something to smash it with. Here, use this."

A silver-tipped cane, discarded in the exodus, was passed up to break the panes, and glass rained down as the chill wind whistled in. Their bid for escape had alerted those on deck, and now hands reached through the gap.

"There's too much broken glass. We'll be cut to shreds trying to get through."

"The life-belts will protect you."

"Not everyone has one."

"Then cover the edges with something. The curtains!

Quick, tear them down and hand them up."

Relieved to be doing something rather than just waiting for the end, Henrica climbed up to help pad the treacherous edges. Now, surely, her companions must be persuaded. Hitching her habit, she climbed up onto the table to try and sling the thick fabric into place. But as she did so her wrist was grabbed by a strong hand from above, and before she knew it she was being pulled through the opening.

"But I cannot leave my…"

"Henrica!"

She looked back down at their upturned faces, and then more hands had her and she felt the icy wind of the storm as she found herself on deck, or what little of it remained. Everything below the funnel was completely submerged, and the section she was standing on rose out of the sea like a wooden rock. The wind whistled and the sea roared, and all around her people shouted and cried, urging each other to come here, where it was higher, or there, where there was something to be tied to. Above her head, she saw that some had climbed the rigging, passengers as well as sailors, where they were clinging on as best they could. Even as she watched, a young man lost his grip and fell with a scream. He narrowly missed the rail of the ship, plunging straight into the sea before the eyes of those who uselessly held their hands towards him. Henrica froze to the spot, transfixed by what she had seen, and impervious to those who were calling out to her to be sure she held onto something, to take heed of the next wave, to look out for…

And then it was upon her, hitting her so hard in the back that she knew as soon as the impact came that there could be no escaping. Her immediate thought was what a waste it had been to come so far, only to lose the battle by a simple oversight now. Her companions would think they had been right after all. She wondered what it was going to be like, to be pitched into the sea with no hope of getting out, to be turned and spun in the dark and the cold. Holy Father, receive me into your kingdom of glory. Her feet were off the deck. Then came the impact, a sharp crack on her head and shoulder – how could liquid be so hard? – and the ice-cold shock of it. Jesus receive my soul. It was hard to concentrate on praying when she was bursting for breath. And oh, the cold tore through her. But it was pointless to struggle, and she was nearly there…

NORTH WALES, 1876

When at last the poem was done, winter was long over and the valley sang with buttercups, dandelions and cornflowers, which Hopkins now noticed as if for the first time.

His ode ran to two hundred and eight lines, across thirty-five stanzas, and he knew that he would not show it to the Rector. This was not the short explanation of the mystery of God's works for the benefit of the ill-educated masses that his superior had requested. Even Hopkins could see that some considerable education would be required to cope with his ornate approach to language. He had gone against his brief, and it would only raise suspicions about his commitment to his calling and his vows of obedience if it was known that he had laboured at such length.

Neither did he intend to show the finished work to anyone else at the college. He had tried small sections on a couple of others – Bacon was one of them, Purbrick another – but their response had been as literal and rigid as Kerr's. To be appreciated, it was clear it required a more literary audience.

Whether his mother and father fitted that description was a moot point, but he had sent them all the verse he had ever written and now he wrote out a copy of this one. His mother had, after all, been complicit in the venture, providing him with the newspaper cuttings in the aftermath of the shipwreck, and it was useful to be able to involve her in these aspects of his life. He had been harsh to his parents at the time of his conversion, he saw now: rushing it through before he even took his degree from Balliol, despite all their entreaties to delay. In his excitement to go over to Rome, and knowing how badly they would take it, he had even ducked telling them in person, breaking the news by post instead.

He still vividly remembered the letter he received by return.

"Oh Gerard, my darling boy. Are you indeed gone from me?" his mother had written.

He had read it dry-eyed at the time, but the phrase had gnawed at his conscience over the years, and he could not think of it now without guilt.

He hoped that sharing the poem with them might also continue to heal some of the wounds with his father. At the time of his conversion, with the memory of Papa's more intolerant phrases ringing in his ears, he had not listened with any sympathy to the latter's angry complaints about the harm to their position that the scandal would inflict. With the mellowing of the years, he could understand that damage more easily now, and he knew that his father had not exaggerated. He felt a measure of remorse, and if he were doing it again he would at least attempt it with more tact, even if the outcome itself would be no different. Nowadays he made a point of writing alternately to both parents, even though his natural inclination had always been to correspond only with his mother, and as he grew older there were more subjects where he found common ground with his father. Verse was not the least of these. Although it hurt his own varsity-man's pride to admit it, his self-schooled father had far more poetry in print – three volumes, no less – than Hopkins himself had ever achieved. And while the Catholic content of his own writing was bound to jar against his father's sensibilities, the subject of the present poem could not fail to be of interest. Like his father and grandfather before him, Papa knew everything there was to know about shipwrecks, by virtue of the family business. As the eldest, Hopkins ought to have followed in their footsteps, rather than exiling himself beyond the social pale. By taking a literary interest in this kind of matter, he might at last give his father grounds for a shred of pride.

The poem was so long that it was a labour just to write it out, made all the harder by a maddening nib that scratched and blotted, and it took him a week of snatched moments to get it finished. Then he fretted that Papa would get the stresses wrong when he read it aloud. Poetry like this was pointless unless it was spoken, but a reader who misunderstood the principles of 'sprung rhythm', as he had resolved to call his new metrics, might botch it completely.

He spent another *ad lib* hour devising a proper system of notation to aid the reader. This consisted of the normal acute accent, a circumflex, a rounded circumflex with a dot inside, a tilde, a rounded circumflex without a dot, a long arc over three or more syllables and a long upside-down arc. Each sign corresponded to a particular stress. He then set about marking up the text itself. It needed care, because there was a danger of an arc or a tilde blotting out a word to make it illegible. But he was pleased with the result when he had eventually finished. It was straightforward and foolproof, and he was confident that any reader would be grateful for the guidance it offered. He could even see this system catching on, like a phonetic alphabet or musical notation for metrics, with futures generations of schoolchildren perhaps using it to declaim in the classroom.

There was one final copy to be made. Vanity and self-promotion were of course to be avoided; but having laboured for four months, was it so unreasonable to entertain a hope of publication? Not in his own name, Heaven forbid, nor in any showy place for all the world to see. But the Society had its own monthly journal, a very decent one, in which Dr Newman himself had published verse. By a stroke of good fortune, Hopkins had known its editor as long as he had known anyone in the Society – longer, for he had met him before he even joined. He had written to him a few weeks earlier and been flattered to receive an immediate response saying that, while there could be no guarantee of publication, any contribution of his would of course be given very favourable consideration. That meant he could be confident that his work would be read, rather than languishing at the bottom of a publisher's pile, as he knew happened all too often if you didn't know anyone. It helped that, as well as being a Balliol man, Coleridge bore one of the most distinguished names in English poetry. He would read Hopkins' ode with an educated eye, not with the blank incomprehension of a Purbrick or a Kerr. He would understand. And he would doubtless appreciate the notation.

That further copy took another week. When it was finally finished, Hopkins vowed to throw himself back into the life of the college, paying proper attention to sermons and essay-readings and being generally less distracted in his dealings with his fellow theologians.

But he also had some phrases about that kestrel circling in his head, so it might not do any harm to get them down on paper and start some notes for a sonnet…

North Wales, the Present

It is a pleasant autumn Saturday afternoon, and Tim is serving a party of cyclists who have stopped for a break at one of the wooden picnic tables he has set up in the car park. Their lightweight racing bikes are lined up alongside the outside wall, and the riders have taken off their spiked shoes, which are lying around in the grass. A couple of them are still wearing their helmets, which seems bizarre to Tim, and it's probably an indication they won't be staying for another after they have finished the round of bitter shandies he has just brought them. But their bright Lycra jerseys give the place a bit of life, and Tim is actually whistling as he carries his tray back inside, having ventured what he hopes are friendly wisecracks about saddle-sores.

The tables, like many new developments at the Red Lion, are Chloe's idea.

Since that first visit she has come back every other weekend throughout the summer, taking to the life with the enthusiasm that emigrant townies are always meant to have for the countryside. It is an enthusiasm that has eluded Tim himself until now, but some of it is beginning to rub off. She has searched for the entrance to the prehistoric caves over the hill on morning walks; she stops at farm gates to buy new-laid duck eggs, home-cured ham or fresh-pulled lettuces, none of which Tim has ever noticed on his way to Morrisons; and in the evenings she is happy to help out behind the bar, or more accurately take it over. She says it takes her back to her barmaiding days as a student, although it must have been a woeful student bar if the Red Lion is anything like it. And she does have a brightening effect on the place, literally so, with her flaming pony tail bouncing about as she humours Alun Gwynne, stoops to make a fuss of the slumbering Macca, treats anyone else who happens to wander in as a long-lost friend and generally cheers the place up. Slowly but surely, her presence helps the business improve, and there are some Saturday nights when you need more than one hand to count the customers.

That doesn't mean the place is anywhere near viable. Despite her initial reaction to his copy of *The Poussin Conundrum* – now stashed safely away – Tim hasn't given up on his project to put the valley on the map for high-spending, treasure-hunting crazies. He just needs to find the right way to sell it to Chloe. If he can persuade her that their rural love nest would be even more idyllic if they were flush with cash from tourists on the Grail Trail, rather than on the verge of bankruptcy, and that he is doing their local man's memory a favour by introducing him to the masses, he doesn't see why he can't continue with the plan.

He is particularly confident given his ongoing exchange of emails with Barry Brook – he has splashed out on a new laptop – about the nuns, the college and the treasure that never eyesight got. There's a temporary stumble when

Brook wants photographic evidence of the inscription that Tim says he found on the terrace steps, and Tim says he tried his best to get one but was thwarted by the security guards. This overstates the role of the woman in the tweed skirt and the gatekeeper at the lodge, and the inscription is of course a figment of his own imagination, but it's certainly true that the place doesn't welcome prying lenses.

However, this failure to present evidence seems to make Barry grouchy, and now he starts echoing Alun Gwynne.

If these nuns were carrying secret Vatican cargo, surely any treasure hunt should focus on the ship itself, not some backwater in Wales, he writes in an email.

At this, Tim loses patience. In his own reply he lets rip, advising Barry to remember that: (a) the treasure doesn't actually exist; (b) the point is to give his readers something to get their sleuthing teeth into; (c) if those readers are going to follow a trail, it will be a lot more practical for them to do so on dry(ish) land than on a treacherous North Sea sandbank; (d) he (Tim) is only working for a "modest tip fee" which isn't even definite; and (e) working out how it all fits together is Barry's own job. In a final blast, he observes that if he were capable of turning all this into four hundred pages of the kind of drivel that stupid people think is profound, then he would be the gazillionaire pulp novelist, not Barry.

After pressing send he realises he has gone way over the top and he will probably never hear from the guy again. Another triumph for Notso Cleverley.

But the response comes straight back:

Dude, cool it. You're right and I get it. I'm up for this, really I am, and I'll be on it as soon as I've wrapped up my current project. Please, don't give it to anyone else. I love the idea and I'm looking forward to working together on it. The tip fee doesn't have to be quite so modest!

Tim opened that three or four days ago, and it has put him in such a good mood for the rest of the week that he has been rehearsing possible ways of broaching the subject with Chloe.

Unfortunately Alun Gwynne beats him to it.

"Oh yes, it's a good scheme all right," the old fool is saying as Tim comes in from serving the cyclists. "If you can get this fellow Barry Brook to talk the place up by turning our boy into a sort of poetic Poussin – yes I like the sound of that, don't you? – then this valley could become a touristic goldmine."

Of all the various ways of bringing the subject up, this is the worst possible option. That is confirmed by the look on Chloe's face, which goes from bemusement to disbelief and then to outrage in the time it takes Tim to set his empty tray on the bar counter. He has a mental image of himself standing on top of a tower of chairs, clawing frantically at the air as Alun Gwynne kicks the bottom one away and the tower begins to topple.

"Wait, wait, wait," she's saying, oblivious to Tim's presence. "Explain this to me properly. You're saying the poem is about the *Holy Grail*?"

"No, it's not actually about the Holy Grail – but if you could make people *think* it is…"

Tim has managed to scoot round the back of the bar behind her and is now making frantic cut-throat gestures at Alun Gwynne, who looks from one to the other nervously.

"I m-may have got it wrong," he says.

"Yes you may," glares Tim, but Chloe waves at him over her shoulder to shut him up.

"I don't understand. What possible connection is there?"

"Well, I'm sure I don't know rightly. You'd have to ask… erm…"

He shoots another nervous glance at Tim, who is willing him to have a heart attack and die on the spot.

But Chloe still wants answers, and she is more persuasive than Tim – especially when she is flushed pink and her blue eyes are shining with anger.

"Well," Alun stumbles, "as I understand, there's an argument, so to speak… or a case to be made… that the ship in the poem may have been carrying something more important than passengers. That could have been why the poet made such a fuss of it. Only he couldn't spell it out, because he didn't want everyone to know, which is why the language is so tough to understand, do you see?"

Chloe still hasn't looked at Tim. "And this nonsense is going to be in a new Barry Brook thriller?"

It sounds so ridiculous, maybe she'll just laugh. That would be nice, to see her laugh and laugh, and then he and Alun will join in and maybe everything will be all right.

"Well, I can't say for certain," says Alun. "It's not settled,

I don't think."

"You just said that was the idea. To persuade him to write it so his readers will all believe it and then they'll come and despoil the valley."

So much for laughing. She now turns on Tim, eyes blazing.

"Why didn't you tell me about this?"

Oh well. They have had a good few months, and it was too much to expect to have it all. Not with his own anti-Midas capacity to turn all that is golden into lead.

"Because I, erm…"

"So you did know about it!"

Know about it?

"And you're just prepared to stand by and let them get on with it?"

Her hands are on her perfect hips as she stares accusingly into his face.

A pinprick of hope begins to glimmer. Let *them* get on with it. Whatever the doddering old idiot has said, he has somehow missed out the crucial part about it all being Tim's idea. Emboldened, Tim can see a way out.

"No, if you'll let me get a word in, I didn't know about it. Where did you say you heard this?"

They both turn on Alun, and Tim makes more cutthroat signs behind Chloe's back. Alun swallows.

"I didn't. I mean, I don't know. I just heard it on the … grapevine, as it were."

"We can't let it happen."

Chloe is more passionate than Tim has ever seen her.

"There must be copyright, literary executors, something

like that. Or the authorities in the college…"

"St Vowelless's?"

"If you must call it that, yes. They'd help put a stop to it, wouldn't they? But we also need to know which cynical bastard is responsible for the whole idea. Are you sure you don't…. Wait!"

She has wheeled round and is pointing at Tim.

"You had a copy of that stupid Poussin book!"

So the reprieve was illusory and this is it, the moment when it all falls apart and he is revealed as an unprincipled, money-grabbing philistine without the slightest interest in literature or the natural heritage of the valley, and he loses the hottest, nicest, sanest girlfriend he can ever hope to find. Notso has surpassed himself.

But, by some miracle, that's not what she's saying.

"You remember? I found it on the bar and you said a customer had left it. Who was it? You haven't exactly got many regulars and hardly anyone else ever comes in, so you must be able to remember. Come on, it's important. Try to think."

"Oh… y-e-e-e-s!" mugs Tim. "I do *vaguely* remember… But what would we do if we do know whose it is?"

"You go and talk to them, of course. Tell them it's not on, despoiling someone's good literary name for commercial advantage."

She really is a good person, there are no two ways about it. He doesn't deserve her. If he gets through this, he will honestly – he will swear it on any and every conceivable deity – *try* to be worthy of her.

"And if you won't, tell me where they live and I'll do it myself. Now come on, try and remember. Who does that book belong to?"

"Truly, I don't remember. I found it on a table. You're right, I don't have many customers. But come on, I can't be expected to remember who was in and where they were sitting on some specific night six months ago, which is probably what it was. I know you're angry, and so am I, of course I am. Very angry. But I don't think this is going to help us."

She is still all for launching house-to-house enquiries. It takes him a while longer, after Alun Gwynne has made himself scarce and Tim has locked up, to persuade her to let it go, for tonight at least.

She eventually goes upstairs, and he says he will follow her up. But instead he lingers at the bar, tippling his uncle's special single malt and contemplating how close he has come to self-destruction.

This is what comes of trying to have his cake and eat it.

It is now vital to keep Barry Brook as far away from the place as he possibly can.

LONDON, 1876

From his open third-floor window, Henry Coleridge watched the hansoms clattering down towards Berkeley Square and wondered what on earth he was going to do about Hopkins.

He had known him, how long was it, seven years? No, it must be more like nine or ten, and he had always had a soft spot for the odd, earnest little chap. He felt a degree of responsibility for him, even. That was what made the present situation so awkward.

He could still recall their first encounter, when they were both on retreat at Newman's place. He himself had been the preacher, and on the afternoon of his arrival he had been walking in that shady red-brick cloister the old man had built to make everyone think they were in the Florence of the Cinquecento, rather than the Birmingham suburbs, when an elfin boy-man, with a wispy beard that was comically out of place on his fresh, pink face, hopped out in front of him. It was funny how that verb suggested itself. It was because of his name, of course, because it wasn't as if the little fellow actually bounced around on one leg. But he did have an abrupt, nervy sort of gait that put Coleridge in mind of an early-morning blackbird, propelling itself about a dew-damp lawn and stretching worms out of the soil. He had a jerky movement of the head, that was part of it, cocked first this way and then that in deepest contemplation, without any thought of how the world might perceive him. That was what warmed you towards him, of course, his utter lack of guile. And it was bold of him to put himself forward like that, for all his shy demeanour.

"Excuse me, is it Dr Coleridge? I'm Hopkins, on the teaching staff here, you know. I think I was at Balliol with your cousin Ernest. We were great friends, but I haven't seen him for a while. Do you? See him, I mean. How is he?"

Coleridge told him such tidings of young Ernest as he had, although they were only second cousins and there was a large age-gap, so these were fairly limited. They went on to exchange pleasantries about the finish of the building, the standard of the pupils and so forth, while Coleridge inwardly cringed at the thought of this delicate creature at the mercy of a class of unruly boys. In the evening they took a cup of coffee together, and on the second night they talked more. He remembered being taken aback by Hopkins' stridency on the subject of country walks.

"Imperceptiveness about nature is like wilful ignorance of God's presence," the little fellow had insisted, his eyes blazing up at Coleridge.

He proceeded to rail on the subject, as if he were reliving unsettled arguments from the past. For someone of such hesitant physical manner, he was remarkably firm in his opinions.

But it turned out that what he really wanted to talk

about was his very recent conversion and the distress it had caused his family, who were blameless, if narrow-minded, Anglican folk. The father was in trade, marine insurance, if memory served, and Hopkins was not just the eldest but also the prodigy of the family, an Oxford man who was likely to be the only one of his several siblings to enter any university. So he was carrying the burden of great expectations, and he was now predictably accused of squandering his education and throwing away his prospects.

"My mother blames me for springing it on her, and it's true that I didn't take her into my confidence earlier. But how could I? It would have upset her for nothing if I had ended up deciding against it, so I had to be certain of myself before saying anything. But now she's saying I came over on a whim. I can understand why she thinks so, because I was so careful not to give them any inkling until I was sure it was the right thing. But of course it's not true, not for a moment."

There was no question of second thoughts, but Hopkins was fretting about the further distress this lady would suffer from his next thunderbolt, namely that he planned to seek holy orders.

"Coming on retreat this weekend was a way of testing myself, to see if I really have a vocation. Of course everything would be so much simpler if I hadn't. But I'm afraid I really have, and it's weighing very heavy on me."

Coleridge was not sure what advice to offer. His own conversion had been calmly received, but the middle classes took this sort of thing much harder.

"Perhaps you could delay, to give them time to come round. If you have a vocation, you will still have it next year, or the year after."

"No, I will not delay." Those eyes flashed again. "None of us knows how long we are put on this earth, and it would be disrespectful not to follow the calling, now that I know I have it. But it gives me no satisfaction to wound my people at home like this, honestly it doesn't."

In the event, of course, there was even worse in store for the young man's poor parents. Not only did their firstborn become a priest, he also joined the Society of Jesus, a step which must to them have seemed an act of the most wilful extremism. And some of the blame must attach to Coleridge himself, he later learned, because he was the first member of the Society that Hopkins ever met. He had put a human face on the order, apparently, and effectively put the idea into the little fellow's head – even if Coleridge was not sure that "human" was the first epithet his nervous young assistant Barry would use of him.

Everyone crossed everyone else's path fairly regularly in the Society, and it was no exception with himself and Hopkins. The most recent occasion had been when he led a retreat at that damp Welsh outpost where the chap was now a theologian. He still looked absurdly young, but at times he had the air of an old man. His eyes bothered him, as did his feet, and he groused about these ailments no end. That he did not fit seamlessly into the community was apparent from various glances and smirks that Coleridge detected; but as a fellow convert, he himself had always prized difference and did not wholly share the Society's disapproval of singular personalities. He would not call himself this strange, intense man's friend; that would be going too far, and in any case friendship was not really permitted within their ranks. But he was happy to acknowledge a genuine affection.

The object of this affection had never given the slightest hint, so far as Coleridge could recall, of literary ambition until a letter arrived out of the blue a few months ago, and even then he had gone into little detail. He had simply said he was working on a poem about the maritime tragedy at the mouth of the Thames the previous winter, and asked if he could send it to the magazine in due course. Coleridge had written back to say he would of course be delighted to take a look at the finished work. Had he perhaps even said he was looking forward to it? He hoped not, but he wouldn't put it past himself; he had been known to give authors false optimism.

On the desk behind him, on top of a detailed analysis of the Ritualism trials by an elderly priest in the Midlands and a flamboyant poem in neat iambic tetrameter from an Oxford undergraduate by the name of Wilde, the dot- and dash-spattered manuscript glared reprovingly up from the top of the pile nearest his blotter. Young Barry had devised a system of these piles, understood only by himself. He occasionally tried to explain it to Coleridge, who took as little notice as possible. All he knew was that Hopkins' extraordinary… whatever it was… seemed to appear at the top of one or other of them roughly once a fortnight. It would be much easier if he could summon the courage to plant the wretched thing definitively on the pointed spike on the far corner of his desk, but he could never bring himself to go that far.

He glowered at the street below, where a hansom driver had got a wheel stuck in a tram-rail and was engaged in a furious set-to with a tram driver. Coleridge had looked down from the same window when they first introduced these public trams. Back then they ran on wooden rails, which just sat on the surface of the road and caused havoc for everyone else. Only later had they been dug into place so that other vehicles could drive over them, and he well remembered the disruption that had caused, when for a while it seemed that every road in the city was being dug up. The row was getting louder now, as passengers on the top deck of the tram added their own encouragement to the hansom driver to get his carriage shifted. A gaggle of street-boys were adding to the chaos by trying to make the horses shy. Finally a policeman appeared, blowing a whistle, which dispersed the boys. It was remarkable how fast they vanished when they put their minds to it.

He slid the sash down to shut out the noise of the disturbance. Not only was Hopkins' submission at the top of the pile once more, but today there was also a letter from the chap himself, asking when it would appear in print. Not whether, mind, but when. The elderly editor sighed and picked up the manuscript. Perhaps it had mellowed in the weeks it had been sitting there. The handwriting was still ghastly, and the dots and dashes execrable. But he would do his best to ignore all that and focus on the text itself.

The exclamation mark at the start of the second line was horribly ugly, and a dreadfully accurate harbinger of all that was to follow. The rhyme scheme was clear enough, but the rhythm was utterly senseless. Even if you indulged the riotously irregular line lengths, you still couldn't get it to scan and, despite the absurd notation, he had no idea how any of it was meant to sound.

The second stanza was just as bad. The first half was histrionic but comprehensible. Then the syntax seemed to get so frenzied, it lost all self-control, rendering itself both dizzying and nonsensical – an unforgivable combination. Coleridge was prepared to allow that the heart might be trodden hard down by the sweep and the hurl of God, if he had any idea what the hurl of God actually was, and that such a heart might swoon, but whose was the horror of height? The circling structure of subordinate clause upon subordinate clause was so bewildering, it made his head spin. He could see it was an achievement of sorts for the phrase *horror of height* actually to induce vertigo. But it was a demonic kind of trickery that had no place in decent literature.

On he struggled. There were the sentences that didn't end where the stanza did, but came to an abrupt halt halfway through the first line of the next one. This, he supposed, was modernity. If so, he didn't like it any more than he liked the clattering of the trams outside. What was any rational person to make of four syllables in the first line and *fifteen* in the last? As the ghastly work wound on, there were rhymes so vulgar they belonged better in the music hall than in a piece of religious poetry.

The word *leeward* (which he knew was pronounced in nautical parlance *loo-ard*) was matched with the run-over rhyme *drew her/ Dead*, and then with *endured*. Was that meant to be a joke? Any schoolboy producing doggerel like that could expect to be beaten for brazen irreverence. No wonder Hopkins had made such a hash of his own teaching posts.

There was also the question of what the man was doing writing poetry of this length at all. The college rector would surely never sanction it. Hopkins was writing like a madman, and he was almost certainly breaking the rules of the Society. Oughtn't Coleridge to alert someone?

But that felt horribly disloyal. It would be snitching, a betrayal of literary confidence, and he would never do it to a friend. Feeling a headache coming on, he decided there was only one course of action for now. Gathering the sheaves of the perishing manuscript and tidying them into a neat pile, he shoved Hopkins' poem at the bottom of Barry's farthest and tallest stack, where he wouldn't have to see it or think about it again for a very long while.

North Wales, the present

Tim seems to have averted the immediate crisis. In the initial uproar of Chloe's discovery that some Judas has been planning on selling the poet's name for thirty pieces of Barry Brook, he is in a frenzy of panic and self-recrimination. In the ensuing days, he tries in vain to think of ways of putting Brook off – unfortunately lines like *it's all been a terrible mistake* or *I'm sorry I made it all up* won't do any good when it was all so obviously made up in the first place – before concluding that his only real option is not to encourage the guy any further. But a couple of weeks on, there has been no further word from Brook, Chloe is not in quite so warlike a mood – she has stopped talking about interrogating everyone in the valley – and Tim is no longer convinced that he has destroyed the best relationship he has ever had through greed and stupidity. He has had a damn good try, but luck and – if he says so himself – a degree of nimble-wittedness seem to have carried him through.

But as the panic abates, and he no longer fears so urgently for his new-found domestic security, Tim begins to reconsider his situation. In this calmer, more balanced light, he is no longer the author of his own near-destruction and is instead the victim of an over-scrupulous moral code.

"It's not fair," he complains to Alun Gwynne one quiet weekday afternoon when Chloe is safely in Manchester, emphasising the word with all the satisfaction of someone lighting on *le mot juste* after a painstaking search. Now he sees it clearly, the unfairness is spectacular and Chloe's literary piety is downright unreasonable, especially considering all the initiative that Tim has shown, and the effort he has expended, to get to this point. Hooking in Barry Brook is surely a massive achievement. Anyone else would see it as grounds for congratulation.

"Women are difficult creatures, landlord. Always have been, always will be," says Alun.

Tempted as Tim has been to tell the old fool never to show his face in the Red Lion again, as punishment for revealing his Grail scheme to Chloe, he can't afford to bar his best customer – particularly when Alun is also his best and only confidant. He also knows the stupid bastard may have done him a favour by allowing him to see the strength of Chloe's reaction before he blurted out something himself.

In that ghastly moment when it all came out, and he saw his relationship unravelling before him, he was completely prepared to abandon his Grail scheme if it meant not being dumped by Chloe. He was panicking at the prospect of losing her, and holding onto her was the only thing he cared about. Being rich and happy would be nice, but if he could not have both, domestic fulfilment was the option he instinctively preferred.

Now, however, he is not so sure. Examining his situation more calmly, he doesn't see why it's so wrong to want to be both rich and happy. And if Chloe herself is the main impediment to the former, is there any guarantee she will help him achieve the latter? Angry as he has been at Alun, he can now see that the old boy knows a thing or two about the opposite sex.

"What is it about me and women?" he says morosely, pulling another pint of special for each of them. He knows it's not sensible for a publican to seek solace via his own beer taps, but for the moment he is past caring.

Alun reaches down to hand Macca a biscuit.

"Were you married in the past, landlord?"

"Haven't I mentioned Nadine?"

He can't believe he hasn't. Then again, Alun Gwynne never mentioned his own wife, and Tim never used to get lubricated in his own bar.

"Well, I wondered if there had been someone. But I didn't like to pry."

"No secrets there."

"What was she like?"

Tim shrugs.

"She was warm, affectionate, she would donate money to anything, especially if it involved animals. The problem was she was also daft. Just not very bright, you know, in a harmless kind of way, but it got on your nerves after a few years. And she believed in all that Poussin stuff. Fell for it big-time. That's where I got the whole idea. I thought I'd told you."

"So that's why you parted? Literary differences?"

"No!" Tim snorts mirthlessly. "Differences over something else. Marriage vows."

"So you…?"

"Me? No, not me. I was faithful. Always had been. I took it seriously. She was the one who wasn't."

"I see," says Alun Gwynne, taking refuge in a sip of beer. He seems to realise these are dangerous memories. "Did you love her?"

Tim is not used to this kind of talk with anyone, let alone with Alun Gwynne. The easiest thing would be to pull away now, start sluicing the floor and make it clear these cosy confidences are not going to happen. But he hears himself saying: "I did once. I'm sure I did. By the end, though? No."

"It doesn't sound like you did. So in a sense…"

"Yes?"

"Well, in a sense, she freed you from your own vows."

Tim opens his mouth to say something, then thinks better of it. It didn't feel like being freed at the time.

Alun Gwynne seems to anticipate him. "But it still made you angry?"

"I nearly killed the guy. He was…"

He wants to go on, but it's hard, even after all this time.

Alun is waiting, and Tim forces himself. "He was my best friend. His name was Pete. Best man at our wedding. So I lost both of them. You can see why it hurt." He starts wiping down the bar so Alun can't see his eyes glistening. But to his surprise he feels strangely unburdened just by getting it out in the open. For years he has not even been able to say Pete's name, even in his head.

"I'm sorry for you, landlord, truly I am. It was a betrayal and it caused you pain. But if you didn't love her? She released you, however much it may have hurt at the time. If it hadn't happened, you would never have come here and met Chloe. Everything happens for a reason, do you see?"

Tim usually despises people who say that everything happens for a reason, and of course Nadine used to say it a lot. But, for the first time, he can understand the truth they are groping for. Every action has a reaction, every event has a consequence and, without a random series of interactions, the present as we know it would not exist. Whatever good stuff happens now, the bad stuff probably played a role in it. It's a useful insight that surprises him. He hopes he will still remember it tomorrow. But it doesn't solve his present problem.

"If I hadn't met Chloe, I'd be getting ready to welcome Barry Brook and looking forward to transforming the fortunes of this valley."

"You only wanted to transform the fortunes of the valley because you had a gap in your life. And now you haven't."

"I had a gap in my bank balance, and I've still got it."

"Oh come on, landlord. You're a romantic. I can see you are – even if you don't know it yourself. And you can see yourself that Chloe can help you get this place working. It won't happen immediately, but it might not happen immediately with Barry Brook either. The whole thing is still just a fantasy, remember, and there's no guarantee it will make you rich, even if he does write a book about the place. The only thing you know for certain is that you'll lose Chloe if she finds out you were behind the whole thing."

"Which she would never have done if some loose-tongued old fool hadn't blabbed."

"I've told you a dozen times I'm sorry about that. I just assumed you'd have told her about it already. In any case, I truthfully think you're fretting about nothing. If you keep mum and don't encourage him any further, I bet you all the tea in China that this character Brook will give up on the idea, and you'll never hear from him again. You mark my words. And even if he does write the book, it won't come back to you, because he doesn't have the slightest idea who you are. In fact, that might be the best of all worlds for you – win/win, as they say – because you'd get the tourists coming anyway. Your lovely lady may not like it, but she'll come round to it when she realises she's sitting on a goldmine. And she'll never know you had anything to do with it."

He chuckles at the thought and takes a sip of beer, as if to toast this perfect outcome. Then he wipes his mouth and continues:

"As long as he doesn't actually turn up here, which I really don't think will happen. And if you want to keep her, which I think you do, you must not have any more direct contact with Barry Brook. That would be most unwise, in my opinion."

Tim thinks on this for the rest of the week and comes round to the idea that the old boy is right. It's true that Nadine did him a favour. Either because of an old-fashioned respect for his vows, or maybe just because he was too gutless, he would never have ended the marriage himself. Of course it hurt to lose the two most important people in his life at the same time, to imagine them together, not just physically but also in comradeship, conspiring against him and laughing at him – that had hurt his pride. But looking back on his years with Nadine, on the rage he had felt because she didn't see the world in just the same way as he did, he cannot ever recall feeling the kind of contentment to which he now looks forward every weekend, the warmth he feels just to be in Chloe's company. That warmth makes him see the world differently: she is softening him, he can feel it already, otherwise he would never have opened up to Alun Gwynne like that. It's odd to feel himself changing, but he likes himself for it, far more than he liked the old Tim.

By the time Chloe arrives the following weekend, he has decided there is indeed a choice between riches and happiness, and happiness is the better route. He plans a walk for them on the Saturday morning before he opens the pub, and in the evening he watches her radiate charm at their slowly enlarging clientele. He even finds himself reflecting some of it in the form of genuine bonhomie. He is all the more convinced that he has made the right decision when, at the end of the evening, he watches her denim-clad rear climb the creaking stairs ahead of him. Yes, he will emerge from this escapade with his relationship intact, even if he must kiss goodbye to his dream of filling the valley with Grail-trailing punters. Keeping her is the main thing, he is certain, as he watches her emerge from the bathroom in a skinny robe that barely covers the tops of her milky thighs.

He is about to get into bed when he notices a message blinking on his phone.

His blood runs suddenly colder when he sees who it is from.

It reads:

Dude, change of plan. My current project has just been shoved back a whole six months so I've got time on my hands. Seems like the perfect opportunity to come check out this place of yours and talk some more about these nuns, no? I'm arriving the back end of next week, so we can finally meet. But I still don't know your real name or where you are. Let me know how I can find you.

BB

Dublin, 1886

Hopkins had been trying to decide which was more bruised, his arm or his dignity. When he removed his undershirt to inspect the damage in the flickering gaslight of his room, he was surprised to find there was barely a mark. Maybe it would flare in the coming days, but for the moment the dignity had it.

All he had been trying to do was get his class more engaged. The witless creatures only ever saw the verse as a chore, dead lines on a page they were translating because they might be examined on it, not an account of flesh-and-blood events that had once moved listeners to tears. He yearned to create that impact once more, to make it sing for them. Of course it was harder when the music of the words came in a difficult ancient language. That was why he had hit on a more theatrical approach.

"You sir," he had said to a mousy boy with buck teeth who always sat in the front row and was one of the few never to chatter, cat-call or cheek – more from lack of spirit, he suspected, than good manners. "How would you like to come out here and be the gleaming-helmeted Hector for us?"

The boy looked alarmed. "What would I have to do, sir?" Even his voice was slow, with a country drawl, although what part of the country Hopkins could not say;

he had not been in Ireland long enough to tell. He hoped he never would be.

"Nothing too taxing. He has just been slain, remember, so for the moment all you need to do is position yourself on the floor, recumbent, about here…"

He moved his table away from the front desk so that the Greek victors, when he had chosen them, would be able to get a clear run around it. When he looked up, the toothy boy had not budged.

"Come on, man."

"What, lie down and that?"

"Yes, yes, sir. Come on, the floor is quite clean." A white lie was permissible in the cause of bringing Homer to life.

"I'd rather not, sir."

He was momentarily at a loss. There was no going back now, but what if there was no going forward either?

"I'll have a crack at it, sir," came a breezy voice from the back.

Hopkins peered near-sightedly through a blur of faces to see a hand semaphoring in his direction.

"Who's that?"

"Me, sir. Craig, sir."

Now he could see. Craig was built like a bull, with manners to match. Hopkins had no idea how he had ended up at a university, even such a sorry one as this.

"Any other volunteers?" He vainly scanned the benches, up, down, across and back again. "No? Very well then, Mr Craig. Down you come."

Craig was remarkably compliant, and they were all

entering into the spirit now. Having cast his Trojans, Hopkins toyed with the idea of making them stand on the table, but he decided that would be too precarious.

"You could turn it upside down, sir," suggested Craig, and it wasn't such a bad idea. So he cleared away his papers and books, and Craig and a couple of the other meatier ones up-ended the desk, allowing the grieving Trojan party to take its smirking place within the legs.

All that was left was to appoint a swift-footed Achilles, mad to avenge the dead Patroclus. A rat-faced young man called Byrne put himself forward to play the warrior hero. It was hard to imagine anyone less appropriate, but there were no other volunteers.

In the text, Achilles pierced Hector's heels to pull him along.

"I'm not sure that's very practical here," said Hopkins. "You'll have to make do with grabbing him by the feet."

Byrne did as he was told, and now there was laughter. Hopkins could not actually see Craig's face, but he assumed there was mugging going on. Byrne pulled and strained but failed to shift Craig an inch.

"You'll have to swap," said Hopkins.

Now Byrne too started fussing about not wanting to lie on the floor, and they seemed to have reached an impasse.

"Why don't you play Hector, sir?" piped up a voice from the back. "Show us how it's done."

And in his keenness to make it work, not to abandon the whole idea, he went along with it, arranging himself on the floor and allowing Craig to grasp his ankles. It was only when the whole lecture theatre erupted in a delighted, Vesuvian uproar, and he saw the room spinning above him as he was trailed in ever faster circles around the upturned legs of the besieged city, that he saw the full, catastrophic extent of his folly.

At some stage his arm hit the table leg, but the ordeal only stopped when the door opened.

"Who was it that came in?" asked his friend Curtis, when Hopkins related the story a couple of days later. It was painful to relive any of the scene and he would have preferred to block it from his memory completely, but he was aware that hiding it away would only worsen the sense of shame. His colleagues were probably all laughing about it behind his back anyway, so facing up to it was the best thing to do.

"You really haven't heard it from him already? It was Darlington."

"No, I swear, I didn't know any of this until now."

"Decent of him not to tell, then. But it was degrading. I thought when I came here that teaching undergraduates would be an improvement on schoolboys. But these ones are just as unruly. I don't object to their cheeking me personally, but I do mind their being rude to their professor and a priest. And I confess I dread facing them again."

"Brazen it out, old man. Don't let them see they're winning."

He and Curtis, who taught mathematics, had been friends since their arrival at the university. Curtis was ten years his junior, with pale blue eyes set beneath a wide brow, and a sportsman's physique that belied the fact that he suffered from epilepsy and avoided all undue exertion. A couple of hours' walking was about the limit of it, and today they had been out to the park, a lonely but beautiful place with deep woods, dells and drives where Hopkins would spend more time, if only it were a little more accessible.

He had imagined this would be an elegant city, and clearly it once had been. There were some fine buildings, a Corinthian colonnade here and a couchant lion above a doorway there, and he had seen richly ornamented interiors. But the whole place had fallen into a sad decline. Few buildings were as wrecked as their own, which had once been a showy gem but now crumbled around their ears. He had entertained notions of walks in the new-laid garden square across the road from the house. But even this was full of vagrants who seemed to have set up home there, and he had not been back after the first time. The fog was thicker than in London, but the worst aspect of the whole confounded city was the ever-present stench. It got stronger the closer you came to the river, and he avoided crossing this open sewer at all, if he could help it. His own preferred route to the park involved crossing it higher up, but Curtis, who had lived here all his life, had set out the most direct way today, and Hopkins had not liked to give offence by objecting. He made do with pressing a handkerchief to his face as they crossed the bridge.

"They hold it against me because I'm English."

"There may be some of that, I'm afraid. Nationalism is growing ever stronger, especially with the archbishops putting their oar in. But there is also..."

Curtis hesitated, passing his hand nervously through his short russet beard.

"Go on," said Hopkins. "What is there also?"

"Well, it's your syllabus. You don't teach to the examination."

This again! "How can I teach to the examination? I set the questions and I mark all the papers. One thousand, six hundred and fifty-two scripts last year, let me remind you, and probably more this. So, as I keep telling everyone, it would be quite improper, *utterly* improper, to give my own students an unfair advantage…"

"Don't work yourself up, old fellow. All I mean is, the rest of us aren't perfect teachers either, far from it. Most of us are complete idiots, if truth be told. But we teach what we think will come up, so they pay attention. It stands to reason, doesn't it?"

"But none of the rest of you has to set an examination!"

"But for heaven's sake, you can teach to some of it! The reason they lark about so much is they know that nothing you teach will ever come up. Don't you see?"

"But don't *you* see…?" Hopkins was trembling. It made him so furious when people refused to acknowledge the impossibility of his position. They didn't have the terrible burden, the Sisyphean labour, of marking papers. He wouldn't mind having to go through the hundreds of scripts if he felt he was furthering the cause of learning, but the process merely confirmed that nothing could be further from the case. The thought of it wound him into a further bate, and it wasn't until he felt Curtis' touch on his arm that he realised they were standing outside the railings of the soot-blackened townhouse where his friend's parents lived.

"Shall we call in for tea?" said Curtis with a conciliatory smile. "It's nearly time, and you know how Mother loves to see you."

Hopkins was not yet in a mood to be conciliated, but his chilblains had flared from walking, and a rest would be very welcome.

North Wales, the present

Tim and Chloe are on the sofa in his little sitting room watching the evening news. Chloe is curled up, her shoes kicked off and her small white feet tucked neatly behind her thighs, as she rolls herself into a feline ginger ball. Tim sprawls with one leg on the rug and the other slung over the coffee table, just clear of their empty supper plates.

The headlines are depressing: wars, terrorist bombings, job losses.

"What kind of world are we living in?" says Chloe. "It just seems to get worse and worse."

Tim nods, sensing that a moment has arrived. Closing his eyes, he recites:

"No worse, there is none. Pitched past pitch of grief,
More pangs will, schooled at forepangs, wilder wring…"

He pauses, as if to suggest he's savouring the power of poetic expression, although it's actually to cover the fact that he can't remember the next line. He could do it yesterday, but now he can't for the life of him remember what comes next. *Mary, mother of us?* No, there's something before that. Bollocks. Why is he always so useless?

He has decided it is important to convince her that he is a genuine devotee of the poet, rather than the mercenary fraud he really is. During the days when he is alone at the Red Lion, he has been looking through some of the other poems in the *Collected Works*. Most of them go way over his head – sometimes he can understand the first few lines and then he gets lost, other times not even that – but this one has caught his eye. It's short, the language isn't too weird or obscure, and in his present mood of self-flagellation, having come so close to messing up the best thing that has happened to him in years, the sentiment seems pretty relevant. He has been trying to get enough of it by heart to recite casually during the weekend, as if lines of poetry are always flowing from his soul, and he has simply never got around to expressing them before. Mindful that this is not the most obviously romantic poem, he has been waiting for a suitably bleak moment to perform it. The present opportunity one is perfect – but now he has managed to balls it up by forgetting the words.

He risks opening his eyes, and finds she is smirking at him.

"It's not 'worse', it's 'worst'," she says, muting the TV to leave the newscaster mouthing gravely on in silence.

"*No worst, there is none. Pitched past pitch of grief,*
More pangs will, schooled at forepangs, wilder wring."

And then, of course, she continues. She is more competitive than any man he can think of – and unlike him, she doesn't dry after two lines.

"*Comforter, where, where is your comforting?*"

How could he have forgotten that? It's not exactly hard – one line made pretty much entirely from the words 'comfort' and 'where'.

She isn't stopping. Why would she? She rattles off the other eleven lines perfectly – he has learned them well enough to recognise that, even if not to successfully recite them himself. He starts to applaud – she is seriously good at it, knowing how to put the accent on certain words so that lines which are obscure on the page suddenly acquire a clarity – but now she's explaining it to him as well. It's a good job he likes her so much.

"Do you see the difference in that first phrase?" she is saying. "If the line went 'no worse there is none', he'd be saying his life couldn't possibly get any shittier than it was for him at that moment, wouldn't he? But he's actually saying it's even worse than that because, however bad things get, they can always surprise you by getting even worse later on. There are no limits to the crap life can throw at you, basically."

"Cheerful."

"Well, you're the one who started quoting it. Is your life so bad at the moment?"

"Of course not."

He leans over to kiss her on the lips. She's right, he is certainly not complaining about this part. But out of the corner of his eye he can see the light of his phone blinking away, to remind him how close to relationship doom he has brought himself.

In the past two weeks he has received no fewer than nine emails and tweets from Barry Brook. They start relatively calmly:

"Hey dude, I'm getting on a plane tomorrow and I still haven't heard back from you. Let me know where you are so I can come and find you, okay? And give me a number so I can call you!"

Then they become more frantic:

"I've been in your goddamn country three whole days now, and I still haven't heard a word from you. Do you want me to write this book or not??!"

And they end up downright furious:

"Just remember YOU were the one who got in touch with ME and I've come four thousand freaking miles for you, so have the decency to send me a darn reply!!!"

Those are just the ones that Tim has opened. He tells himself the guy can't do him any harm even if he could find him, which he can't. But throughout the weekend, that winking red eye of the unopened messages serves as both a rebuke and a menace, reminding him how badly he has messed up, and how much messier it could still get.

He eventually checks them after Chloe has left. Only one is from Barry; the other two are spam from an insurance company and a forlorn suggestion from a garage back in England that he should have the Suzuki serviced. But the ominous silence after a final angry outburst from Brook is, if anything, even more alarming.

The worry gnaws at him. Over the next few days, he finds himself prickly and irritable. He loses his temper in traffic on the way to Morrisons, and he picks a fight with customer service when his trolley won't give him his pound coin back.

"It's like he's here somewhere, and I don't know where or when he's going to pop out," he tells Alun Gwynne.

"You've no reason to think he's actually here," says the old boy.

"Apart from all those messages saying he's arrived?"

"But did he actually say he was coming *here*? He said he was coming to this country, by which he probably meant England not Wales, so he's probably in some fancy hotel in London."

Tim tries to remember what he told Barry Brook about their location. He was careful not to give his own identity away, so he certainly didn't mention the Red Lion. But did he mention the village, the valley, St Vowelless's? Thinking back, he is pretty sure he didn't. But that's not much consolation, because it wouldn't be hard for Brook to work it out from any online biography of the poet.

He explains that to Alun, who just shrugs and says: "I'm sure we'd have heard if he had been here."

"Really? He's an author, not a film star. It's not like he's recognised everywhere he goes. Do you know what he looks like? I don't think I do."

"I might. I saw him on TV once."

Tim makes a mental note to google Barry Brook to see if he can find a picture.

"But I really don't think he'll come any where near this corner of Wales," Alun continues. "I bet you at this very moment he's eating cucumber sandwiches in Harrods. Americans love that sort of thing, don't they?"

Tim is not entirely sure that rich American tourists eat afternoon tea in Harrods, but before he can say so they are both distracted by the scrape of the heavy front door on the flagstones.

In the doorway is a small, round man of about sixty. He removes a pair of aviator shades and squints as his eyes still don't adjust to the gloom.

"Afternoon, sir," says Tim with a queasy feeling. He wishes Alun Gwynne and Macca didn't look quite so much like extras from *The Wicker Man*, turning round to stare at any stranger.

"Good day to you," says the newcomer.

He's wearing a pink Lacoste polo shirt over long shorts, with matching pink socks over gleaming white trainers. It's a strange ensemble, but of more obvious concern is his unmistakably American accent.

"I'm looking for a room to stay a few nights, and I saw your sign. Do you have vacancies?"

Cleaning up the battered old board advertising bed and breakfast has been another of Chloe's schemes, and they have bought new bedding and towels and little tabs of guest soap. That's one reason that Tim doesn't immediately tell the American he's sorry, but all the rooms are taken: it feels wrong to be turning his first-ever customer away, particularly when he needs the cash so badly. Also, he reckons the visitor would see through that right away. This doesn't look like the kind of pub where the accommodation is all taken. And there are two hundred and fifty million Americans, so the odds are stacked heavily against this being the only one of them he specifically doesn't want staying under his roof.

"Certainly, sir. Just a single room, will that be? And if I could take a name for the register?" He tries to open his brand new guest book in such a way that the guy can't see that his will be the first entry.

"Yes of course. It's Brook."

Tim feels his stomach turn over. He signals urgently

with his eyes to Alun Gwynne not to say a word.

"Would that be Brooke with an 'e' or Brook without?"

He knows he is clutching at straws.

"Without. B-R-O-O-K."

"Without. Got it."

"And that's initial F," adds the visitor.

Tim looks up, perhaps a little too delightedly. Is there a God after all?

"…for Finbar."

"Of course," says Tim as he inscribes it. "Why wouldn't it be?"

"I beg your pardon?"

"I mean it's, erm, a name you don't come across very often."

"I'm from an Irish background," says the visitor.

"Oh yes, I see. Marvellous. Now, if you wouldn't mind just signing here…"

Tim's face is fixed in a rictus smile of hospitality as he offers his guest a pen.

But he is actually thinking how right the poet got it.

No worst there is none.

DUBLIN, 1886

Hopkins truly understood how bad his living conditions were the day he was summoned to the kitchen by a chorus of female screaming. It was not long after his arrival, when he was still trying to comprehend the cultural vandalism of the bishops who had previously run the university and had departed with all the books. He and his colleagues had been trying to rebuild a collection, but since the bishops had also confined their sorry institution to the top two floors of the crumbling building, there was barely anywhere to put the few volumes they did have. These works were now shelved on odd bits of spare wall around the stairs and hallways. He had been trying to reach down an Aeschylus from a high shelf when the alarm was raised.

He turned to find the older of their two cooks, redder in the face than normal and wild-eyed with panic.

"I'm sorry to disturb you, Father, but can you come?"

"Whatever is it?"

"Would you just come?"

Another wail reached them from the kitchen, followed by a plaintive: "Would you hurry up, Mrs Brady?"

The cook looked imploringly at him, kneading a tea-cloth in her calloused hands.

"Very well," he blinked, although he wondered if this was quite his jurisdiction. Was it an intruder of some kind? As Mrs Brady bustled ahead of him, he plucked one of the house umbrellas from the hall stand and gripped it tight. Could she not have found someone else – Father Delany, or one of the resident students?

His guide had reached the doorway, and now stood aside to let him see. Whatever he had expected, the sight that greeted him was not it. The younger cook, a broad-faced creature with a lazy eye, was perched on a chair in the middle of the room. Whimpering, she had her one good eye fixed on the corner opposite the door.

"It's still there," she hissed. "I've had me eyes peeled the whole time." She risked a glance in their direction and registered Hopkins' presence. "Was that the only Father there was?"

He drew himself up to his full five feet two.

"Come, my dear. Tell me what on earth is going on here."

The girl on the chair pointed at the range.

"It came out of that stewpot. I just took the lid off to give it a stir, and it jumped out at me. Dirty great huge thing, with teeth and everything."

Hopkins suppressed a smile. He liked mice and had never been able to fathom female hysteria over them.

"And where is it now?"

He hoped his calm tone might reassure the girl.

"Over there, behind them buckets."

She nodded at a cluster of mops and pails.

"Well, then. We'll soon get him out of there. No need to distress yourself any further. I'm certain he's far more afraid of you than you are of him."

He was rather enjoying himself.

"Now, all we have to do is move this one here…"

He was expecting the fugitive to bury itself further within the pile and not emerge till he removed the last item. It might even have found some skirting-hole to squeeze through already. He was *not* expecting to be charged by a foot-long monster, if you counted the tail, its fur slick with whatever gelatinous concoction had been in the stewpot. The girl screamed again, and Hopkins uttered a yelp of his own as he leapt to avoid it. He wheeled round to see the rat disappearing under the low legs of a stout dresser against the opposite wall.

"Get it out, Father! Get it out of my kitchen now!" cried Mrs Brady. "I swear by the Blessed Virgin I'm not going near that stove until you do."

Hopkins discovered he was trembling. He had no idea how to proceed. He was professor of Greek, for pity's sake, not a rat-catcher.

"Isn't there a man for this? Whom do you usually call on for practical things?"

He was ashamed to find himself so ignorant about how the place worked. Back in Wales, he would have known which member of the household to summon, at least as a first resort. But this wasn't that kind of community.

"That would normally be my brother, Father. But he's after breaking a bone in his foot and he's laid up this last month. Should we go for Father Delany?"

This acted as a spur. Was Hopkins really so unequal to the task? Shaking his head and indicating they should stand back, he hitched his cassock into a fold so that it gave a double thickness for a cushion at the knees, and lowered himself to the floor. With his palms flat on the cool slate slabs, he cautiously brought his face down to the same level.

"Careful, Father. You don't want it to bite."

"No, Mrs Brady, I most certainly don't."

He had hoped the rat might have found some means of escape under the range, but no such luck. There it was, every bit as large as it had seemed at first encounter, staring straight at him with mean little eyes. What on earth was he meant to do? If it charged him again, it really could bite, with possible consequences that did not bear thinking about. Perhaps they ought to fetch Father Delany after all. He backed slowly away and stood up.

"There must be a rat-catcher locally," he said. How could they not have one when the place was so infested? "Other than your brother, I mean. A proper rat-man. You must send for him today. But first we must get rid of this one." He mopped his brow with the sleeve of his robe. "Mrs Brady, could you fetch me a jar? No, that's too small. Nothing bigger? It should be as tall as you can find." He spotted a row of earthenware flasks on the shelf next the sink. "One of those will do. What's in it, flour? Tip it into a bowl, that's it. And now we need some bait. Have you some cheese? Put it in the bottom, like so, and let's lay the jar down… gently now, we don't want to scare him away. But give me that chopping board first…"

It was ingenious, even if he said so himself. Whether it would work was another matter. With the older cook stooping behind him to offer moral if not practical support, he rolled the jar gently into position so that the neck was level with the rat.

"Give him a prod from behind," offered the younger cook, still on her chair. "Force him out, like."

"No, that will send him to ground." He was impressed by his own certainty, whether or not it was true.

He positioned the mouth of the jar as close as he could to the gap at the base of the dresser. But he realised he would have no way of knowing if the rat had gone inside, so he pulled his makeshift trap back an inch or two. Then he waited. With no sign of movement, he lowered himself down again as gently as he could and brought his face down to the floor. The creature was in the same place, with just a glint of those black eyes to show it was observing everything that was going on.

"Maybe we should go for Father Delany," said the girl on the chair.

"Sh!" he hissed, irritated, because now that he had come this far, he did not want her to be right. He waited on, but nothing moved. He sighed and was about to admit defeat when the snout of the rat appeared, gingerly at first and disappearing from view again. Then, to his delight, the whole creature skittered forward and into the jar.

"Now!" he cried, grabbing the lip of the jar to right it, and slamming the chopping board over the neck. His heart beat fast as he pressed the board down, and he could feel a trickle of sweat running between his shoulder-blades. He had done it.

Together they bore the jar downstairs and out through the front door, dodging the carriages to cross over into the square. To think that when they first offered him this chair of Greek, he had seen himself striding across a college green with his hands behind his back, like some latter-day Jowett or Pusey, deep in learned argumentation with the brightest of his pupils.

"Maybe you've found your calling at last, Hopkins," said Darlington at dinner that night. He joined in with the laughter. But it was a stark reminder of the gap between what he had aspired to achieve in his life and career and what he had actually achieved.

Every night after dinner their small community repaired to what served as their sitting room, its ornate plaster reliefs now chipped and soiled, its walls hung with cheap reproductions of the saints. Hopkins never joined them. The tall windows were rotten at the top, which meant draughts whistled in. In the grip of a murderous head-cold the previous winter, he had found it was easier to stay warm in his own room on the top floor, and since winters seemed to last until at least May in this country, he had lost the habit of sitting with the others at all.

His Englishness isolated him too. It wasn't just his views on Home Rule, which in any case had mellowed since his arrival. He knew that his colleagues also resented the appointment to the teaching staff of anyone from the English province – they had made that clear by having an open row about it at the time of his appointment. For them, a Catholic university was primarily about nationalism, not religion.

But he would never break down the hostility if he did not make the effort to mix. Ten years ago in Wales, he had been the one to come up with word games or make everyone laugh with comic doggerel. Companionship was part of the reason he had chosen the religious life rather than take a parish, so it made no sense to shun it now.

He saw his opportunity a night or two later. The old Frenchman Mallac, who taught Logic but seemed to have little use for it in his daily life, was creating merriment with his latest medical fad. He had developed a fascination for a European system of medicine involving tiny globules taken in water. Hopkins had tried it a few times and had been none the worse for it, even if it would be a stretch to say it had helped; Curtis, on the other hand, had a fit the night after he took his first dose.

"Not that quackery again," the latter said now.

Mallac made a show of looking hurt, which fooled no one. "No, this is a new one," he said.

"A new quackery?"

"A new system."

"Go on then, you'd better tell us," said someone else. "You're going to anyway."

"Well, if you really want to know it's based on the same principle…"

"Quackery?"

"It's called homeopathy." The old man glared from under his shaggy white eyebrows, but there was a twitch of amusement at the corner of his mouth. He was never wholly serious. "Only this time it is applied with electricity."

That made the smiles disappear.

"You're not serious?"

"Deadly!"

"I should say it is!"

That was Curtis again, and Mallac reached across the table in a mock swipe.

"Let me explain how it works."

"I think you should."

There were several kinds of electricity, apparently: red, blue, yellow, green and so forth. This system used the white kind, which you took from a battery. You used it with a liquid applied with cotton wool to the parts affected.

"It comes from a shop in Paris, two francs a bottle. It should arrive next week." Mallac beamed like a child.

"Well in that case," said Father Delany, "someone ought to try it."

"Not on your life," said one of the resident students.

"Don't look at me," said Darlington.

"Does it work for chilblains?"

A mass of faces turned to Hopkins in surprise.

"It is recommended for all manner of complaints."

"That's not what I asked."

He was sick to death of the pain and was open to anything, and it might help his standing in the household if he showed willing.

"Can you assure me it won't hurt?" he pressed.

The old man's blue eyes laughed at him.

"Of course not. But tell me – do the chilblains hurt?"

"Certainly they do. Which is no reason to subject myself to additional pain."

"It would be, if the extra pain is a means to eliminating the original pain."

"Well, obviously. But you haven't established that."

"That's what you should have asked about, then. You need to know if it will work, not if it will hurt."

"And will it?"

They had made their way out of the dining room and were at the sitting room door now.

"We won't know until we try it, will we?" Mallac winked.

Hopkins had decided to come into the sitting room too. Volunteering for the treatment was a way of pulling down the wall he had erected between himself and the rest of them, and joining them after the meal was the natural next step. Because it felt so natural to him, it did not occur to Hopkins that it might not be so obvious to everyone else. There was no malice in Mallac as he opened the door for himself, without standing aside for Hopkins to go first or holding it for him to follow. He doubtless intended no rebuff when he said: "I'll let you know when I've got the battery working and the tincture arrives. For now, my brave friend, good night."

The old man could have little idea how much it hurt when he closed the door behind him, still chuckling, leaving Hopkins with no choice but to continue his lonely climb to his own room.

As he opened his own door, the sight of the piles of papers on his desk filled him with desolation. There were his notes for an essay on the Dorian measure that would never be published; the start of another on Homeric study, ditto; a letter to Bridges that he had been working on for a fortnight; a few pages of music where he had been trying to work up a melody that had come to him on a walk... It all seemed so pointless. Somewhere at the bottom of one of those piles was the manuscript of his poem about those poor wrecked nuns. Nothing had ever become of it, and he had given up trying to get an answer out of Coleridge. Where was the point of any of it? He couldn't see any use continuing with any of these doomed, lonely projects. None of them would ever see the light of day.

He sat on his hard wooden chair, frowned for a moment at the picture of Dolben on the *carte de visite* that the boy had sent all those years ago, then took a sheet of foolscap from the drawer and dipped his pen. He had the opening words of a sonnet, at least.

"No worst; there is none..." he began to write.

NORTH WALES, THE PRESENT

Tim helps fetch his American guest's luggage from his hire car, a colossal black-windowed Lexus that looks like it could be armour-plated, and leads the way upstairs to the better of the two rooms, in that it has a view of the valley rather than the car park. It has its own wash-basin, in a primrose shade that seems horribly dated to Tim, but Chloe has managed to make a feature of it by finding bedding and towels in various beiges and browns to set it off. Because having guests is all so new, Tim is flustered anyway, trying to remember all the things he ought to be saying about where the bathroom is, how to work the shower, what would his visitor like for his breakfast, and so on. And all the while his mind is racing though the implications of what is happening. He wonders if he should acknowledge it, come straight out and ask if the guy is Finbar Brook as in Barry Brook, the world-famous writer. Is it odd that he isn't doing so, like he's deliberately avoiding mentioning it? But since the guy hasn't said he's called Barry, mightn't that be even more suspicious, as if Tim has particular reason to be thinking about Barry Brook?

"I'll leave you to, erm, settle in," is all he says, leaving his guest to admire his uncle's ancient oak desk and a car-boot sale watercolour of Rhuddlan Castle, and backing out like an anxious flunky. At least Brook won't notice anything too odd about that last part: he probably thinks it's completely normal for the British serving-classes to be feudally polite.

He wonders if there is any point at all in entertaining the flimsy hope that Finbar Brook may not actually be Barry Brook. He is in a mood to clutch at any straw he can find. But Alun Gwynne shatters that possibility when Tim gets back downstairs by saying yes, he recognises the guy from what he remembers of his author picture. And Brook himself banishes any remaining doubt when he reappears in the bar ten minutes later.

"Could either of you good gentlemen point me in the direction of Saint... now I don't think I can pronounce this, but I have it written down..." he says, producing a Post-It note on which the name of St Vowelless's is printed in neat capitals.

It's all getting to Tim now, and he is sure the beads of sweat on his forehead must be visible. But Alun Gwynne seems more than happy to play the role of quaint, garrulous local, telling their guest the way and asking if he has business at the college. He has to repeat himself a lot, and Tim is momentarily diverted to see that Brook is struggling with the old boy's Welsh accent. But eventually Alun makes himself understood.

"No, no," says Brook. "I'm interested in the poet who used to live there, is all. Do you know his work? I guess everyone in these parts is real proud of him."

"I've barely read any of it," says Tim. In his mind the phrase *No worst there is none* is playing on loop.

"Me neither," says Alun Gwynne. "For me he's just another English incomer. No offence, landlord."

"None taken, Alun," says Tim with a frozen smile.

"But some people round here might be real experts, right? I mean, they could have all kinds of, like, theories about his work?"

"Oh, not really," says Tim. "That's to say, I've never heard anyone talk about him. Certainly not in here. Have you, Alun?"

"Not a soul, landlord."

Even Macca seems to shake his head in solidarity. If Tim gets out of this mess intact, the mutt can have a bag of pork scratchings on the house every day. Well, maybe every week.

"Okay," shrugs Brook. "I just wish I could find the son of a bitch who lured me here to tell me all about him, and has now disappeared into thin air."

Tim and Alun Gwynne tut sympathetically, but then Tim has to turn away because he can feel a muscle below his left eye begin to flutter uncontrollably. He bends behind the bar as if he's attending to a beer keg.

"Well, thank you gentlemen, I'll make my way over to Saint … how do you pronounce that actually?" says Brook, and Alun Gwynne demonstrates. The American tries it himself a few times. His version is probably execrable, but Tim is in no position to cast the first stone.

Halfway to the door, Brook turns back. "Just one other thing. You guys both know the landscape around here real well, right? Is there any particular hill that looks to you like a forehead?"

Tim, who is emptying an overflowing drip tray into the sink, spills most of it down his jeans.

He has offered his visitor a full Welsh breakfast, assuring him that everything will be free-range and locally sourced. Brook says he always likes an early-morning stroll before eating, which gives Tim the chance to nip down to Morrisons. There he locally sources a dozen eggs for one pound thirty-two, sausages and bacon on buy-one-get-one-free, and sell-by-date mushrooms from the discount counter. With a nice grind of rock salt and black pepper, a sprinkle of dried herbs and some fancy bread, the guy will never know the difference. He grabs some wild flowers out of a hedgerow on the way back and it all looks authentically rustic by the time it all gets to the table.

Brook seems appreciative enough. He doesn't volunteer whether or not he has found St Vowelless's the previous evening and Tim doesn't ask. He does ask if his visitor knows how long he'll be staying, but the answer is vague.

"I'm doing some research in the area and I don't know how long it's going to take me," says Brook.

Perhaps that's meant to be a cue for Tim to ask what kind of research – oh you're a writer, hey wait, Finbar Brook, you're not actually *the*… in *my* pub! well I'll be…! But if it is, he ignores it and his guest is in no mood to chat. In fact the American doesn't appear particularly relaxed around Tim and seems to be much more comfortable talking to Alun Gwynne. Tim decides that's a sign of insecurity: he's happy patronising the rude Welsh mechanical but can't cope with an equal.

After breakfast, Brook makes himself scarce, and Tim imagines him driving along the valley, sizing up each outcrop from every possible angle to see if it looks like a human brow. For a wistful moment, he allows himself to consider what a result this would have been in any other circumstances: one of the world's most famous writers wandering around the lanes of North Wales researching a new book entirely at Tim's behest. It is a case of sod's law: if Tim was still desperate for Brook to come, and Chloe was not in the equation, he could be sure his guest would still be in America now, refusing all blandishments. But there is no point thinking like that, because Chloe *is* in the equation and that's a good thing. Instead, he should thank his lucky stars that she isn't coming this weekend. Having her around would make life seriously difficult.

At about lunchtime he gets a text, although he is out at the back when it arrives, so he doesn't notice it till mid-afternoon.

Hey handsome, good news! I managed to move things around so I can come down this weekend!! The weather's meant to be awesome so I couldn't resist :) Hope that's okay, let me know if it isn't, otherwise I'll get going as soon as I've grabbed what I need from home. Can't wait to see you Cxxx

As a wise man once said: Fuck, fuck, fuck, fuckity fuck.

Tim rules out the most obvious excuses. He's got a lot of work on. He's skint. He's organising a stag do for his best/second-best/not-so-close-that-you've-ever-heard-of-him mate. Any of those would be bad, and putting Chloe off will do more harm than allowing her to come – especially since she leaves work early on Fridays, and is almost certainly on her way by the time he sees the message. So it's a case of damage limitation. He needs to convince her he has no idea that Finbar Brook is actually Barry Brook, and somehow he also needs to ensure that she doesn't inflict violence, physical or verbal, on his first paying guest. With both those ends in mind, his immediate priority is to make sure that Brook and Chloe are never alone together. This can't be too difficult, and he resolves to stress the importance of it to Alun Gwynne as soon as he appears. It will give the old bastard a chance to make himself useful. But the main thing is to be vigilant himself. Given that he has little else to do but stand behind an empty bar, that can't be too difficult either.

There's no sign of his guest for the rest of the day, and Tim begins to fantasise that the American has done a runner. The more he thinks about it, the more attractive this prospect seems, and he even lets himself into Brook's room to see if the guy has secretly removed his luggage. Sadly, he hasn't. All his bags are still there, and alongside the crisply folded shirt and neat rolls of socks there is a pile of books on the oak desk, including an American edition of the *Complete Works* and a biography of the poet, his portrait peering sadly off the cover. Tim has never seen a picture of him before. He looks like a boy of fifteen with droopy eyelids and a straggly beard.

There is also no sign of Alun Gwynne all afternoon. This is unusual, and Tim is wondering where the old boy has got to when his phone rings.

He doesn't recognise the number.

"Is it Red Lion?"

"Yes, this is the Red Lion."

The accent is East European and the tone is peevish.

"What the hell this language everywhere? I lost, I take wrong road, I get stuck. You come help now?"

He has forgotten that he is due a brewery delivery. One advantage of not selling much beer is that he doesn't have to deal with deliveries very often; the disadvantage is that there isn't a regular driver and the irregular ones persist in following sat nav routes that turn out to be unsuitable for heavy vehicles, rather than the perfectly serviceable road signs. The present one is now jammed under a low railway bridge up near the coast road. It doesn't sound like he's coping well with the stress, and the Welsh language signage seems to have added to his bad temper, even though the signs are all in English too.

Tim tries to calm the driver down, but it's difficult with the language barrier, and it's clear that he is going to have to go and help. Fortunately it's fairly obvious where the guy is – that bridge is a notorious trap – otherwise just working out his location over the phone would be a nightmare.

Sure enough, finding the lorry isn't hard. But extracting it turns out to be complicated. With one lane of the road completely blocked, there is traffic backing up in both directions and Tim can see why the guy, who turns out to be Latvian, needs another body just to make the angry queue behind him keep its distance, and then give him the space to reverse and turn round. The logistics are tricky, but once it's clear what is needed, a couple of car drivers help out too. Eventually the truck is free and pointing in the direction it has come, so Tim can escort the guy back along the route he should have taken if he had bothered to read the signs. Instead of being grateful, the driver seems to think the whole mess is Tim's fault, and is complaining that he is way behind schedule. It's a relief when Tim gets back in his car to lead the way: at least he doesn't have to listen to the moaning.

He notices that Barry Brook's Lexus is back, but with the delivery driver still stressing about his schedule, Tim has to go straight round the side of the building to open the cellar hatch. It's only when they have finally got all the barrels unloaded and the driver is pulling out of the car park that he sees Chloe's yellow Fiat. It must have arrived when he was down below. Heart pounding, he races inside, clinging to the hope that Alun Gwynne will have turned up and fended her off, or that Brook will be up in his room.

No chance of that. The first thing he sees as he steps inside is his guest and his girlfriend sitting side by side on stools at the bar. They seem to be sipping gin and tonic.

Even then, not all hope is lost. Maybe, just maybe, she won't have worked out who he is.

"Hey, handsome," says Chloe, turning on her stool with a broad smile. "Why didn't you tell me you had a famous writer staying with you?"

So much for hope.

Tim does an elaborate double-take, praying his facial twitch or his sweaty forehead won't start up again to give him away.

"Because I didn't know," he says.

He looks from Chloe to his guest, as if inviting one of them to enlighten him.

"This is Barry Brook!" she says. "You know, who wrote *The Poussin Conundrum*. He's only, like, one of the best-selling authors on the planet and he's staying in your best bedroom!"

"No way!" says Tim, willing it to sound natural, but without any great faith that he's succeeding. "I mean, I saw 'Finbar' and I didn't make the connection. I never knew the name Barry was short for anything."

He is rambling.

But Brook chuckles: "People don't."

Chloe has really put him at his ease. But that's what Tim is having trouble fathoming. She hates the guy's books and everything they stand for, and a couple of weeks ago she would have done anything possible to prevent him setting foot in the valley. So what is she up to now?

"I didn't know you were such a fan," he says to her.

"How could I not be? It's *Barry Brook*. Like, *the* Barry Brook!"

A mad fantasy briefly crosses Tim's mind that she is so star-struck to meet the guy in the flesh that there may be hope for the Grail Trail scheme after all. But the way she says it, emitting a little squeak that he can't remember her ever making before, and giving the American a playful punch on the arm, puts paid to that. She is acting a role, that much is clear, and it makes him very nervous, because he has no idea how much she knows and where all this is going. Meanwhile Brook himself is lapping it up. To Tim's distaste, the guy actually blushes at the arm-punch.

He is wondering at what stage he needs to start asserting himself. It's important not to get up Chloe's nose and make her think he is being proprietorial. But Brook also needs to know she is off limits. Tim lifts the flap of the bar so that he can get behind it and try to position himself between them. Unfortunately, Chloe seems to have other ideas.

"Babe, can you do me a huge, huge favour and get my bag out of the car?"

She holds out her keys and gives him an icky little pretty-please smile that, again, he could swear he has never seen before. Tim calculates that he is in no position to refuse. He continues to run frantically over the possibilities as he goes out to the Fiat. She doesn't appear to be mad at him, which she certainly would be if she thought he knew he had Brook staying with him, and that he had tried to keep it from her. So maybe she does believe Tim when he says he didn't know who the guy was. But then the mystery remains: why is she determined to be left alone with a man she has always said she despises? Any doubt that this is her intention is dispelled when Tim comes back inside with her bag and finds them both on their feet, with their jackets on.

"Babe, Barry hasn't seen the 800-year-old yew tree yet, so I'm just going to pop out and show him," she says.

She hasn't quite got her arm through Brook's as they walk out of the door, but it's pretty close.

Tim is shaking so badly that he has to sit down. Christ on a bike, what the hell is going on?

Dublin, 1889

Not for the first time, Hopkins wondered how the very old endured it. Here he was, still in middle life, plagued by bodily woes that he could never have imagined as a young man. Sore eyes, aching back, screaming feet; agony passing solids; shaking at the knees going up or downstairs; and now this attack of rheumatic fever that made sleep all but impossible. If the ailments piled on at the same rate, he would be a wretched sack of pain by the time he was sixty, let alone seventy or eighty. The elderly grumbled, for sure. But they made nothing like the fuss they ought to make if they were suffering at twice or thrice the rate he was, which was perfectly likely. Maybe you got used to it, and you forgot that there was ever a time when you expected to go about the world in ache-free working order from head to toe. In that case, perhaps this middle period of life really was the worst one, when you could still remember being able to do that and you weren't ready to stop. He was not sure that was much consolation.

"Why didn't you tell me sooner?" said Mallac, when Hopkins privately told him how bad he was feeling.

He had now been in Ireland three years. To everyone's surprise, the barbaric treatment for his chilblains for which he had volunteered back in his first year had actually worked. But he was no longer prepared to expose every ailment to general scrutiny for the entertainment of the house, and he declined the Frenchman's offer of further help.

"I just… wanted to tell someone," he said vaguely. "I suppose it will pass."

But it did not. Every morning he woke with his night clothes so damp that they had to go straight to the laundry. When it was no better after a week, he went to the doctor, an angular figure of about his own age called Redmond, who had consulting rooms just along the square.

"It is most likely a fleabite," Redmond pronounced after a perfunctory examination. "I'll give you a draught to take every morning and every evening, and you should see an improvement very soon."

The vile-tasting tonic made Hopkins drowsy but had no effect on the muscular ache or the fever. After two weeks of it, he was feeling just as ill, if not worse. He wondered if he had been too hasty to dismiss Mallac's quackery.

"I have some beads for you," the Frenchman said. "You must dissolve them in water and they will make you feel better in no time. As I always promise, your money back if it doesn't work – and I've never had to pay anyone yet."

"That's because you never take money from anyone in the first place."

The Frenchman gave him one of his winks. Mallac did at least lift the spirits.

Hopkins took the beads trustingly. But if faith in the method was part of the process, it was not enough on this occasion. The treatment made no difference.

All the while, he struggled on with his teaching, knowing that he would soon have an examination to set. The prospect always filled him with dread, but this time it took physical form: the nausea and headaches that came on when he thought about this task were real enough and, on more than one occasion during his working day, he found himself checking where the nearest vase or bucket was, in case of emergency.

In the end, it was Mrs Brady who put her foot down.

"You need bed rest, at the very least," she said in front of everyone at the luncheon table, hands on hips to brook no dissent. Ever since their adventure in the kitchen, she had made a particular fuss of him. "You've eaten less and less every day this week." She turned indignantly to Father Wheeler, who sat at the top of the table beside Delany and was technically responsible for the welfare of the house. "Will you look at the poor little fellow? He eats like a bird at the best of times, but today he's had no more than four spoonfuls of soup, and he has not touched his meat at all. He's really not well, Father."

Having caught sight of his own pale, damp face in the hall mirror on the way to table, Hopkins knew he certainly looked the part.

"You'll up to your room this instant, and I'll send young Bridie after you with some beef tea. And if that doctor isn't here to see you again first thing tomorrow, he'll have meself to answer to. Wouldn't you say so, Father?"

"I would say so, Mrs Brady, I would indeed," said Wheeler, letting his napkin slip to the floor as he came round the table to offer Hopkins his arm. "You're quite right, and you put the rest of us to shame. We'll get you tucked up now, Hopkins old man, and we'll have that doctor back first thing. And we'll all pray that you have a better night tonight."

He passed it fitfully, by turns shivering and then throwing the covers off when he woke drenched with sweat. In the morning Redmond reappeared. This time he looked much graver, running a bony hand through his thinning chestnut hair. His change in manner was unnerving, but Hopkins told himself that it must be a consequence of the roasting he had doubtless received from Mrs Brady. The doctor put his hand on Hopkins' brow, asked about the pains in his back and limbs, and wanted to know precisely how much he had eaten (virtually nothing) and drunk (gallons). He then instructed him to unbutton his nightshirt so that he could look at his chest and press the cold brass of his stethoscope to it.

"Have you any ringing or buzzing in the ears?"

He had not.

"Any rigor or shivering?"

"Well, yes. When the chills come I shake all over. And then in no time I'm hot and feverish again." His own voice sounded weak and thin, and he could see Redmond straining to hear him.

"And what about energy?"

"I'm utterly exhausted. I could barely climb the stairs back up here last night. But I expect that's the lack of food as much as anything else."

The doctor nodded. Now he wanted to see the patient's tongue, and his teeth. All the while he made little clicking noises to himself. When the examination was over, he told Hopkins he could fasten his nightshirt. This was an effort because his hands were heavy and his fingers and thumbs unwilling to do his bidding. He became engrossed in the task, and it took him some moments to realise that Redmond was waiting to deliver his verdict.

"The news is not good, Father."

"Oh?"

"I'm afraid you have typhoid." He said it very slowly and clearly, as if to allow no misunderstanding.

Hopkins was conscious of passing suddenly, without a by-your-leave, into a domain hitherto reserved for others.

"Are you quite sure?"

His own voice sounded distant, even to himself. He was conscious he must make an effort to take the news manfully – but could not guarantee he would succeed.

"I'm afraid there can be no doubt. The symptoms did not present themselves so obviously last time we met which is why, er… But this time they are unambiguous. Nevertheless there is no need for despair. You are still a young man, Father. What, thirty…?"

"I am nearly forty-five."

Redmond looked genuinely surprised; it had not been flattery.

"Really? Well in that case…"

"In that case I am not quite so young and resilient after all?"

It was meant to be a pleasantry, but his facial muscles seemed reluctant to smile.

"Not a bit of it," said Redmond earnestly. "Nature

is clearly on your side and you can overcome this. You have every chance. Now I'm going to leave you another tonic…" – he started pouring out grains from a jar that he took from his leather bag – "which I want you to take twice daily. It's sulphate and quinine, and I've seen it work wonders on patients much worse afflicted than you." He looked over his shoulder. "Is the other Father still there? I'll need to tell him how to make the tonic up and how he should best look after you…"

Hopkins was left alone to absorb the news.

So he might be spared the horrors of ageing. All of a sudden they did not seem so bad.

North Wales, the present

If nothing else, Tim is developing a powerful fellow feeling with the poet. The guy had it just right when he said *No worst there is none*: every time you think things are as bad as they could possibly be, they go and get a whole lot worse. What's amazing is that their man managed to express all that in five words of one syllable. Tim is also pretty amazed at his own bone-headedness in missing this simple point the first time round, when he was trying to learn it and got the first line completely wrong. On top of it all, he is aware of a cruel irony: the pain and humiliation of being caught pretending to have a poetic sensibility, when he was in fact a complete philistine, has awakened a genuine poetic sensibility that he never knew he had – but it has come too late to do him any good.

As well as being devastating, this is a Notsoism of the first order.

Not that Chloe has confronted him yet, but it's only a matter of time. She has now been out with Barry Brook for two and a half hours, which has given Tim the leisure to rehearse the collapse of his life half a dozen times over.

She doesn't know for certain that Tim is @Wreckileaks, and since he himself has given Barry Brook no clues, there is nothing that his girlfriend and his American guest can say to each other to establish beyond doubt that Tim is the cheap chancer who has enticed the great conspiracy theorist to this valley. In that sense, he is in the clear. But it isn't that simple, it can't be. Chloe knows, because she isn't stupid, that Tim was well aware he had Barry Brook under his roof, and she knows he chose not to tell her. If she thinks that is suspicious behaviour on his part, she is absolutely right. And she must know more than she is letting on, otherwise she wouldn't have gone to such elaborate lengths to pretend that she is Barry Brook's greatest fan. She is therefore up to something, and whichever way he looks at it, Tim cannot see it ending well for himself.

The not knowing is an agony, made worse by the fact that he is alone in the Red Lion. It is unusual for Alun Gwynne not to be propping up the bar of an afternoon, and while it was maddening that the old boy was not there earlier to keep Chloe and Barry Brook apart while Tim was dealing with the Latvian delivery driver, he is now desperately missing his confidant. He is about to lock the door and run round to Alun's house to see if he's there, when the old boy and Macca finally turn up. They have been to the vet for the mutt's annual check-up. Tim is absurdly pleased to see them both. He pulls the old boy a pint on the house and opens a bag of scratchings for the dog, and then brings Alun up to speed.

Alun Gwynne professes himself as baffled as Tim. He can't see any obvious explanation for Chloe's extraordinary change of heart, cosying up to a writer the mere mention of whose name has previously disgusted her – bar one.

"You wouldn't call the fellow good-looking," he muses.

"But he's got more hair up top than you, landlord, and of course he must be filthy rich. He's worth millions and millions, wouldn't you say. Tens of millions. Women like that in a man, even when they say they don't."

"Thanks for that, Alun. Very comforting."

"Maybe even hundreds of millions."

"You've made your point."

Tim feels a sudden ebbing of affection for his customer. He also has half a mind to take the scratchings away from Macca, who is already poisoning the air with pork-flavoured farts.

Before he can do so, the front door scrapes noisily open and the two tourists appear.

"Sorry we were so long. We took a detour so I could show Barry the oldest brick-built house in Wales," says Chloe, glowing like a newly-wed. The detour is a low blow. She is definitely punishing him.

"Ah, the oldest brick-built house," says Tim uselessly. "How was it?"

"*Fasc*inating," beams Chloe.

That's even lower. She is clearly trying to rub salt into his wound. But Tim is determined not to show that it hurts.

"Another gin and tonic for you, Mr … er… Barry?" he asks, with as much landlordly cheer as he can muster. "Alun, did you know that our Mr Brook is the famous author Barry Brook? I had no idea, did you? Who would have thought we'd have such a distinguished guest in the humble old Red Lion?"

He is aware he may be laying it on a little thick,

but only now does he notice that Brook does not share Chloe's happy glow. The American is looking distracted. He is frowning heavily, avoiding looking anyone in the eye and pulling at his fingers in an agitated manner. In fact his face is a picture of misery. He is either no fan of sightseeing, or else the yew tree and the old house have fallen badly short of expectations.

"No thank you, sir," says Brook stiffly. "In fact if you'd be so kind as to prepare my bill, I'm going to have to check out right away. Of course you must bill me for tonight – I'm more than happy to cover that for your inconvenience. But I'm afraid my plans have, ah, changed and I need to go pack."

"Yes, of course, no problem. But… has something happened?"

He glances at Chloe, who smiles innocently back.

"No, no, it's just that… Well, I have to be on my way. Won't you excuse me?"

Brook manages a grim smile and disappears in the direction of the staircase.

Tim's imagination is running all over the place. He has been desperate to get rid of the guy ever since he arrived, so he ought to be pleased. But the abruptness of it all is alarming.

"One thing about that fellow," says Alun Gwynne at a discreet volume. "For all his fame and his money, he doesn't seem very happy in himself, does he?"

Tim glowers. If Alun were concentrating on his role, he would have remembered that he wasn't meant to know that their guest had any fame and money at all until five minutes ago. At this point he should still be reeling in astonishment at the discovery, not slagging the guy off.

But Chloe seems not to have noticed. She appears to be taking sadistic delight in looking inscrutable.

"What's going on?" Tim hisses. "What did you say to him? Why's he leaving?"

She puts a pale finger to her nose and winks.

The three of them wait in painful silence, with the only sound coming from Macca destroying his final scratching.

"Don't forget he needs his bill," she says.

Tim had indeed forgotten. He is grateful for the distraction.

Finally Brook comes bumping back downstairs with his luggage.

"Let me get that for you," says Tim, seeing him struggling.

"No, no!" says the American, so sharply that Tim backs off and holds his hands up to make it clear he has no intention of touching the guy's stuff.

"Is my bill ready?" says Brook.

"Yes, of course. Here you are, sir."

It takes Tim a while to work out how to use the credit-card machine, and he can see Brook growing more and more impatient as he fumbles with it. When the payment finally goes through, his guest gives him a cursory handshake with little eye contact. Alun Gwynne gets a slightly longer one and Chloe a proper squeeze, with hurried thanks that sound heartfelt.

Tim tries to get the door for him but Brook insists on doing that himself too. It scrapes closed behind him and then there's a silence as the three of them wait to hear the Lexus purr to life. It crunches softly on the gravel as it turns round, and then it is gone.

"Okay, what just happened?" says Tim, turning to Chloe.

Alun Gwynne and the dog are staring at her too.

She seems to be trying not to laugh, but she is clearly in no hurry to share the joke.

"Aha," she says.

NORTH WALES, THE PRESENT

As she drives back home at the end of an exhilarating weekend, Chloe recalls her resolution when she started seeing Tim. Didn't she tell herself she wouldn't put up with him if he turned out to be a manipulator, because that is the one quality she really can't stand in another human being? So by rights she ought to have dumped him. But she knows she's not going to.

Without being sure of every detail, she has long had a fair idea of what Tim has been up to. Working this out has not been hard, mainly because he is such a hopeless liar. It has been clear for a while that he and Alun Gwynne know far more about Barry Brook and his interest in the valley than they are letting on, and she wouldn't put it past the pair of idiots to be up to their necks in the entire hare-brained scheme. She has suspected that all along, but her arrival at short notice this weekend to find Brook himself staying under Tim's own roof – a development, crucially, that Tim has neglected to mention to her – is all the confirmation she needed.

At that point, all she needed to know was whether Tim's crackpot scheme was still live. That was why she needed to get Brook on her own, and proposed showing him the local sights.

"Would you prefer to walk or take the car?" she asked

him, with her most winning smile, as she closed the door of the Red Lion behind them.

"Oh, I prefer to walk, if it's not too far."

"Me too. It's a lovely evening. So tell me, what brings you to North Wales?"

"Kind of a long story."

"I'm a good listener. Tell me."

And so he told her all about the local man – or possibly woman, he couldn't be sure – who had contacted him with the germ of an idea for a new book. The idea was complicated. It related to the famous poet who used to live up the road – had she heard of him? – and it sounded pretty crazy at first. But, as a subject for the kind of thing Barry writes about, it might actually have legs. So he wrote back and got a dialogue going with this local informant, and they seemed to be getting on pretty well, right up to the point where Barry announced he was up for the idea, was prepared to reward his contact for it, and proposed to come and visit.

"That's when the guy – let's just assume it's a guy – like, disappears."

"No!" said Chloe.

"I swear. I'm, like, emailing and messaging and doing everything I can to say I'm up for this, so c'mon, buddy, talk to me. But the guy is, like, blanking me. No response. Zip."

"How mysterious. And rude. That really is no way to behave."

"I know, right?"

"Tell me: when was this, roughly?"

"Let me see. The first approach must have been the middle of May. I remember, because I'd just come back from a trip to New York. And then we talked, and that must have gone on for, I don't know, two, three months."

"When did you last hear from him?"

"That would have been a month ago, maybe a little more. That was when he stopped replying."

"Shocking."

As he talked, she tried to match the dates with her own milestones: meeting Tim at the lecture; coming over for her first visit; then getting together with him and spending lots more time at the Red Lion. Barry Brook's local informant – Chloe prefers to call him "Tim" – seemed to have been in effusive communication during most of that time, and only stopped replying fairly recently, long after Chloe's own arrival. Wasn't it around a month ago that Alun Gwynne first blurted out all that stuff about Brook, when Tim made a ridiculous attempt to pretend that this was the first he had heard of it? She counted back in her head. Yes, exactly right. That was the night when she herself went bananas. Tim had clearly thought better of the whole thing since that moment. Bless his little heart.

She finds herself laughing out loud at the memory, as she eases into traffic on the fast coast road that will speed her back towards Manchester.

Once she was sure that Tim was no longer encouraging Brook, she knew she wouldn't have to dump him, and that was a relief. After that it was easy work to put the frighteners on Brook and make him get out of the valley as fast as his Lexus would carry him. Tim's face as the guy walked out of the Red Lion was truly a picture, and since then he hasn't let up asking what she said to make him leave. He can ask all he likes, she doesn't have the slightest intention of telling him. Not yet, anyway.

If she is planning on staying with him, does that mean she has changed her mind on manipulators and her standards are slipping? She wonders about that as she flicks on her wipers to deal with a sudden shower of rain. It would worry her if that were so. But no, that's not quite it. It's true that Tim has embarked on a cynical scheme for entirely mercenary ends that would have hoodwinked huge numbers of readers into believing utter claptrap, and he came astonishingly close to pulling it off. But he seems to have repented, which is a good thing, and even though he came so close to success, there is still something loveably inept about the whole business.

Maybe that's it: she can cope with someone a little bit sneaky provided she can always see right through him.

Nevertheless, he cannot be allowed to get off completely free. He still needs to be punished, which she plans to do in the most entertaining way she can find. All she has to do now is think of how.

DUBLIN, 1889

Hopkins was now in a ground-floor sick room, to which he had been moved so that he could be properly nursed by the women of the parish. Curtis had packed a small bag of personal items for him – his rosary, his Bible, letters from his mother and brother Arthur, volumes of published verses by his friends – although he had not the focus or the inclination to open any of them. He had asked also for his portrait of Savonarola, which he was still carrying around with him after all these years. The monk now glared down at him from the wall opposite his bed. The only treasure he had not dared request was his picture of Dolben, which remained untouched in the top drawer of his writing desk. It too had accompanied him on move after move, and it had always comforted him in times of distress. If he had been packing his own bag, he would have tucked it into one of the books, but the attachment was a private one, locked away deep in his memory, and revealed to no one in all that intervening time. Even now, when the idea of keeping secrets seemed so unimportant, he was not ready to bare that part of his soul.

He could remember the first snowdrops shivering over Christ Church Meadow on the morning twenty-four years earlier when he first encountered that strange, entrancing boy. He had arranged to go to Bridges' rooms to meet the famous young cousin visiting from school. He had hastened to get there, fearing he was going to be late, but the boy himself was much later. Dolben kept the pair of them waiting a full two hours before he finally appeared, and then he seemed completely unconcerned about it. The discourtesy ought to have been maddening, but Dolben's detachment from the trivial reality of concerns like punctuality somehow added to his allure.

Having heard so much about this young eccentric, Hopkins was disappointed to find him in conventional dress – albeit a scruffy form of it, with dust all over his top hat and his collar wildly askew. Tall and pale with a delicate face, he was by no means conventionally good-looking. But there was something immediately attractive about his faraway expression. It gave him an other-worldly manner.

Bridges was late for the river, so it was up to Hopkins to show the boy around. Dolben had his heart set on Balliol, which was Hopkins' own college, so Bridges thought they would get on well. Dolben was a poet too, which would give them something else in common.

Hopkins thought he saw a look of disappointment when the boy realised he was to be handed into his care. He attempted to counter that by showing what a perceptive guide to the city he could be. Conversation was difficult at first, but once they reached Balliol, Dolben became more animated. He was especially taken by the new rose-striped chapel, with its chaotic interior geometry and flamboyant alabasters – a controversial design which was deplored by the enemies of Catholicism. Before Hopkins could stop him, he had even genuflected. Hopkins looked around nervously: he thought they had the place to themselves but you could never be too careful, even in Oxford. He was beginning to understand why this boy created such a stir wherever he went.

Dolben was obsessed with the pre-industrial past, which this dreamy Italianate interior so powerfully evoked. And he was most obsessed of all by the Florentine friar Savonarola, scourge of corruption and excess, who preached with such fervour that congregations fought to get into the churches. They were talking of him when they caught a glimpse of Jowett, who was not yet Master but was already, by dint of the controversies around his name, the most famous man in academe. He was despised by the anti-Catholic zealots whom Dolben most enjoyed upsetting, so it was only natural that the boy would be excited.

They met again the next day, when they walked across Port Meadow to Binsey. And the following afternoon, Dolben's last, they strolled through the deer park and up along the Cherwell. During this time Dolben had spoken without embarrassment of his feelings for a boy at school, who was his best friend but unaware of his passion. Hopkins was not used to such frankness in conversation but was aware that he felt a burning envy for this other, unknown boy – and an indignation that the ingrate should not be aware of the honour bestowed on him.

When they parted, Hopkins expressed the hope that, the next time they met, it would be as fellow members of Balliol. In the event, that was never to be. The boy sent his photograph at Hopkins' request – inscribed "ever yr affectionate D Mackworth Dolben" – but there was no letter, no thanks for his time and attention, his hospitality. The boy was too ascetic to bother with such fripperies, he told himself. Still hoping to begin a correspondence, Hopkins wrote regularly from Oxford, in the summer from Hampstead, from a walking holiday in Snowdonia, dispensing cheerful items of news, begging to be considered Dolben's true and obedient friend, and remaining in hope of receiving some word of reply. Did the boy plan another visit to Oxford? Was he ever in London, and if so would he care to visit Hopkins at home? Sometimes he attached poems, asking for critical comment and offering to perform the same favour in return. He received a cordial reply to one of these letters, focusing on the boy's own news and pointedly not enquiring about Hopkins' own doings. It was encouragement enough to make Hopkins carry on writing for a while, but there was nothing more.

All he could remember of those weeks was waiting on the arrival of the postman for day after day, with disappointment every time. He was deeply hurt by the rebuff. He had carried that pain with him at first, but the appalling tragedy that came not long afterwards allowed the hurt and rejection to mutate into something nobler. He was no longer spurned, but bereaved. Lying with his head on the hard pillows of his cheerless Dublin infirmary, he smiled to recall his own foolishness. He had been bewitched, that was all it was. How could he have spent so many years deluding himself about a lost love that never existed?

The accident itself occurred two summers after their meeting – which had felt a long time then, when they were all so young. Dolben had failed his Balliol entrance after fainting in the examination room. He had been starving himself as part of his devotion to the Rule of St Benedict, a piety of such extravagance that it really was another form of vanity, Hopkins could see now. Dolben's father was furious and the boy was sent to a succession of private tutors to cram. The last of these was a country parson in the East Midlands, a decent member of the English Church who turned a blind eye to the images of the Virgin that his unusual young charge kept beside his bed. This vicar had a boy of about ten who looked up to Dolben as to an older brother and loved bathing in a pool of the local river, even though he could not actually swim a stroke. He would nag Dolben to take him there and would then float on his back, with Dolben towing him along and generally being on hand to save him if he got into trouble. Unfortunately, there was no provision for the reverse possibility. Dolben was a strong swimmer, so the consensus was that he must have fainted again. He suddenly sank within a few yards of the bank. The parson's son was terrified, of course. The only thing he could do was flip onto his back and scream loud enough for some labourers working in the fields to hear him. But the water was deep, and Dolben's body was not found till several hours afterwards.

Hopkins heard all this in a letter from Bridges, who conveyed it as a family tragedy, having no thought – why should he? – for how much it would devastate him. So

Hopkins had dissembled, pretending to be unaffected.

He had always seen that lack of understanding from Bridges and his other friends as further cause for self-pity, but now he could see that they were right. The whole business had been futile, impertinent even. He had felt deeply for Dolben on the basis of a few days' acquaintance, and the boy had felt nothing for him. So his death had indeed been a tragedy – for Dolben's mother, his father, his sister and brother, and of course for the world of letters, because he was never able to fulfil his great promise as a poet. But it had robbed Hopkins of nothing – no friendship, no affection, certainly not love, because those things had all been figments of his lonely imagination. Dolben's death had merely allowed that illusion to stay alive.

How strange to be able to see that only now, a quarter of a century later. The illusion was gone, only clarity remained, and it was a relief at long last to be unburdened of it. It was a peace of sorts, he realised as Mrs Brady wheezed in to mix up his tonic.

"It's good to see you smiling, Father? What's the joke? Have I got something on me face?"

Hopkins shook his head and assured her it was nothing. How could he begin to explain to her the comfort he had just found in realising what a fool he had been?

North Sea, 1875

Aurea had been half out of the skylight too, holding up her hands to be lifted out, when she saw the wave gather Henrica. Their beautiful, kind, wise leader had been standing there one moment, and in the next came a wall of water that forced Aurea to turn her face away as the sea sluiced through the open skylight and into the saloon below. All she caught was the look of surprise on poor Henrica's white face. When she looked again, their leader was not there. She might be safe, simply knocked off her feet and holding on to the rail or the rigging. But Aurea saw from the shocked faces of the men who had been helping them up, looking down at her as if not knowing how much she had seen, how much to tell her – she saw that Henrica was gone.

And now, for the first time, it was real. This was not the kind of danger that would be averted by rescue or by God's mercy. Henrica, the guide she had looked up to and relied upon to put everything right, had been taken from them in the most horrifying way. What hope could there be? All she could see in her mind was what she had not seen: Henrica flying off the deck, veil billowing and hands flailing, reaching uselessly back toward the ship as she was pulled by her heavy robes, tiny and doomed, into the unimaginable cold and dark.

And Aurea screamed, letting all the terror of the past twenty-four hours come howling out.

The others still had no idea.

"What is it?"

"I knew the deck wasn't safe. She has seen something terrible."

"What is it, Aurea? What have you seen?"

At first she could not find the words, even after her three companions had helped her down, and when she did, they came only haltingly, because telling it meant reliving it, seeing it again, the vision that she wanted to blot out and forget that she had ever had. But out it came, at last, and Brigitta too began to keen, while Norberta renewed her frantically whispered Ave Marias.

They were pressed now into the highest corner of the saloon, where the water came to their waists if they knelt to pray. They shivered as they clutched at one another, their life-belts making the embrace clumsy and uncomfortable. Hands reached down from the skylight to pull up the last of those who had decided to escape the brimming saloon. Then the shouting receded, as those above gave up trying to coax them out, and looked instead to their own safety. All the while, the icy sea was seeping higher, the wash through the open skylight adding to the merciless rise of the tide, and Aurea was trembling as much with cold as with fear. It seared deeper into her being than any winter she had known on land.

She had clung all along to the hope that the tide would turn in time, that something would happen to make everything all right. But now she knew it would not be so.

All they could do was pray for Henrica's soul, and their own souls, and hope the transition from this world to the next would not be too awful.

Barbara was speaking.

"We are all four here together, and we will stay here," she said, struggling to control the shake in her voice. "We will not die without human companionship, like poor Henrica. We have the comfort of one another, as well as that of what is to come. And we know, as she did even at the dreadful last moment, that the good Lord is with us always."

Brigitta sobbed uncontrollably.

"Let it come quickly," whispered Aurea in a tiny, terrified voice.

A little later, from his wind-lashed vantage point in the rigging, Otto Lundgren saw a veiled head emerge through the broken glass. The sight of the leader of their party being washed away was not one that he – who had survived the *Schiller* disaster only a few months ago and had already seen so many horrors – would quickly forget. He had reconciled himself to the impossibility of coaxing the other proud, frightened women onto the deck after such a tragedy. Perhaps they had finally changed their minds, the dark waters engulfing their refuge proving a greater terror than the elements on deck. He started to climb down, but others were there first, reaching down to haul her out. Come on, woman, hold your arms up so they can pull you. But she would not.

It was the tallest of them, he could see that now, the

one called Norberta, and she seemed to have no thought of saving herself. With her arms at her sides to resist any attempt to help her up, she flung her head back and shrieked something into the wind. He did not catch it at first, but again she shouted it, and again, and again, so that eventually her desperate, blood-stopping plea was unmistakable.

"Oh my God, make it quick! Oh my God, make it quick!"

But it was not quick. It took hours for the desperate cry to stop, and Lundgren saw people try to stop their ears, even as they held on with cold-red hands for their lives. *Yes, God help me, let it be quick, for her sake and theirs.*

At first light, when the seas had abated, the tide had gone down and the English vessel that had at last come to find them was sending small boats alongside, Lundgren ventured back down into the saloon. He wished he had not. The four robed bodies were strewn about the soaking floor like discarded dolls, lifebelts still around their necks. Three were lying face down but the fourth, the tall nun who had shouted through the night, was facing upwards. It was obvious which one it was from the difference in height, but her face was bloated already from the water and Lundgren could scarcely recognise the woman with whom he had shared a table just two nights earlier – or was it three? He had lost all track of time.

It was all so senseless. Their leader, the bravest of them and the one with whom he had had the most contact, was beyond rescue as she was pitched into the wild sea.

But these four could have been saved. They could now have greeted this dawn and led the prayers of gratitude. Lundgren was no Catholic, but he would certainly have knelt with them. Shivering with cold and delayed shock, he could scarcely believe that he, of all people, was still alive.

"Lundgren! L-look sharp, man. They are ready for us."

It was Meyer, calling for him down the companionway. Lundgren took one last look at the pitiful sight and turned away. It was time to leave the stricken ship.

Whether its horrors would ever leave him was another matter.

Dublin, 1889

In the following days, Father Wheeler was in attendance for much of the time. Curtis was a regular visitor, and the other members of the house also took turns to drop in, so Hopkins could assure his mother when he wrote to her that he was quite comfortable, perfectly happy and there was no immediate cause for alarm. The best thing about his situation was being able to excuse himself without a scrap of guilt from all his forthcoming examination commitments.

But of course he also thought about what would happen if Doctor Redmond's tonic – administered by a sparrow of a woman called Clara, who mixed it up with boiled water every morning and evening so that he could drink it when it had cooled down, and who came back to stand over him to make sure he finished it to the last drop – did not live up to its promise. This was typhoid, after all. It was quite likely he would not recover.

It was odd to think of himself dying before his parents, and it pained him to imagine the sorrow it would cause them – even his father, to whom he had never been close. But he had very little distress on his own account. After the initial shock of the diagnosis, he was surprised by how calm he had become. He did not wish to be ungrateful for the gift of life, but death would have great compensations.

Apart from anything else, it would free him once and for all from the wretched examination burden.

For so many years he had been dogged by frustration that his verse had never got into print, that he was so little understood, that his concept of sprung rhythm had been so utterly ignored, even though children recited nursery rhymes in it every day. He had been deeply wounded by Coleridge's failure to publish his massive work about the shipping tragedy. But that no longer hurt him. He felt bad only for the poor women he had tried to memorialise. Their fate had gripped the newspaper-reading public for a few days, and they had been given a tremendous funeral conducted by a cardinal. But now, fifteen years on, they were doubtless forgotten by most people, and in fifteen more years not a soul would know about the wreck of the *Deutschland*.

Really, though, did any of it matter? It was only posterity, which was another form of vanity while you were alive, and made no difference at all to you once you were dead. He could now see that he had written the poem for himself and for God, and that was all that counted. What gave him far greater concern was the chance that Bridges would be indiscreet with his jottings. He had been copying his verses out for years and sending them to his old friend. What if his lines were rubbish after all, and his attempt to reinvent meter was just laughable? If it reached wider attention, his work might bring mockery to his community. That was far more important than posterity: it would be a legacy, bequeathing ridicule on those who remained in the Society once he was gone.

"Father, if I don't survive…" he said when Wheeler made his afternoon visit.

"Now then, who says you won't survive?"

"We both know I may not."

"No one else is giving up hope, so you must not either."

"I know, but you will put my mind at rest greatly if you listen to me now. Among my papers upstairs… I'm afraid there are a great deal. But if you find scribblings, verses… I'm afraid I have broken the rules of the Society by indulging in many such projects over the years. I beg of you, please put them in the fire. You will be doing me a great favour if you promise me that."

"I promise, old man. I'll use my best judgment and I'll make sure that nothing exists that will put you at odds with the Society. How does that sound?"

"Thank you, Father."

"But it won't come to that, so let's hear no more of it."

Hopkins smiled, and after that he slept soundly.

He spent more and more time sleeping as the days went on, and he began to lose track of time. He dreamed of his mother leaning over to tuck him in, as she had when he was a child. She looked greyer now, not just than when he was young, but also than the last time he had seen her. How lined her face was; if only he could reach out to smooth the furrows away. He fancied his father was there too, pacing and pulling at his moustache, standing over him occasionally, but mainly in the background, which was how Hopkins always thought of him. It was comforting to have them both here, even if they were imaginary.

"I am so happy, so happy…" he whispered to her.

He awoke to find Wheeler where his mother had been.

"What day is it?" he wanted to know.

Wheeler leaned down, bringing his ear close to Hopkins' mouth.

"Say again, old man?"

Hopkins repeated the question.

"It's Saturday."

Saturday. No teaching, at least.

"How are you feeling now?"

Confused, weak, and his head ached. As well as being hard to think straight, it was an effort to speak, because his mouth was dry and his breath in short supply.

"Here, have a sip of water. Let me help you. There you are. Now, if you wait just a second, there's someone here to see you."

He left the room and Hopkins shivered. His headache was worse now. Then the door opened again and there was his mother, with his father just behind. What an extraordinary coincidence for them to arrive now, just after he had dreamed about them. He tried to tell them so, but the words would not come out well, and it was only when his mother had taken his hand in hers, and was mopping his brow with a cool cloth, that he realised it could not have been a dream. He must have been through a period of delirium.

It was so good of them to come, but how had they managed that awful journey?

"I have put you to so much trouble all my life. I'm sorry."

All of a sudden he had a great impulse to weep.

"Hush, Gerard," came his mother's soothing voice. "Don't try to speak, if it's an effort. And it has been no trouble. We came on the packet and it was really quite easy. The crossing was smooth and we were well looked after. Your father will tell you. Here he is, can you see?"

Now he did see everything, only too clearly. They had been sent for. It meant the end must be near.

"How are ... Cyril and Arthur and Everard ... and Grace and Milicent... and Lionel?"

"They are all fine. They send their very best love. They are looking forward to seeing you properly when you are better."

"And Kate?"

How could he have forgotten Kate?

There were tears in his mother's eyes too. He did his best to smile, playing along with the fiction that he would see them all soon, because she intended it for his benefit. It would certainly be a pity not to see any of them again, not to watch his brothers' children grow up, but he was tired, so tired...

Naturally, all his life he had wondered what heaven might be like, but now his picture of it was clear: it was a place with no headaches or gouty eyes, where you could discard the body that caused so many woes, and where there was no need to mark a single examination paper ever again. That would be paradise enough for him. *Sleep, the end of all desire* – wasn't that Dolben's line? It really wasn't bad.

And God would be there too, of course. Having loosened

his hold on life, Hopkins was excited at the prospect of coming into His presence. It was a form of joy, the same as he had imagined for the nuns in his great shipwreck piece: a happy knowledge that God was waiting for them. This was not how anyone ever pictured drowning at sea, but he was reassured to find that dying really could be like this. He might not have been so wide of the mark after all.

He rested his eyes for a moment. When he opened them again, his parents were gone. One of the parish women was by his bedside instead, reading her Bible.

"Your mother and father have just gone to take some air, Father. They will be back soon."

"Not ... too ... much... I ... hope."

"What's that now, Father?"

He couldn't remember seeing this one before. Plump, in an ill-fed way, with broken veins in her cheeks and yellow snaggle teeth, but a pleasant voice and kind eyes.

"I hope they don't take ... too much ... air... It's not ... good..."

It was meant to be a joke, to show he hadn't lost his sense of humour. But she didn't seem to understand that.

"Don't you worry about them, Father. They'll be quite safe. Now let me do your pillows. There's nice, no? Oh and here they are back already. What did I tell you?"

But it wasn't his parents, it was Wheeler.

"It's good to see you awake again, old man."

"Have I been asleep very much?"

"I should say so, yes. Your parents have been here three days, and you've slept most of that time."

"Three days?"

It was extraordinary how time played so many tricks.

"In that case…"

"Yes, old man?"

"I think it's time, don't you? While my mother is out. I don't want … to distress her."

"If you're sure?"

"Do you disagree?"

Wheeler shook his head gently.

"Very well."

Wheeler turned away and Hopkins could hear him getting the unction oil out of its box. Then the priest pulled up a chair beside the bed and made the sign of the cross.

"In nomine Patris et Filii et Spiritus Sancti."

"Bless me, Father… for I have sinned," said Hopkins as clearly as he could, but it was a terrible effort. "I do not know… how many days it is… since my last confession… but for all the sins of my past life… I ask pardon of God… penance and absolution from you, Father…"

"And now the Act of Contrition."

Hopkins said the words in Latin, and he felt the wet dab of olive oil from the cotton pad – strikingly odourless compared to the heavily spiced version they used at Mass – as Wheeler slowly applied it with a touch of his finger to his eyelids, ears, nose, mouth, back of the hands and finally, pulling the covers out from the base of the bed, his feet.

"Dominus noster Jesus Christus te absolvat," the priest recited. *"Et ego auctoritate ipsius te absolvo ab omni vinculo excommunicationis et interdicti in quantum possum et tu*

indiges."

Then came the final words, *"Ego te absolvo…"*

Hopkins summoned a great effort to pull his hand up to his forehead and make the sign of the cross, knowing that he could sleep soon, perhaps even before his mother returned. He would be sorry to miss her, but oh, that sleep would be so pleasant…

NORTH WALES, THE PRESENT

It is a fine spring Friday, the kind of day when this part of the world comes into its own. Tim is on the track south of the village that leads up their local hill. In the months since Chloe moved in, he has taken more and more pleasure in exploring the locality on foot. Today, tasked with gathering wild grasses to arrange in the bedrooms of the four guests who are arriving later on, he is combining that duty with his morning constitutional.

In a few hours, two dozen visitors will converge on the Red Lion. Four of them will stay on the premises – including two in what Tim likes to think of as the Barry Brook Suite – while the rest are billeted in outlying bed-and-breakfast accommodation that Chloe has secured at a discount and sold on at a mark-up to the literary pilgrims as part of their Appreciating Gerard Manley Hopkins weekend package. All guests will receive a welcome pack consisting of their own hand-calligraphed sonnet, which Tim and Chloe have both been working on for the past couple of weeks, plus a large-scale map of the valley and a packet of Welsh cakes done up in fancy ribbon. Chloe has devised, marketed and organised it down to the last detail, so Tim has little left to do but marvel at his amazing good fortune in enticing this creature into his life. Just occasionally he finds himself wondering what it would be like if she applied the same formidable skills to his plans to put the valley on the Grail Trail, but he does his best to cast this unworthy, destructive thought out of his mind. No need to balls it up, Notso.

He has eventually wheedled out of her how she managed to get rid of Barry Brook.

"All I did was take him by the arm, tell him I was a massive fan, and then warn him that someone locally was out to scam him by hooking him into some stupid yarn that not even his readers would be gullible enough to fall for. I told him their plan was to sell the story to the papers in a way that would max out his embarrassment." Her eyes are big, wide and innocent. "I said I didn't know who was doing it, I'd just heard it on the village grapevine. Oh, and I said I wouldn't put it past whoever was behind it to be filming him on a smartphone everywhere he went, so they could package his humiliation on YouTube. They might even be doing it at that very moment. That was enough to make him race back here and check out on the spot. He would have done it with his jacket over his head, but I told him that if he really was being filmed, he wouldn't do himself any favours by acting like a paedophile at the Old Bailey. He didn't know what that was, but he got the general idea."

They both laugh, although for Tim, it's more about relief than the hilarity of it. He has had a lucky escape, and all of it feels too good to be true.

He spends weeks waiting for the catch. But as those weeks turn to months, he tells himself not to be so pessimistic, that good things can also happen to him, and he mustn't expect the worst all the time. You create your own luck, he thinks now. Maybe he's not so Notso after all.

"I wonder who it was," he ventures occasionally, with his best quizzical expression. "You know, the guy hoaxing that loser Barry Brook. I guess we'll never know, but wouldn't you love to find out?"

She nods distractedly when he says this, not really that interested, and he gives himself a sneaky smile inside. Not so Notso, buddy.

Now that the weekend is nearly upon them, he can't believe how little she has left him to do. She has sent him off to Morrisons to get supplies for the lunches and dinners, but Hugh Pugh's granddaughter is coming in to do the catering and serving, and all he has to do is give the rooms the final once-over and then prepare some kind of speech of welcome. They're all due to arrive in the evening, when they'll have beer and local cheeses in the bar and take part in a Gerard Manley Hopkins quiz to get them in the mood.

"We can make it light-hearted," Chloe promises when she first suggests the idea. "It'll be fun."

"If you say so," says Tim.

He's only hoping that she doesn't ask him to set the questions. But she has that covered too, and on the eve of the guests' arrival, she tries some of them out on Tim and Alun Gwynne.

"Okay, an easy one to start," she says. "How many poems did Gerard Manley Hopkins have published in his own lifetime? Was it a) zero; b) less than ten or c) more than fifty?"

Tim smiles in a way that he hopes says this one is so easy it's beneath him, and he offers it to Alun as if he's being generous.

Alun Gwynne scratches his head, casting the usual snowstorm over his trouser legs and stool.

"I think he published one or two, so it would have to be number b."

"Is the right answer!" says Chloe.

She turns to Tim. "Now one for you. This is easy too. I only put it in to make people laugh. Which poet laureate made Gerard Manley Hopkins famous by publishing his work posthumously? Was it a) Robert Bridges, b) Alfred Lord Tennyson or c) John Betjeman?"

Alun Gwynne chuckles ostentatiously, and Chloe bestows on him one of her most appreciative beams.

Tim grasps that one of the answers must be ridiculous, and it's probably John Betjeman. He laughs too, to show that he's in on the joke, then shrugs and shakes his head, gesturing back to Chloe and Alun Gwynne as if to say this one is so hilariously obvious he's not going to dignify it with a reply.

Unfortunately, Chloe isn't having that.

"Well?" she says, putting her tongue into her cheek in a way she has when she thinks she's about to prove something.

Tim begins to panic. The only name apart from Betjeman that he has actually heard of is Tennyson. He didn't know he was a poet laureate, but it sounds like the sort of job he might have had, and he must be vaguely the right era: Tim recalls an image of a massive black beard, so the guy must have been a major Victorian.

"Well obviously it's…"

"…Robert Bridges!" cuts in Alun Gwynne.

How come he is surrounded by such competitive people?

"Is the right answer!" says Chloe again, but through slightly gritted teeth this time. Is Tim imagining it, or did she know that she had him on the spot?

"But that was easy," she adds. "Even Macca would have known it."

The dog yawns by way of confirmation, and Chloe gives him a pork scratching.

"Okay," she continues. "Now, this is a really fun fact and you could be forgiven for not knowing it. Which world-famous writer had their first-ever work published in the very same journal that rejected *The Wreck of the Deutschland*, at almost exactly the same time?"

"Go on then, what are the options?"

"No options for this one, you have to guess."

Alun is frowning.

"It would have to be someone religious. A writer of hymns, perhaps? I'm going to say … er …."

"Oscar Wilde," says Tim, stabbing in the dark with the first nineteenth century writer he can think of. She has said it was hard, so at least he has permission to get it wrong.

Chloe's eyes widen.

"How did you know that?"

Tim scoffs, as if it's beneath him to explain.

She looks at him askance, as if to say that she knows he cheated, even if she doesn't know how.

For his part, Tim is hoping that his luck will hold, and that he can get through this weekend without being rumbled as knowing next to zilch about the poet he is meant to be celebrating.

Now that the day is upon them, he is feeling genuinely optimistic. He stops on the gently rising path to look back the way he has come. The sea is glinting in the distance, as are cars on the road on the other side of the valley. Up to his right he spots a hawk of some kind, hovering motionless and alone in the sky.

Unbidden, lines of poetry flow into his head.

"I caught this morning morning's minion, king-
dom of daylight's dauphin, dapple-dawn-drawn Falcon,
in his riding
Of the rolling level underneath him steady air…"

He laughs out loud, amazed at himself. He hasn't tried to memorise those lines, but he has copied them out four or five times in the past week, and somehow they have stuck. No, not somehow. They have stuck because the rhythm helps fix the pattern. And the words themselves, opposites like 'rolling' and 'level' jammed together, manage to capture in a memorable phrase the wonder of this living creature that stays dead still on a moving current.

The bird is still hovering, but now it wheels on the wind, and once more the lines are in his head, without him even trying to summon them.

"… off, off forth on swing,
As a skate's heel sweeps smooth on a bow-bend…"

Wow.

Tim is light-headed with the discovery that it is possible to observe the world through the eyes of a man who has been dead for more than a century, and to get so much more out of that observation in the process. Is this what it means to have poetry in your soul? He wonders if Nadine will ever know the feeling. For her sake, he hopes she does. And suddenly he doesn't hate her. He doesn't even hate Pete. Alun Gwynne is right: Nadine released Tim from obligations that he wished he didn't have, and now perhaps both of them – all four of them, including Pete and Chloe – will have a chance of happiness. That's surely not too much to begrudge the person you were once married to.

He is still on a high when he gets back to the pub, and it's only when he sees a pile of printed papers on the bar that he remembers the other task Chloe has set him. She wants him to fold and put into envelopes the agendas for the weekend, all ready for the punters' arrival. It's a small thing, and he is not quite sure why she hasn't emailed them all this stuff in advance. But for some reason she has been insistent on him doing it, reminding him twice before going out this morning that she has left them ready for him.

He picks up the papers and takes them to a window table, taking care there are no sticky puddles before he puts them down; it would be sacrilege to mess up Chloe's hyper-efficient handiwork. He pads back to the kitchen to get himself an espresso – there's always fresh coffee nowadays – and settles back at the window table to perform his allotted duty. The pile of agendas is lying face up, and he hasn't actually looked at them yet. He picks up the top one to read it properly, and that's when the sky falls in. The contented smile freezes on his lips. Instead there comes an insistent thumping at his chest and a tightening at the throat. He has caught sight of his own name on the agenda. And it's not just at the top, as in 'Tim and Chloe are delighted to welcome you…' There's a list of workshops and activities, and his name is all over that too.

Hopkins and Nature, workshop leader: Tim Cleverley.

Just below that, *Hopkins in Wales, led by Tim Cleverley.*

After lunch there's a Reverend Something or other on Hopkins and the Jesuit order, followed by a guided walk of significant landmarks in the oeuvre of the poet, led by Alun Gwynne (*really?*).

But then the final session fills him with even greater horror, if that's possible. It's a concluding seminar on *Inscape and Instress*, with an introduction by T Cleverley.

Tim has never knowingly had a panic attack, and has always been dismissive of the kind of person who does. But now his temples are throbbing, he is gasping for air, and the room is spinning around him as if it's circling in for the kill. Questions compete for attention. How could she? What the hell is he going to do? Can he get together one presentation, let alone three, by the evening? Is there any chance she has already told him about this and he has forgotten, or just wasn't listening? And again, how *could* she? After a while, these queries seem a bit specific and they blur into a more general, self-pitying what-the-hell-is-he-going-to-*do*. The only consolation at this juncture is that he runs a pub, which at least means he can serve himself a neat double whisky. He's about to pour a second one when Chloe gets back from the village.

"How do you mean you didn't know?" she says. "You agreed to this weeks ago! Anyway there's no point arguing about it now. We've got guests arriving in a few hours and they're expecting workshops and seminars. Come on, handsome, with your knowledge it shouldn't be too difficult to pull something out of the hat."

Hat? What hat? Tim has never felt more bare-headed.

"But…but…but…"

As the whisky hits his brain, his head is in more of a whirr than ever. He can't for the life of him remember her mentioning it. But she wouldn't get something like that wrong, not someone as efficient and all-knowing as Chloe. So she must have told him, in which case he wasn't listening. And admitting that, in his experience, is the worst thing to tell a woman. But that leaves the problem of what the hell he is meant to say to a bunch of people who know infinitely more than he ever could about a man whose name he wishes he has never heard, and who are paying a hefty fee to be further edified, not to have their intelligence insulted.

He notices that Chloe is shaking. Her shoulders are heaving, her peachy white skin has flushed the colour of raspberries and there are tears in her eyes. Now she's doubling up, creased at the middle and clutching at the furniture to stop herself falling over because she's laughing so much.

"Have you… have you looked at the…" She's finding it hard to get anything out. "Have you looked at the… at the… *date* at the top of that?"

It's there somewhere, it must be up at the top. Yes, there it is, Gerard Manley Hopkins Weekend, April the…

"APRIL FOOL!!!"

She throws herself round his neck and pulls his head down to kiss him hard on the forehead. Her face is purple now, and he is worried she may do herself a serious mischief.

"I can't believe you think I'd really do that to you," she pants eventually. "Look, I've got the real ones here."

And she brings from behind her back another sheaf of agendas, all identical to the ones he has been staring at, except that there are other names, proper ones with professor and doctor next to them, alongside those hideous workshop titles he has been fretting over for the past hour. He ought to be furious – with Nadine he would have been furious – but she's so much cuter than Nadine, especially when she laughs, and it's such a massive, surging relief that he can't hold it against her. Instead they play-fight, and she squeals and laughs even more. Eventually they stop because they're in the public bar and anyone could come in; not just Alun Gwynne, these days, but seven or eight other regulars too, as well as genuine passing trade.

"I can't believe you fell for it," she says, still panting from the exertion. "You really think I'd trust you to run a workshop on Hopkins?"

He smiles, but in the nick of time he remembers he's meant to be a massive Hopkins fan. Now that he's out of danger, that's not a pretence he is prepared to drop. The smile turns to a frown.

"Why shouldn't I?" he says. "I could, if I had time to prepare. It was only that you never warned me."

"What, on inscape and instress? Aren't you more of a sprung rhythm specialist?"

He doesn't like her tone.

"Oh, come off it," she continues, before he can say anything. "You can drop the pretence. You wouldn't know Gerard Manley Hopkins from a hole in the road. I suspected it from the moment I met you, you great wazzock, when you didn't know what a stanza was and you couldn't quote any of the *Wreck* except the first line. You were bullshitting your arse off. I knew for sure when you got *No worst there is none* wrong. It's only his most famous poem after the *Wreck*. No real fan would say *worse* instead of *worst*."

Tim opens and shuts his mouth.

"It's okay, really it is," she says. "I don't care that you don't know anything about him. I've got all I want anyway."

She kisses him.

"Now come on, let me check what you've done with the rooms."

Tim follows her upstairs, not knowing what to say, but assuming that nothing might be a good start. He's a little hurt that all that effort, all that pretence at sounding erudite, has been so completely unnecessary and she has been laughing at him the whole time. He also wants to protest: but I do know about him now! I can quote from *The Windhover* and even understand it! But that would involve conceding that he was bullshitting before, which it may not be wise to do. The main thing is that no harm has been done, and he seems to have emerged not just unscathed, but with a sane, hot girlfriend, and perhaps even the makings of a modest niche business providing themed weekends to well-behaved literary tourists. It's not the kind of life that anyone will memorialise in poetry, and nobody will ever propel him to posthumous fame, but it is beginning to look like a decent, rewarding, fulfilling existence.

And while it's a shame that he won't ever get to enjoy riches of the Grail Trail, at least Chloe never rumbled him on that score. That's surely worth clinging on to.

At the top of the stairs she turns back to him.

"Hey, you'll never guess what I found under the bed."

He stops dead, two steps below her. In her hand, horribly close to his face, is that old copy of *The Poussin Conundrum*. He had shoved it there all those months ago, he remembers now, before she moved in. Why didn't he just chuck it in the bin?

Still, all is not lost. He has got this far by bluffing it out, and he sees no reason to stop doing so now.

"That thing? Yeah, whoever left it never came back. Good thing, I reckon. That's not the kind of customer we want nowadays, is it?"

She's looking at him with a funny sort of smile, the kind that says she knows something he doesn't. Maybe he's just imagining that, and she still hasn't got over the hilarity of April Fooling him. But it makes him nervous, and when he's nervous he talks too much.

"You always said that whoever left it was the same person who lured Barry Brook here, didn't you? I wasn't sure at the time, but I reckon you're right now. It's obvious when you think about it, no? What do you reckon, babe?"

She sucks her bottom lip and narrows her eyes as if she's thinking it over.

"Could be, yeah," she says. "It would certainly make sense. Maybe we should ask him."

"If we knew who it was. And it could be a 'she', don't forget. Let's not make sexist assumptions."

"Mmm. Of course, we would know who it was if they'd done something useful like write their name in the front of the book."

And slowly, calmly, she holds it out.

A chill spreads through Tim's body, starting at the crown of his head and spreading down his neck, then fanning out across his back as if he has been thrown head first into an icy ocean. Did he really do that? He couldn't have. Of all the cretinous, suicidally stupid things to do, that would be the ultimate Notsoism. He doesn't need to open the front cover because, he already knows the answer. But he does so anyway and there it is, in the same hand he has been putting to such good use in the calligraphed sonnets: *Tim Cleverley, North Wales, 2011.*

He looks up at Chloe, utterly lost for words this time and wondering if this is the moment where it all falls apart and she packs her bags, leaving him to deal with the Gerard Manley Bloody Hopkins weekend on his own.

She looks back at him deadpan, and his mouth is dry. Then she winks.

It's just a normal wink, with that freckled eyelid and those long, lovely red lashes. But it's laden with irony and indulgence and amusement. What it seems to mean is that she can see right through anything and everything he will ever do.

She turns away to resume her inspection of the guest rooms.

How much has she known? And for how long? Did she have the measure of him the whole time Barry Brook was here? Or is it more recent than that? Oh bloody hell, *No worst there is none.*

He feels sick to the stomach, and his mood has not improved by the time the guests are due to arrive. Chloe notices, because of course Chloe notices everything. He needs to remember that.

"Honestly, handsome, now is not the time to go sulky on me," she says.

There's a look in her eye that says she means it, and he realises she is right: he needs to snap out of it, because this is their first proper venture together and it needs to go well.

So he takes a deep breath and tells himself that he is the landlord of a nice pub which hasn't gone bust, where several people do actually want to spend the entire weekend and pay good money for the privilege. He can't be a total incompetent.

Then they start arriving, and he's so busy welcoming them and showing them their rooms and talking them through the schedule for the weekend, that he hasn't got time to worry about anything else. Before he knows it, he is actually enjoying himself.

And when one of the new arrivals is making small-talk and addresses Tim as if he's a long-standing Hopkins aficionado, he corrects them without hesitation.

"Most of it goes way over my head, I'm afraid," he says. "Chloe here's the expert. I'm just the publican. Although I have to say I'm slowly getting there, and I'm beginning to see what the fuss is about."

Chloe turns to him and beams. It's not a beam of triumph, but of congratulation.

"Well done," she mouths, and gives him a sly squeeze.

Alun Gwynne comes over in the evening to play the part of picturesque local, along with Hugh Pugh and the others. Later in the evening even Alun's wife comes to join them.

"I've heard this is the place to be nowadays, landlord," she says, and asks for a port and lemon. Since it's the first time she has set foot in the Red Lion on his watch, Tim gives it her on the house – although he makes sure he does it discreetly, so that Alun doesn't notice and want a free pint himself.

Later, when most of the guests have gone upstairs to bed or off to wherever they are staying, Tim finds himself alone with Alun, the two of them facing each other across the bar.

"Just like the old days, eh, landlord?" says Alun. "Just the pair of us."

"Don't forget Macca," says Tim, doling out a scratching.

"I didn't think you had it in you when you first arrived,

but I think you're going to make a success of this place."

Tim decides to take it as a compliment.

"I nearly mucked it up along the way, though. With Barry Brook."

"You nearly mucked it up with Chloe, that's what mattered." Alun lowers his voice confidentially. "How much did she really know, do you think?"

"Don't go there," says Tim. "I don't know, and I don't want to know. All I know is that I tried to bullshit her, she didn't seem to mind, and at the end of the day she actually seems to like me for who I am, not who I pretended to be."

"Let's drink to that, then, landlord."

"Cheers."

"And do you know? Maybe it was worth going through all that nonsense with Barry Brook just to find out that she likes you the way you are."

"Maybe you're right."

"As I always say, everything happens for a reason."

Tim smiles and picks up his familiar old cloth to wipe down the bar. Perhaps it really does.

ACKNOWLEDGEMENTS

Two of the narrative strands in *The Hopkins Conundrum* are based on real lives and events. The chapters featuring Hopkins himself are based wherever possible on genuine incidents and populated with real people. Aside from some necessary simplifications, the sections telling the story of the shipwreck also match the sequence of events as best we know them. My main sources were Hopkins' letters and journals and the newspaper accounts of the shipwreck, but I am also indebted to Robert Bernard Martin's biography *Gerard Manley Hopkins: A Very Private Life*, Norman White's *Gerard Manley Hopkins in Wales* and *Hopkins in Ireland*, and to Sean Street's *The Wreck of the Deutschland*.

The characters in the fictional strand are entirely invented and are not meant to be based on any living persons. The valley they inhabit is real enough, and the identity of the building I have called St Vowelless's is not hard to work out. I have used artistic licence in the nickname Tim gives it: there are more vowels than consonants in the actual name (although that doesn't make it much easier for English visitors to pronounce).

This may be a slim novel, but it has been many years in the making. It owes its genesis to Matthew Hamilton at Aitken Alexander, who noticed that Hopkins was intruding unbidden into another piece of writing and suggested I get him out of my system by giving him a project of his own. From that point the manuscript variously grew and shrank as I wrote and threw away reams of material, including one entire narrative strand that proved to be a research indulgence too far. My City University comrades Glenda Cooper, Maha Khan Phillips, David Evans, Sarah Jane Checkland and Yasmine Lever offered tireless guidance, feedback and encouragement, as did Henry Fitzherbert at the newspaper office where we both spent many years. Other friends supplied historical or technical expertise, including Dominic Janes, Shan Rees Roberts, Ian Lucas, Margaret Tracey and Alan Beck (whose detailed knowledge of nuns' underclothing is remarkable). Georgie Bouz at Marjacq boosted my confidence in the novel and helped me balance its three strands, and the late Gary Pulsifer made the crucial introduction to Lightning Books. I am grateful to him for doing so when he was in thick of his struggle with cancer; I sorely wish I could send him a finished copy.

A large number of other people have given support and advice through the publishing process, including Simon McLinden, Rina Gill, Amanda Cummings, David Free, Liz Curry, Fiona Moore, Martin Edge, Charles Darwent, Neil Bartlett, David Smith, Douglas Board, Arabella McKessar, and the past and present directors of creative writing at City University, Harriett Gilbert and Jonathan Myerson.

I was sceptical when Dan Hiscocks at Lightning said that turning the manuscript into a book would be the fun part, but he was completely right. My working and personal relationship with him has been hugely enriching, and I look forward to our collaboration continuing. My editor Scott Pack worked practical magic to enable the novel I wanted to write to finally emerge, and I am also grateful for the wisdom, enthusiasm and professionalism of Andrew Samuelson, Hugh Brune and Ruth Killick. We are all indebted to Anna Morrison for her cover design.

Supporting a would-be writer can be a thankless and sometimes hazardous business. Douglas Slater was tactful but uncompromising in helping me see the failings of my early prose. The late Peter Burton provided copious moral support, and my former partner Tony Bird dealt with my attempts to learn the craft with great patience.

The arrival in my life of my beloved husband Ezio Alessandroni, a former priest who had lived in similar institutions to Hopkins, gave this project renewed relevance. He made me see the attraction of the religious life to both Hopkins and the nuns of the *Deutschland*, and his love of the Church of his native Rome brought me closer to my characters. He lost his struggle with cancer just too soon to see the finished version in print, but he lives on in many hearts. I dedicate this work to him, with undying love.